THIRST

THIRST

A NOVEL

BENJAMIN WARNER

B L O O M S B U R Y

NEW YORK · LONDON · OXFORD · NEW DELHI · SYDNEY

Bloomsbury USA
An imprint of Bloomsbury Publishing Plc

1385 Broadway	50 Bedford Square
New York	London
NY 10018	WC1B 3DP
USA	UK

www.bloomsbury.com
BLOOMSBURY and the Diana logo are trademarks of Bloomsbury
Publishing Plc

First published 2016

ISBN: HB: 978-1-63286-215-0
       epub: 978-1-63286-216-7

LIBRARY OF CONGRESS CATALOGING-IN-PUBLICATION DATA

Warner, Benjamin.
Thirst / Benjamin Warner.
pages cm
ISBN 978-1-63286-215-0 (hardback) / 978-1-63286-216-7 (epub)
I. Title.
PS3623.A86248T66 2016
813'.6—dc23
2015015311

2 4 6 8 10 9 7 5 3 1

Typeset by RefineCatch Limited, Bungay, Suffolk
Printed and bound in the U.S.A. by Berryville Graphics Inc., Berryville, Virginia

To find out more about our authors and books visit www.bloomsbury.com. Here
you will find extracts, author interviews, details of forthcoming events and the
option to sign up for our newsletters.

Bloomsbury books may be purchased for business or promotional use. For
information on bulk purchases please contact Macmillan Corporate and Premium
Sales Department at specialmarkets@macmillan.com.

For Joanna, my travel partner

The western wave was all a-flame.
The day was well nigh done!
—COLERIDGE

THIRST

EDDIE RAN.

His car was stuck north of the wreck, and though he'd left the horns behind him in the distance, he could still feel their clamor pressing into his temples. For three and a half hours he'd waited—three and a half hours!—his anger mounting as the horns had lulled and rallied like crowd noise. His radio had died; his phone had lost service. At first, he'd opened his door and walked among the other parked cars; he'd put his hands on his hips and commiserated with those standing around in varying degrees of advanced frustration. A man with a red, chapped face had looked into the sun and turned to Eddie. "I could *run* home faster than this," he'd said, and squeezed his fists by his sides.

Those words had glinted for Eddie like a dime waiting to be plucked from the street.

Enough was enough already. He *could* run home faster. He'd had a partial scholarship for track in college. The house was only another ten- or fifteen-minute drive down the highway. Probably eight or nine miles.

So he ran.

Where were the cops? The ambulances? Still, he heard no sirens. But the running did him good. With each stride, he felt his anger dissipating like dust beaten from a carpet. He laughed out loud. Oh, God, he thought, I'm abandoning my car on the highway. It wouldn't be there for long, though—not on that stretch of road. When the emergency crews finally came, they'd send one of those long flatbed tow trucks he'd seen in medians after wrecks. He imagined Laura having to drive him to an impound lot. He could picture rows of cars behind chain-link fencing.

How many had been in the pile-up? By the time he'd reached the collisions on the bridge, people had left their cars to stand dazed on the asphalt, their hair on end from either wind or shock or when they'd pulled it in frustration. Eddie had listened to the edges of their quiet conversations. There'd been no screaming. Not even the faintest moan. Too much time had passed for that. Glass and colored plastic had spilled across the four lanes, and he'd woven through a line of cars pushed up against one another like spent dominoes.

Eddie kept running. There'd been no point standing around to gawk. When the emergency crews showed up, they'd have to clear the gawkers out of the way, too. Once he was home, he could charge his phone and call 911. It would be moot by then, of course, but he would call anyway. A hundred people would have called by then.

Laura would be worried. Maybe she'd heard about the wreck on the news. When she worried on the phone, she bit hard at the thumbnail of her empty hand. Eddie always thought she might draw blood.

If he kept this pace, he'd be home in just over an hour. He continued south, running in the middle of the road now, following the broken white lines. They formed a rhythm in his head. *Stride, stride, stride, break.* The day was bright and blue ahead of him, and he tried to free his mind into it. He'd sat in his office all morning, imagining he'd be on his back porch by now, setting up the grill. On summer Fridays, they got off a little early.

Back in his car, before the jam and before the radio had clicked out, he'd caught the tail end of "Like a Rolling Stone"—a song he loved—and by the end of a summer day like this one, when dreaminess washed away all consequences, he might just shout along with Dylan. Traffic was clear here, as if it had been cut off down below, the highway big and open—three lanes across in each direction—and the lyrics still tumbled in his head. He belted out a line as if releasing a weight that slowed him down, but the silence behind him swallowed his voice and had the effect of making him feel small. He listened, but still he heard no sirens.

The important thing was to get home before Laura did. If he'd stayed with the car and been stuck out there until all hours of the night, she'd bite her thumb down to the bone. He could see her setting the phone on the kitchen table and staring at it—as if by the strength of her concern, she could make it ring.

Sweat began to run down his sides, and when he inhaled, his chest felt full of straw. It was hot, and he was wearing loafers. He stripped to his undershirt and balled up his button-down, chucking it to the side of the road. When he tried his phone again, the call still wouldn't go through.

This stretch of Route 29 was choked with green, and he tried to think of only that—that the highway was a trail going through the woods. He stared into it, a patch so thick it could have been jungle. The trees were well after bloom beyond the pull-off lane, and there were suburban developments behind it, but still.

Soon, an embankment rose to the left and the road graded up. The retaining wall was made of stacked landscaping stones, giving it a scalloped look. Beyond it was a strip mall. Nothing was moving up there. A traffic light swung over the off-ramp, but it was out. Eddie's undershirt clung to him, and his feet were rubbing raw. He hoped that what he felt inside his shoes was only sweat.

To keep from stopping, he lengthened his stride. The straw in his chest was starting to ignite, but it wasn't as bad as the marathon he'd run his senior year of college. He'd been off the track team by then, but he'd thought his wind would hold. He'd never run a marathon before; it was Laura who'd egged him on. He could still hear her saying, "You track stars. You never get out of shape."

You track stars. It thrilled him to remember it.

The last five miles he'd thought he'd die, but Laura had come with friends to meet him at the finish line. It was the fear of humiliation that had kept him going. At the end, he'd seen the crowd of people and grown confused. Several of them had looked like Laura, but as he approached, they became strangers. One woman had widened her eyes as Eddie ran to her and soundlessly fell into her arms. He'd regained his senses with Laura standing above him in the medical tent.

Up on his right was a McDonald's. The golden arches were attached to a high pole so they could be seen from the highway. Beneath were signs for a Subway and a Ross Dress for Less. He was making progress. His house was only a couple of miles away.

There was construction work ahead—an overpass that curved and stopped midair, the rebar sticking out. An apparatus holding halogen lights stood unmanned and dark. Eddie had driven this stretch at night and seen the dome of white light exposing workmen in their hard hats, like they were repairing the inside of a glass bulb.

He stopped and put his hands on his knees, sucking air in through his nose and pressing himself into the nubby stones of the retaining wall. But he didn't rest for long.

Route 29 narrowed to two lanes here, and he passed the brick mill with its historical signs and trail maps for the park that stretched behind it. There were hiking paths back there that curved from this road back into his neighborhood, following a stream that ran south all the way into the city. He stopped again and considered taking a trail home, but the trees to his right were dark and strange. He squinted to try to see them better. Back where they met the park, they were black and burnt-looking. Usually, the stream poured over a spillway there, but that wide slope of cement was dry. Over its edge, where the water would have pooled, was only whitish sand. Eddie stood on the stretch of road beneath which the stream should have disappeared and then become visible again on the other side. But there was no water on the other side of the road. A thin rust-colored scar ran through the sand where it should have flowed.

Something had ignited—had ripped through the whole path of the stream. A chemical spill, Eddie thought. He could see the charred points of treetops curve into the distance where the stream cut through the woods.

Just up ahead, an aluminum guardrail along the side of the road opened up into a path, and he took it, walking carefully down an embankment where a trail ran into the park. He'd crossed into the park here before, using stepping-stones to traverse a small tributary. Now the stones were dry. Ash was clumped along the edge of the streambed, and Eddie brushed the toe of his shoe over it, spreading it out the way he might the soft remains of a campfire. His head ached suddenly. He'd run too far too fast and felt woozy. For a moment, he believed he was hallucinating. He looked hard into the dry streambed as if to clear his thoughts and see it run again.

Then the toe of his shoe touched something hard—harder than the ash he'd been walking through. It was a burnt tuft of hair at the crown of a dog's skull. The eye sockets were hollow, and what remained of the fur on its cheek was singed and rough as stubble. Eddie bent to see, and then jerked upright, seeing the animal's stomach, still intact and sticky with brown blood.

He swallowed the bad taste in his throat. A pain stabbed once again at his temple, as if puncturing a hole there, and a helplessness seeped in. It filled his limbs right down into his swollen fingertips.

It was dim where he stood, but a clear light filtered through the ragged trees. Ahead, the park rose to a wooded hill. Eddie looked up into it. His head throbbed sharply and he winced at the pain.

Up on the hill, a boy was standing—as still as a spooked deer. Eddie followed his gaze to the carcass at his feet. The wrecked belly seemed to tremble in the clarity of the light. When he looked up the hill again, the image of the boy fluttered, too, like a mirage.

"Hey!" Eddie yelled.

The boy stared back. He was filthy, head to foot, like some kind of urchin in a movie. His hair stood on end.

"Is this your dog?" Eddie called to the boy. The life was rushing back into his limbs. "Were you here when it happened?"

At the largeness of Eddie's voice, the boy jolted and ran back through the trees.

"Stay there!" Eddie chased him up the hill, but his foot caught and he fell against a trunk to catch himself. The heels of his hands broke away charred hunks of wood. His palms were black with it.

"Hey!" he called again, but the boy was gone, and the trees were silent.

Eddie walked back and stood in the stream—the stream that was no longer there, no longer where it should have been. The ash along the bank was gray, almost milky gray, and it had collected along the steep sides of the channel.

When he was up on the road again, the helplessness trickled back into him, but this time it didn't fill him up. Whatever had burned the stream had happened quickly, and now it was over. It would be dusk soon, and he jogged ahead, only now he moved a little gingerly. He tried not to think about the boy.

This was the stretch of road where the speed limit dropped to thirty-five and it got neighborhoody. This was *his* neighborhood. There was a grocery store on his left. A few cars were still in the parking lot. The Best Auto lot was full of bodywork jobs. A minivan pulled out from Edgewood Drive, and Eddie had to wait for it to cross the southbound lanes. He wanted to rap on the windows, but it was already gaining speed. He jogged onto Kerwin Avenue. The homes were nice here, nicer than where he and Laura lived, but only by a little. Giant sycamores rose up next to the sidewalk at intervals that gave each house a canopy, and a few station wagons were parked with their two side tires up on the curb to give passing traffic room. A huddle of people stood in a circle in front of a driveway. Some of them were still dressed in work clothes.

He wanted to run hard again, to sprint past them and make it back to Laura—to grab her and press his lips to the side of her face at the relief of being home. He could already smell the skin along the edge of her ear, could feel the cold nick of her earring. But he couldn't run—not now after this group of neighbors had spotted him.

He'd seen some of them before, but he didn't know their names. He hadn't learned their names in the five years he'd lived there.

"There's an accident on Twenty-nine," he said as if he'd heard it on the radio. He wasn't breathing as hard as he had been before.

"Yeah? Power's out here. All the cell service is down, too." The man speaking to him wore a wide-brimmed hat with mesh ventilation above the band, the kind a scientist might wear in the field. Both his shirt and shorts were made of the same quick-drying material and had many pockets. He carried a two-million-candle flashlight the size of a car battery.

Next to him was an older woman whom Eddie had seen posting signs about community street sweeping. He'd seen her, in fact, pushing a broom, raising dust along the sidewalks. "I tried to check the power company's site, but my Internet's down," she said.

"Mine, too," said someone else.

"You'll get used to it," said one of them, a pretty, short-haired brunette. "My husband and I do this once a month. A technology fast, they call it. We don't check our e-mail all day."

"So we walk around like cavemen? My husband would like that, too."

"No, really," the woman said. "It's therapeutic."

"Where's the accident?" someone asked.

Eddie stood there dazed in the swirl of their conversation. A silence descended over them.

They were looking at him, and Eddie's voice jumped up in his throat. "Just past Briggs Road," he said. "On the bridge. There was a pile-up."

"You were there?"

"Yeah."

"Is it bad?"

The trees in the neighborhood were fine, but he could still picture the ones near the spillway, the powder of ash that his feet had kicked up. Though the boy had seemed unreal, the memory of him came back clearly—as if Eddie had looked at his reflection in the water and been told he had it in reverse: that what he'd thought was an illusion was in fact the truth.

"Just a wreck," he said.

The dry stream, the burnt trees, the dog, the boy—those pieces of information would have given his neighbors new variables to work with, but Eddie didn't offer them up. They were panic variables, the kind that would demonstrate that all other variables were moot, and he felt the delicate wealth of their being only his.

"And you ran all the way here?"

"We were waiting for hours and no one came," Eddie said.

"But they must be clearing it up by now."

"I saw smoke," said another, "over by the park. There are power lines over there."

"The spillway's dry," Eddie said, allowing it to slip through. He held his breath and waited for someone to clear up this confusion—for some know-it-all to say, *Of course the spillway's dry. The spillway is always dry this time of year,* but they said nothing about it, as if they hadn't heard him, and so Eddie stood there quietly and said nothing about the burned-up trees.

"You left your car?" the woman who'd endorsed technology-fasting asked.

Eddie recognized her then. She had a walking route that went right in front of his house. How many Sunday mornings had he stood at his picture window and watched her pass, knowing she couldn't see him through the reflection off the glass?

"I had to leave it," he said. "I would've sat there all night."

"What do you think will happen to it?" she asked. "I'm just thinking about my John—he takes Twenty-nine home, too."

The man in the science getup said, "It'll be towed. Just

one more thing for them to clean up." He said this without looking at Eddie, and Eddie again felt the shame of having left it there.

"The Beltway's jammed up for miles, too," continued the man. "I walked down to the ramp and saw. If there was an accident where you're coming from, there must be a pile-up down there, too. *All* the traffic lights are out."

Eddie tried to dam up the thought that Laura was stuck out on the Beltway, that her car was sitting motionless amid the horn blasts of the coming night.

"It's gotta be something directly at the power plant," said another man. This one had a beard. He wore jean shorts that were out of style for anything but organic gardening. "This wide a range, it makes no sense. If it were localized, then a tree could have taken out a line."

The man in the science getup clicked on his flashlight. "Has everyone gotten home?" he said. "I mean, who else are we still waiting on to get home from work?"

"The Lawrences' cars aren't here. They're usually home by now."

"My husband's in Cincinnati," said a woman. She looked at the man in the science getup as if to apologize for her husband's work trip. "I was talking to him when the phones died."

"My wife," said another, "is stuck in it."

The technology-faster had been studying an imperfection in the road's resurfacing. When she looked up, she said, "Alex is missing."

The woman beside her reached over to rub her shoulder and mouthed *Her dog* to the others.

Fear beat in Eddie's chest.

"Do you have a son?" he asked.

The technology-faster looked at him, her eyes beginning to well up. "Why would you say that?" she said.

"I saw a boy—" he started.

"Jonathan's upstairs," she snapped. "Why would you say that to me?"

Eddie shrank into the silence that followed. He found no comfort in these neighbors—these likewise inconvenienced people.

"Excuse me," he said.

He turned and started running again, listening for them to call after him, but none of them did.

The cars parked along the street were only half as many as there should have been, and maybe less than that. No lights were on in any houses, though some people were in their yards. They stood at the edges and talked to one another and some-body shouted at Eddie to ask him why he was running.

Laura's car wasn't in the driveway. He felt himself saying "Come on come on come on come on" before he realized he was saying it aloud. He stood at the front door and prodded his empty pockets. His insides didn't know what to tell his outsides to do. His house key was attached to the ring of his car key, and he didn't know where his car key was. It could still be in the ignition. It could be on the side of the highway.

He pulled on the knob and threw his shoulder into the door. He did the same at the back of the house and at the basement. At the basement door, he kicked with the heel of his shoe and felt a twinge in his knee.

There was a pile of smooth stones the size of softballs beneath the back porch stairs, and he palmed one and hit at a glass pane in the back door, but the pane didn't break. He hit it again and again, and on the fourth time, it shattered. He used the stone to punch out the shards, and reached through to unlock the door.

"Laura!" he called.

The inside of the house was already too dark to see. The switch was dead. He knocked through the kitchen drawer where they kept the flashlights.

The beam darted over the walls, past the sink, and into the empty living room. She wasn't in the bedroom, either.

He called her name again and let the flashlight drop. Neither of them had made the bed that morning, and, in a panic, he dropped down into it.

When he stood, his knee buckled. It was like one ligament had twisted around another. He limped into the kitchen and put a glass under the faucet. When he lifted the metal arm, nothing happened. He wrenched it up and down, and a clunking sound arose from the plumbing. He tried in the bathroom, too, turning the knobs.

The house was dry.

Once, when they'd been visiting Laura's parents during a hurricane, Eddie had watched her father fill their tub as a precaution. When he'd finished, Eddie had stood there with him in the silence of the small guest bathroom, watching him look sternly at the water as though an important task had been completed. Eddie hadn't known what to say to Laura's father— he was not his son and couldn't ask the questions a son could ask. It seemed to him he'd met Laura's father too late in life.

Eddie was a man by then and felt her father would have liked him better had he still been a boy or at least a younger version of himself—and so he'd kept a stern expression on his face and watched the tub with him for a long moment before Laura's mother called to ask what they were doing.

Now Eddie went to the basement door and gripped the wooden handrail, stepping lightly down the stairs. There were two plastic water bottles down there with the camping gear, and he went to the utility bathroom and dipped each of them into the toilet tank. As an experiment, he flushed, and the water went down but didn't refill. He screwed the caps on top of the water bottles and put them in the bottom of the closet.

He didn't want to call the water company only to have them ask if he'd checked the water main, and it took him a moment to remember where it was. There was an old TV stand against the wall, and as he bent and moved it, a few old issues of *Sports Illustrated* slid off. Behind it was a wooden panel. He spun a metal latch to take it out. Inside, he tried to turn the valve, but the valve was all the way open, and so he put the panel back in place.

Above him was a shelf where they kept his five-thousand-meters trophy from high school and Laura's silver pom-pom. She'd been a cheerleader for a year after a guidance counselor had suggested extracurriculars. In spite of herself, she'd made friends in the pyramid, though where they were now, she didn't know. When she got into one of her cleaning moods, Eddie would sometimes surprise her with the pom-pom to cheer her on as she scrubbed the grout above the bathtub. He brought it down to his face and inhaled it the way he might her shirt, though the plastic strands were odorless.

Back upstairs, he thought to fill more bottles from the toilet in the bathroom, but he was being ridiculous. There was a container of apple juice in the fridge, and he lifted it and drank in big, greedy gulps. It overflowed his mouth and ran onto his chin. He stopped only when he had to gasp for breath and could feel the liquid sloshing in his stomach.

There was beer left in the fridge, too, and he took one out and opened it. Then he went outside and sat on the stoop. He felt silly for breaking the window. He could have sat out here and waited for Laura to come home and let him in.

She would ask him if he'd checked in on any of the neighbors. Her own family took care of people that way. When she'd first brought Eddie home, they'd all walked down the block to deliver a plate of dinner to a ninety-year-old woman who still lived by herself. Laura's father had cut the chicken into bite-sized pieces and covered it all in plastic. After they'd rung the bell about a dozen times, the woman had opened up in curlers, and mumbled something of recognition and gratitude.

Laura wanted *them* to be like that, taking trays of food to people. To care about the neighborhood. Who were their friends now? Sometimes it felt like it was just the two of them on their own, but Eddie didn't mind that.

A retired couple in their seventies lived across the street from them. Mr. Mathias was a religious man—he'd been a preacher or minister or something. His wife had been a nurse.

Eddie walked across the street and knocked, the beer still in his hand.

There was no answer. Both of their cars were parked on the curb, and he knocked again.

This time, he heard shuffling inside, and Mr. Mathias opened the door. He had on a red baseball cap with the curly *W* of the Nationals, and a thick cloth neck brace.

"I'm your neighbor," Eddie said, and felt the falsity of the gesture: the truth was he didn't want to be standing there. He wanted to be waiting for Laura—to watch her drive up the road so he could walk from his stoop to her car to greet her. "Ed Gardner. I'm right over there," he said, pointing across the street.

"Yes, sir." Mr. Mathias had an accent that might have been Caribbean. His head was cocked to the side in an uncomfortable-looking way.

"I'm just checking in. With the power out and all. You folks all right?"

"Oh, we okay. We okay, yes," Mr. Mathias said. "We got the candles going. Thank you."

"You holler if you need anything. I'm right over there." Eddie pointed again. Mr. Mathias closed the door before Eddie turned to leave. There were old-timers all over this neighborhood. Old-timers and young couples like him and Laura. Many of them had children.

The house next to his was the Davises'. Patty Davis had wobbled out onto her deck and Eddie could smell cigarette smoke. In the dark, he couldn't see her face, only the shape of her body. She was overweight by a hundred pounds, at least, and had a short pageboy haircut. When she walked, she looked to be wading through deep water.

He started to call to her, but his voice had no strength and died before it left his mouth. Laura would find all this amusing—how worried he'd become.

When he was close enough that he didn't have to shout, he said, "Mike Sr. home yet?"

"Nah." Her voice was big and round in the night air. "He's stuck with the rest of 'em."

"You get any calls out?"

"Nah."

"Lines must be down everywhere," he said.

"I got put on hold at about four o'clock, when it first went out. Then I got cut off in about two seconds."

"The power company?"

"Yeah. They must know. In two thousand eight we were out six days."

"The water company, too, huh?"

"Couldn't get through."

"Your phone's working? I'm trying to call Laura."

"She's stuck out there, too?"

"I guess. But if your phone is working, I can try her again."

"No, I don't have any service."

Eddie walked up to her side of the lawn. A chain-link fence divided the properties halfway up the driveway, and he leaned against it. When his hands touched the metal, he felt that they were shaking.

"Six days?" he said.

"Yup. I was cooking spaghetti and meatballs on the grill. That was in a snowstorm."

"The repair crews better get here soon," he said.

"At least they got good weather to work in."

Even in the dark, Eddie smiled to be neighborly. He put the beer to his mouth and drank off about half of it in a gulp. His knee ached in a serious way, but he didn't care about it then. There was a drunkenness to the way the night had come down so thick and black. The air swirled above them loosely on a breeze. Eddie felt his mind begin to pitch. He sat down on the grass.

"I had to run home," he told Patty. He stretched himself out and the top of his head touched the fence. He kept his knee bent and it felt better.

"You okay down there?" Patty asked.

"Yeah. How about Mike Jr.? He get home from daycare?"

"Wore himself out riding his bike," she said.

"No training wheels?"

"Not since he took them off last weekend."

"That's good." Eddie looked at the sky. "He's a little athlete." He got the sense the stars were swirling toward a single point, as if going down a drain—that even the air resting on his face was pulling in that direction. "A good athlete can make friends for life," he said.

Patty was silent, as if contemplating the idea of her son in the future.

"Hey," she said after a moment, "make sure not to flush."

Eddie's imagination had leaked into the starlight. It was only he who'd been contemplating Mike Jr. all grown up; Patty was thinking about the water in his toilets.

"Was the water out in oh-eight, too?" he asked.

"The water, nah. Must be something else. They'll send people for it."

"The water company knows when they have problems with the pipes," Eddie said. "They have sensors that can tell when one's about to break."

"Yeah, I heard of that."

"It has to be something with one of those big water mains. I saw on the news that they're over seventy years old. There's only so much patching up the county can do."

He stopped to listen to the air. There was no sound of the peepers in the trees. Just a thrum in his ears.

"You have enough to drink in there?" he said.

"Sure. I have a gallon of milk I just bought . . . I've got prune juice, not that anyone but me would drink it. I've got a little wine spritzer in case me and Mike Sr. feel like celebrating."

Eddie stared up at the sky.

"Poor Mike Sr.," she said. "He's got bladder problems. Probably ready to piss himself by now. Oh, well. He'll have to use a Big Gulp cup."

Eddie didn't want to think of Laura peeing into a Big Gulp cup. Wherever she was stuck, it was closer to the city—farther south than he had been, running through that suburban no-man's-land—and she could at least leave her car and get to a restaurant or grocery store or one of the gas stations.

He tried to think of other things instead.

In college, he'd taken an English seminar. Dammit, if he could only remember one thing, he'd remember that line from Dickens. It was about Wenman or something. *Wemmick.*

That was the character's name.

The professor had been reading passages. He could still see him standing on the stage of the lecture hall. Eddie had been up high in the seats, alone.

"Wemmick," the professor had read, "had such a slit for a mouth that he didn't so much *eat* his food as *post it*." He'd paused after that and let the hall fill with shuffling. Fat and gray-bearded, the professor had been, with a pleased expression on his face. "The magic of literary description," he'd said. "Close your eyes." And Eddie had closed them. "Now. Picture Wemmick. Do you see him?" Eyes closed, Eddie had nodded. He had seen the man.

"What color shirt is he wearing?" the professor trumpeted. "Does he have on pants? How thick is his hair?"

Eddie hadn't been able to answer. Each attribute he'd given—a red sweater, for instance, or a shining, bald head—was false; it was not Wemmick. In his mind, Wemmick's shirt was both there and not there. Wemmick's entire body—even his mouth, which could not have possibly looked like a post office slot—existed without dimension.

When he pictured Laura stuck out there in traffic, the lanes had no depth, no beginning or end. The cars around her were both there and not there—a catastrophe and nothing.

He went inside and lay down on the bed. His clock radio had a battery backup and was illuminated to 9:33. The numbers cast the room in dull blue. When he closed his eyes, he could see the boy in the woods so distinctly that he snapped them back open. It took Eddie a moment to recognize the room. The clock read 1:07.

"Laura?" he called.

He ran a palm over the sheet next to him and felt her absence there.

In the kitchen, he saw through the window that there were no cars in his driveway and only Patty's car next door. He tried the sink again, and again there was nothing. He sipped from the apple juice in the fridge and allowed his mind to continue buzzing.

His neck was stiff, and he rubbed his thumb into it. Then he went outside into the warm night. She'd have come around from the east on the Beltway, up six miles on 295 from her office in the city. She'd have been on her way out around the same time he'd left his car.

He walked back onto the street, the way he'd come through the neighborhood earlier. Someone had started a fire in a little pit and sparks popped in the air. As he got closer, he heard the murmur of voices. One of them laughed, and others joined in. They had a grill going. He could smell the meat. They were making burgers past one in the morning.

He did not want to be called over. He did not want to be stopped and asked to have a beer with these people. He jogged up the street, passing by their yard on the opposite sidewalk, and didn't turn his head to look at them.

At the dead stoplight, he went right, back onto Route 29. It was called Colesville Road here, and Eddie crossed over to walk on the grassy median, which had been mown close to the ground. The road was empty, but up ahead was the intersection with University Avenue, and he could see where cars had come in on the eastbound lanes and were stopped.

There were restaurants ahead: a burrito place and a Peruvian chicken shack. A gourmet pastry shop. He'd bought Laura's birthday cake there last winter. People stood in front of the chicken shack speaking Spanish. Peruvian chicken, but all the Spanish speakers here were from El Salvador. The *Post* had done a piece on how terrible the gang violence was down there. If you had a certain kind of tattoo, you could never go back.

He jogged left at the intersection for University. Cars were parked three lanes across going toward the ramp for the Beltway and as far back as he could see down the eastbound lanes. In the other direction—the direction Laura would be coming home—the lanes were empty. The other accidents, wherever they were, must have cut off the exits leaving the Beltway.

The median ended and there was no sidewalk. He could have moved much more easily up the deserted westbound lanes, but their emptiness was like a prohibition keeping him away.

He jogged between the cars. Though he knew that none of them could have been Laura's, and that it would only make him crazy to look inside their windows, he looked inside them anyway. Seats had been reclined all the way back, and people were sleeping or at least closing their eyes. Others came out from the woods and opened their doors, illuminating interiors. Farther up, people were sitting on their hoods and whispering like stargazers.

There was a woman standing up ahead, leaning against her side mirror. She wore a white dress. Maybe that's why he ran to her—glowing in the dark the way she was.

"What are you doing?" he asked.

"Stretching my legs."

Eddie was shocked by her voice—that she'd responded to him at all, that she wasn't an illusion.

"What *can* we do?" she said as Eddie stared at her. "Unless you got news, you can go back to your friends." She jutted her chin to a car somewhere behind him.

"I'm not here with my friends," Eddie said. "I'm new."

"*New?* I swear to God, this is the worst emergency I've ever been in."

"I mean, I just got here."

"Yeah? Well, I've been here all night." When she looked at him, her face softened, as if she felt she'd been unfair. "A lady up there has sodas in her trunk," she said, "but they're probably gone by now."

"What's happening?"

"Beltway's jammed. This is all jammed. I haven't seen one cop the whole time. I heard sirens about three hours ago, but that's all."

"People are just sleeping in their cars?"

"What are they gonna do? Walk home? We got trees right here. You don't have toilet paper, do you? If you got toilet paper, you'll be a hero."

"No," Eddie said.

"A few of these idiots were playing their radios before. Probably drained the batteries."

"How will you get home?"

"Same way as you. Wait it out. You think they're gonna fire everyone who doesn't make it to work in the morning? I'd like to see them try."

Eddie walked ahead. A few boys were kicking a soccer ball in the pull-off. They were good players, juggling it on their feet before passing. Someone's headlights were lighting them up and dust swirled in a dramatic way.

The on-ramp was only one exit away, and when he came to it, cars had filled it up two across. A truck had run into the wall at an angle, and in the space between the wall and the truck's tailgate, the nose of an Audi had shoved in between. Eddie turned sideways and had to brush against the grit on the door to get past. No one was inside any of the cars on the ramp. It rose and turned sharply, and beneath him, Eddie could see a long stretch of the Beltway. Traffic stood still in both directions, and dome lights blinked on and off as doors opened and closed. Laura drove a blue Civic, but it was impossible to tell what color was which from where he stood. He knew its shape—compact, wedgelike, too sporty for her. They'd bought it used from a lot.

He walked down the ramp as it twisted and leveled off again with the Beltway, and crossed the median into the westbound lanes where Laura would be coming from. People were walking through the cars—maybe walking home into the city. It would take them all night from here. He looked for the Civic. There were a few he passed, and he looked inside them, but they weren't hers. People pushed by him in the space between driver's-side and passenger doors. A father held his child at his chest. Eddie thought about calling Laura's name, but no one else was talking. The strange silence acted on him like a rule. It made him feel deaf. He began looking into the windows of all the small cars he passed.

He walked for half an hour, maybe more. Suddenly, he felt the pavement shiver beneath him, and then the breath of a runner's body so close that he stumbled, catching himself against the hood of a car. The heels of his hands made a muted *pock.* A second and a third person ran by. He looked at the backs of their heads. Laura had jet-black hair, and so he looked for heads that were only barely visible in the darkness.

The highway rose in the distance, and headlights shone at its apex. As he approached, he saw a clog of people standing there, the headlights crisscrossing to illuminate them. Even in the relative calm of where he stood, the crowd charged the air with current. It was like walking toward an electrical storm. Eddie thought to turn around, but didn't.

He walked. The group seemed to be standing together just to keep from falling over—their limbs hanging dopily with fatigue.

Somewhere down the hill behind him, a door slammed. The sound was like a bag popping in the night. Eddie imagined a boy grinning and holding the blown-out plastic. Another pop and another. The bleating of interior alarms—keys still in ignitions. Someone shouted, but Eddie couldn't make out the words. Closer, doors opened with a rhythmic clicking. He turned to look down the hill behind him where car interiors illuminated and extinguished like fireflies, more and more of them in the night.

People were coming up behind him—jostling him into the crowd ahead. He was caught in the center lane and had to shoulder his way through the bodies to get to the side of the road, where a woman was encircled. She was sitting on a bucket. A man was grabbing at the long bottle of water she held, but she hung on with both hands.

"That wasn't even *two*!" the man yelled.

The woman yanked and rose a little off the bucket. She swayed back and forth.

Someone in the crowd was responding to a question, or simply narrating the event. "She wants to charge five dollars for three sips," he said.

"Just give it to him," came a voice. "He's thirsty. He's got a kid."

"*I'm* thirsty."

The woman didn't respond. The skin around her eyes and nose looked like old newspaper. She gripped her lips against her teeth and tugged on the bottle. The man grabbed her by the arm and pulled her off the bucket, and she landed on the road. She wasn't there for more than a second before Eddie's view was obstructed by bodies lunging for the bottle, and she was lost in them.

"Laura!" he cupped his hands around his mouth and shouted into the riot. "Laura Gardner!

Glass broke behind him and someone yelled, "He's got a hammer." Then a hand was on his shoulder, pressing him forward, and a flash of pain went off inside his knee where it banged into a fender. He grabbed at the person behind him, but whoever it was had disappeared into the crowd.

The Beltway became a bridge up ahead, and he could see the dark well of space that opened up beside it, how the trees there were skeletal and sloped down into the chasm. He pushed himself to the edge of the highway, lifting his leg up and over the guardrail. On the other side, the woods were quiet. The noise of people cramming over the bridge was already distant.

He went into the trees and sat in the dirt. Branches broke behind him and there were footsteps in the leaves. He crawled to where the land dipped, and as he got closer to the edge, he looked into the sky and saw the stars. The trees overhead were leafless.

Then he was going down before he'd made up his mind that he wanted to. The land sloped quickly and his heart caught in his chest. He was sliding. He felt rocks and sharp sticks dig at his legs. His hands flailed at his sides until he caught a root and stopped himself. There was more noise above him—the quick, rhythmic swishing of pant legs. There were voices, too, but both the voices and the swishing stopped abruptly. Eddie could tell they had paused right above him, and he let go of the root and peddled with his feet and used his hands to brake behind him.

In this way, he arrived at the bottom. The light was dim there, and he thought that maybe dawn was breaking. But half the sky was still starry above him, the other half black. It was the underside of the Beltway.

His raised his palms and saw that they were black, too.

There were shrubs where the trees ended, and when he touched one, it disappeared. Eddie froze where he was. His heart was still racing. When he touched another shrub with his toe, it, too, crumbled into ash. Beyond the shrubs was a wide stretch of sand. Its emptiness brightened the night. He walked out onto it and knelt down and shoved his hands in, bringing them up so that the sand poured through his fingers. Hard pieces that felt like glass were in there, too. He held one up against the sky and saw it twisting like an icicle. The other pieces he pulled up were smaller. Eddie felt exhaustion rise over him as though the streambed had been full of a current he'd waded into.

The noise from the Beltway above him was only the faintest sound. Whoever had been mucking around in the woods hadn't followed him down there.

He walked back to the bank and the skeletons of undergrowth dissolved against his legs. Beneath the shadow of the Beltway, he lay down between the trunks of some trees that were close together. The ground was soft with a thick layer of ash, just as it had been around the spillway. He would rest here, and when the sun rose, he would go back up and look for Laura. He felt sure it was almost light, and that he wouldn't rest for long.

He could feel his blood pulsing, his own temperature seeming to flood the plane where the water had once been.

It was important not to resist sleep entirely; that was his strategy. He would indulge it quickly and then be on his way. But soon, the mosquitoes were on him. The way they struck all at once, they seemed to have only just found their way down the hill, or the scent of his body was the only animal scent remaining. He had to bury himself—heaping the ash over his legs, then his chest, then spreading it on his face using his fingers to mush into the creases of his ears—to keep from being eaten.

HE FELT THE light before he opened his eyes, and then he saw a blur of orange above him. There was a man squatting just beside his head. He was close enough for Eddie to grab the corner of his shirt, and when he did, the man stepped back and Eddie pitched forward, sending the pile of ash from his body into the air around them.

"Whoa!" the man said as Eddie clung to him. His head was throbbing; the ache arrived together with the memory of the day before. He used the handful of shirt to pull himself to standing. The man strained backward and beat his own thigh with an open hand. Then he held it up it by his face in a way that meant "Just stop." Eddie could smell his licorice breath. There was nothing violent in his eyes. He released his hold on the shirt, and the man coughed and rubbed both sides of his throat with his index and middle fingers. He left black streaks of ash there.

"Jesus," he said. "All I saw was a head. I thought maybe you were down here when it happened."

"When what happened?"

"When it went up. I saw it. I was under the bridge up there, I'm not ashamed to say. A man's got to get out of the heat."

He had gray hair that looked gelled back but was probably slick with grime. He wore a green flannel shirt beneath his orange one. His pants were a mess—they might have been khakis once, but now they were blackened. Eddie let his eyes adjust. He was at the edge of the streambed; the sand was tawny and cut through a landscape of trees that were foreshortened to charred sticks.

"What happened?" he said.

"This whole thing was on fire."

"The whole valley?"

"It started on the river. I couldn't believe it. But I heard about it happening once in Cleveland."

"And you were under the bridge? How come you're alive?"

"I was all wedged back where the concrete meets the ground. There were flames all around me, man."

"Are there still people up there?" Eddie bobbed his head up toward the Beltway.

"I suppose there are."

"The medics come?"

"You need a medic?"

"No."

Eddie started climbing back up the hill. When it got steep, his legs went out from under him, and he had to use both hands to break his fall. He grabbed at trees, and they came away in cinders.

"Get around under the bridge," the man called out from beneath him. "It's easier over there."

Eddie bent down and used his hands to half-crawl to the bridge. The pain in his knee reached into his hip. Under the bridge, the ash was thin and there was dirt and trash and he could grip and stand up fully. Near the road, he saw where the man must have been when the flames came up. He imagined that slope of cement, how tightly he must have pressed his back into it as the air raged red around him, how it must have felt like it would never end or that he'd died and ended up in hell.

He pulled himself over the guardrail and had to squint against the light.

He looked for the Civic and saw a few, but no dark blue ones. People were still asleep in their cars. Or else they were sitting in them with the seats dropped back, resigned to stillness. He needed to get home. Laura would have headed home. She'd have been there by now if she'd kept a steady pace.

Eddie made it to the far lane and saw on the asphalt the green diamonds of shattered glass. A minivan had its windshield spiderwebbed from a blow to the passenger's side. He understood that the world could mirror the inside of his mind—that there were enough broken pieces and enough whole pieces to exhaust his racing thoughts.

He took the highway exit back to University Avenue and then crossed through the cars parked there and over into the empty lanes. There was a two-story thrift shop with words painted in Spanish that people were coming out of with hangers of clothing. Eddie went in. No one was working the cash registers, and he watched as men and women walked down the dingy rows of dresses and pants and took what they wanted and left without paying. He had never been in this store before, and the air smelled of dust and cedar. Near the checkout, a refrigerated case had been emptied and its door hung open.

On the next block was a 7-Eleven gas station. In front of the glass doors, a group of men were arguing. Eddie looked at the images of giant sodas printed on plastic signs above the windows. There were other men with tools standing around. One had a shovel, which he held with the tip up, and one stood with both fists just beneath the metal head of a sledgehammer. When Eddie tried to go in, the man with the shovel sidestepped in front of him and lowered it diagonally with one hand. With the other hand, he tapped Eddie in the chest and shook his head. *"Usted no puede entrar,"* he said.

"I have money. Look." Eddie took out his wallet and edged some bills up to the surface.

"No," said the man, shaking his head. "No."

Eddie tried to walk in past him, but he moved again and used the edge of the shovel head to press him away. They were making a small disturbance away from the other men, and the man with the sledgehammer came up next to Eddie, too. He said something and used the sledgehammer to point down the road.

Eddie moved on, limping, his tongue not yet resigned to sticking inside his mouth. He rolled it around, feeling the residue that clicked when he passed it over his upper palate.

At the dead traffic light, he watched a teenager wearing an old Bulls jersey and low jean shorts surveying the line of cars sitting in the eastbound lanes.

Eddie had seen kids hanging out on this street before, selling bottles of water at red lights.

He hustled closer before he caught the kid's eye.

"What do you have?" Eddie said.

The kid waved him over to the sidewalk. He lifted a bottle of water from where he'd stuck it in the waist of his pants.

"How much?" Eddie said.

"This my last one."

"How much you want for it?"

"Thirty."

The kid was tall and had the long veined biceps of a high school athlete.

Eddie took out his wallet.

"I've got twenty-six," he said, handing the cash over.

The kid gave him the bottle and nodded beyond Eddie to another kid down the street whom Eddie hadn't seen. The other kid carried a crate with both hands, his arms straining beneath the weight. Eddie could see the white plastic tops of all the "last ones" lined up within it.

He tipped the bottle to his mouth and drank. The water hit his stomach like he'd poured it into a metal bucket. He had to squat and put his head between his knees to keep from throwing up. Even then, the world went swimmy. A woman walked by him and stopped. Eddie was forced to stare at her feet. She wore parsimonious shoes. When he looked up at her, the sun blacked out her face.

"Here," he said, and thrust the half-full bottle at her. She took it without speaking and put it in her purse.

When he had the strength, he got up and started to walk again. The house wasn't too far off. Maybe another mile and a half.

From the sky behind him came the distant rhythmic thumping of helicopter blades. Eddie watched as the heads on the street all lifted in the same direction. The sound died away and in its absence he heard crying. Someone said, "They'll be here soon, anyway. They've got to get to everyone."

Eddie tried to jog, but jogging wasn't possible. His knee was kinked, even when he walked.

He watched a man go up to a house and knock on its door. He was carrying an empty gallon jug. When no one answered, he went down the walkway and over to the next house and tried again. He saw Eddie, and his face broadened in a way that made Eddie stop. The man came up and stuck out his hand, and Eddie shook it. The jug hung from his other hand like a bubble of thought not yet raised.

"I'm Bill Peters," the man said. "You live around here?"

"No," Eddie said. "Not right around here."

"I can follow you," Bill Peters said. He smiled like a salesman. "What do you need?"

"Our water's still out. I just need to fill up this jug."

"Mine was out when I left, too."

"When was that?"

"Last night."

"Maybe you can check again."

"Everybody's is out."

"Yeah, but when it comes back on, it won't all be at once."

"I'd help," Eddie said, "but I'm out here looking for my wife right now."

"I've got a little boy with a congenital heart defect. I don't mean to give you a sob story, trust me, but I need to get some liquid in him. It's not for me, understand?"

"It's for your boy."

"He's got to be hydrated. I don't have a car."

"Let me check on my wife."

"I can follow you," he said again.

"Let me check on her first."

"What's the address?"

Eddie looked at the man's dopey collared shirt, which he'd tucked into his pants. The skin on his hands had sunken spots between the bones in a way that made him appear desperate.

"Give me a little while, and then you can come by," Eddie said.

"I can just follow you now and wait outside."

"Just give me a while, okay? Don't follow me now."

"What's the address?"

"It's up on Greenbriar."

"What's the number?"

"You don't need the number."

"I won't know where to go."

"Sixteen twenty-seven."

"Okay, then. Sixteen twenty-seven." He closed his eyes, committing it to memory. "And what's your name?" he said.

"Ed Gardner."

"Okay, then, Mr. Gardner. I'll see you soon. Good luck with your wife."

Eddie walked the streets of his neighborhood. When he looked over his shoulder, he could see that Bill Peters was following at a distance. He stopped and waved him away. At the next block, he turned and saw he was still coming.

"Come back later!" Eddie shouted, but Bill Peters just stood straight where he was. He was far enough away that Eddie could barely see the milk jug.

There was a path behind one of these houses that he and Laura sometimes used on their walks. It went by a garden full of tomato plants that an elderly couple started from seed each spring. In the summer, if the old man was out tending them, he'd hand Laura one of the cherry types. Eddie cut through that path. The tomato plants were about a foot tall, and since he'd last seen them, the old man had filled the bed with straw. Eddie limped up the short block ahead and then cut down another street, up another. He walked a block beyond the turn to his house, and didn't see Bill Peters behind him any longer. To be safe, he went in a circle—four right turns past his neighbors' houses. There was a woman unloading groceries from the trunk of her car there. Eddie had seen her before.

"Get to the market while you can," she said, smiling.

"You haven't seen my wife, have you?" Eddie said. "Her name is Laura. She's, like, this tall and has black hair."

The smile left the woman's face, and she put the bag back into the trunk and walked to Eddie to touch his arm.

"Where did you come from?" she said.

"I was stuck out in the mess for a while."

"And your wife's still out there? The side streets are cleared up. She'll make it back soon."

"Yeah," Eddie said. "She's probably out here looking for *me.*"

The woman looked down briefly at her driveway, then raised her eyes with a pained expression. "Maybe she's already waiting for you back home. My family made it back, too. There are others not so lucky. You can see the jam if you're driving on Randolph. It's backed up for miles still."

Eddie didn't say anything.

She clutched her hands behind her back and her nose and lips began to quiver. Her face flushed red.

"I need to sit down," she said.

Eddie moved quickly to help her to the grass. She shook her head back and forth.

"I'm a Christian," she said, pressing her fingers into the corners of her eyes. "I stole all this."

"The groceries?"

"There was no one there to pay. You have to steal. But that doesn't make it right." She looked up at Eddie, and her face seemed to clear. "Go on," she said. "Take whatever you need. Just look in there and take it."

"I need to get back to my wife."

She nodded to him, serenely. "Go to her, then," she said.

LAURA WAS HOME—as though the woman saying so had made it true. He wanted to run to her, to throw his arms around her like he used to, to take her to the ground and smother her with his body. He wanted to squeeze his eyes shut in such a way that there would be nothing in the world but her chest beneath his own.

When she saw him, her hand went to her mouth but not fast enough to trap a sob. They had barstools at the kitchen counter, and she stepped behind one as if to protect herself from him.

"Eddie," she said. She took a few breaths to keep her expression from breaking. Her forehead was scraped, but not so badly.

Then she stepped out from the barstool and hung her arms around his neck. Her nose pushed against his throat, and her skin was warm, except for the tip of her nose where it made contact. She was crying. The urge to tell her about the boy in the woods was rising somewhere in his chest. But telling her would do no good. It made no sense to make her worry. He wasn't even sure he'd seen the boy. He could no longer describe him to himself.

"How did you get here?" he said, but she didn't answer. She stayed there, hugging him silently, and now he could breathe her in—the faint chemical lilac trapped inside her clothes. He put his hands on her waist and held her as though he were holding her aloft.

"I should call the police," he said, pressing away.

"Everyone's trying," she said. "Where were you? You look like a ghost."

Eddie looked down at himself. His clothes and arms were streaked with ash.

"I was looking for you."

"Oh no," she said.

"I spent the night outside, but it's okay. We're okay now."

"What's happening?"

"I don't know," he said. "I heard helicopters, though. We'll have the power back on soon."

"Will you clean yourself up, please," she said. "I can't look at you like this."

"How long have you been back?"

"Just now," she said. "I sat in my car until four in the morning. I left when people started leaving. Everybody was leaving. I left the car, Eddie."

He squeezed her arm. She was shaking. "I left mine, too," he said. "It's okay."

"No, it isn't. I had to pull a woman off another woman's child last night. She was hitting him. You know why? She said he stepped on her."

"You walked the whole way?"

"Everyone was stepping on everybody. We all walked. I was in my flats, thank God."

"You must have walked right past me."

"You were on the Beltway?"

"I went back out to look for you. Where'd you leave the car?"

"Just a couple of miles before the exit. There were people walking a lot farther."

"It'll be fine. They'll tow some of the cars, but they can't tow everyone. When things clear up, I'll walk back down and get it."

"I don't care about the car, I guess."

"I don't want you to worry," he said. "There was nothing else you could do. Did you try the phone?"

"I tried to call my parents, but I can't get a call to go out. Thank God you're back, but I'm worried about them."

Eddie went to the sink and tried the faucet handle again.

"Your parents are nowhere close to this. They're three counties over. This is just a power thing."

"How do you know that? There's no communication."

"They're fine. They're probably worried about *us*, is all."

"You have no way of knowing that."

"Do your parents leave the house? No. So they're sitting at home just like we are."

"I'm going to cry," she said, though she'd been crying already. "I've been wanting to cry all morning. I couldn't do it last night, not with all those people. I had to be a good person and be on the lookout for women hitting other people's children."

Eddie went to her and held the back of her head so that she could cry into his chest. He felt her cheekbones against his ribs, the hollowness of her eye sockets.

"What's on you?" she said.

He looked down at the ash on his shirt. It was too much to tell her. He didn't know what he should say. There was enough to deal with right there in front of them.

"I was in the woods," he managed, but he said it softly—a mumble—and the words didn't register.

"Go," she said. "You need to clean yourself off."

Eddie went gamely to the bathroom and turned the knob in the tub. He pounded on the opening of the faucet with the heel of his hand and waited. Then he sat on the edge of the tub and allowed his mind to wander.

She liked to bathe in the dark, and he would come in and flip the switch to brush his teeth and see the water flash in oscillating white plates above her body. He would see the tuft of her pubic hair floating like grass beneath the water.

The memory calmed him.

He remembered handing her towels and helping to pat her dry, feeling the warmth of her breasts and shoulders coming through the cloth. Smelling the cleanness of her skin.

He stood to collect himself—that was a different time from this. He peed a yellow stream into the toilet bowl. Without thinking, he flushed, and the water gulped down but didn't refill. He took the lid from off the tank and the ceramic scrape jarred him to attention like a bell. The tank was empty. His gut clenched. He should have saved the water from this tank, too.

There were wipes beneath the sink that they used on the porcelain, and he wiped his arms and face and the back of his neck. He took off his clothes and put them in a pile and got his chest and most of his back. Then he went into the bedroom and put on a fresh T-shirt and a pair of shorts. In the kitchen, Laura was quiet. She was sitting on a barstool, staring down into the marble of the counter. There was a bowl of fruit there, and Eddie took an apple and extended it beneath her face.

"Eat," he said.

"I'm not hungry."

"Just eat it."

There was a knock on the door, and Eddie put the apple down. Laura looked up at him, and he raised his hand for silence.

The knock came again.

He listened and could hear footsteps around the side of the house. From the kitchen window, he saw the top of someone's head. It was Bill Peters's head. He'd forgotten about Bill Peters. He watched the head through the windows. It moved around to the side of the house, and he heard the hollow sound the man's feet made on the wood of the back porch steps. The screen door groaned on its hinge and slammed as he walked across the boards. He knocked at the back door this time.

"I met him outside," Eddie said. He went to the door and looked back to Laura before he turned the knob. She lifted her eyebrows in a way that cautioned, but didn't tell him not to.

Eddie opened up a couple of inches.

"I'm here," said Bill Peters like a game show host. "Just like you said."

"Our water's still off," Eddie said. He moved his body fully in front of the opening in the door.

Bill Peters stuck the milk jug in the opening. "I'll take whatever. It doesn't have to be water. We just need to get something in him."

Eddie felt anger flood his body. He'd dealt with people like this before, petitioners who wouldn't take no for an answer, pressing him for donations until he was too flustered to deny them. "You know there's a grocery store a mile from here," he said.

"Have *you* been there? There's nothing on the shelves. I know they're human beings, but they're behaving like animals."

Eddie squeezed through the door, forcing Bill Peters back out onto the porch. He closed the door behind himself. When he spoke, his voice came out sharply.

"I need you to get away from my house," he said.

Bill Peters's face slackened. Then he smiled and shook his head. "I'm not trying to take advantage of you here," he said. "This is for my son. My son is sick, you understand? Are you a father?"

Eddie stared at him. His clothes were a huckster's clothes.

"I'll take you down to see him if you don't believe me," he said.

"That's not necessary."

He held up the jug. "Whatever you have," he said.

"Did you try anyone else?"

"No one else told me to come by their house. *You* told me that. I could tell you were a good man right away. You've got a good man's face."

"That was before I knew the extent of the outage."

"You have any juice or anything in the fridge? We normally give him apple juice."

The mention of apple juice pinched at Eddie's nerve. He felt briefly panicked and shifted in front of the door—as if protecting the apple juice they did, indeed, have in the fridge.

"We've got nothing," he said. "Go to the store and buy some juice. Get him to Holy Cross if you need to. They'll take care of him there."

"Fine," said Bill Peters. He crossed his arms over his chest so that the milk jug protruded from his armpit. "You're a liar, then."

"Leave, please."

"You're a liar and you feel bad about it, don't you? I've got a sick kid, and you're a healthy man. You should be ashamed."

"I've been patient with you," Eddie said. He felt his voice rise and tried to steady it. "We're all in this together. Just wait until they come."

"Your wife is in there, isn't she? Does she know she's married to a liar?" He came up close and tried to peer around Eddie.

Eddie caught his arm and turned him around. He pushed his hand into the small of Bill Peters's back. He hardly weighed anything at all. "Come on," Eddie said between his teeth.

Bill Peters stiffened as Eddie pushed him toward the screen door. At the top of the steps, he lifted at the man's collar and shoved. Bill Peters tripped and landed in a pile in the driveway.

He didn't get up, and he didn't turn his head to look at Eddie. He reached to pick at one of the desiccated day lilies that lined the asphalt and crushed the crisp flower in his fist. "I know where you live now," he said.

"What the hell is that supposed to mean?" Eddie called down to him.

"You know what it means."

There was a table on the porch where Eddie and Laura sometimes ate dinner in the twilight, and a thin glass vase where he put flowers. The vase was empty, and Eddie grabbed it by the neck. He let it dangle at his side as he stood at the top of the steps. Bill Peters got up. The jug had fallen into an azalea bush, and he retrieved it and went walking down the block. When he was a few houses away, he raised his middle finger in the air and held it up behind his head.

Eddie put the vase back on the table and went inside.

"You fought with him?" Laura said.

"He threatened us," Eddie said, immediately regretting it.

"What did he say?"

"He thought I was holding out on him, is all."

"That's not what he said."

"So if you know, why are you asking?"

"You could have filled up his bottle."

"Listen to me," he said. He put both hands on her shoulders. "Don't give away anything we have in the fridge."

"It's not like there are people lining up."

"Just don't. Promise me. Let's just save it until we see what happens." He went to the refrigerator and took out the bottle of juice. A quarter of it was left and he poured it into a glass.

"Here," he said. "Drink this."

"I thought we were saving it."

"Drink it."

"All the water's out, right?" she said. "I only tried the kitchen sink."

"Please."

He held the glass out to her and she took it and drank down the juice in big, vocal gulps.

"Okay," she said, finally breathing.

"We'll be fine until it comes back on."

"Wait," she said. She bunched her thumb and fingers and pressed them to her forehead. "The woman down the street."

"Who?"

She squeezed her eyes shut to concentrate.

"Mrs. Kasolos," she said.

"I'll check on her."

"We'll go together."

"Let me. I feel fine. Which one is it?"

"It's the one right on the corner. On our side of the street."

"And *how* do you know her?"

"I'll go if you don't want to."

"She knows you?"

"Eddie . . ."

He went outside and was buoyed by the sunlight. The sidewalk was as bright as a washed plate. There was no sign of anyone up the street.

He walked to the corner and knocked on Mrs. Kasolos's door.

Mrs. Kasolos called, "Who is it?" from deep inside.

"It's Ed Gardner," he said.

"Who?"

"Laura Gardner's husband. Eddie Gardner from up the street."

There was a muffled sound of footsteps on the other side of the door. The dead bolt thunked across.

She opened up a crack and stared at him.

"I'm just checking to see how you're doing," he said.

"Your wife thinks old people are cute, doesn't she? Tell her not to worry."

"You have things to eat?"

"I've been feeding myself for years."

"I mean, with the power out."

"I have a pork chop from Thursday that's still good. It takes me a while, but I'll eat it."

"How about to drink?"

"Come in here," she said.

She opened the door up fully, and Eddie stepped inside. There was a long dining room table padded with thick brown squares that lay askew. A bunch of bananas in a bowl sat on the table. A breakfront held a series of presidential plates in wooden stands, the largest of which had G. W. Bush's face painted on one half, G. H. W.'s face on the other. More plates—a row of them with blue Chinese designs—had been affixed to the wall.

"Look at that," she said. Her face soured, and she pointed to the other side of the room, as if identifying where it had been vandalized. Her finger shook as she held it up.

Eddie's eyes adjusted to the dim light. There was a water-cooler there.

"Oh," he said.

"That's five gallons. I have a man who comes to replace it every three weeks. They brought me an extra in the beginning, so I have one in the basement, too."

He stood there, silently, until she said, "Well?"

"If you need any help . . . my wife and I are right down the street."

"I have my daughter coming down. She lives in Burtonsville, but she checks on me."

"When is she supposed to come?"

"She's never on time. She works a job with the government and they run her to the ground."

"There's a lot of traffic. She might be held up."

"Tell your wife not to worry. I've survived worse. You don't get to be my age without being able to make it."

"I'll be back to check on you."

"Don't bother," she said.

"I'll be back."

BILL PETERS HAD been right. The grocery store was picked over. Sections of shelves were hollowed out where the sodas and sports drinks had been. There was still cereal. One of the aisles had suffered a fracturing of tomato sauce jars. Laura put an arm against his chest to hold him back.

"Glass," she pointed.

They each wore a backpack. "There's no milk?"

Laura shook her head.

It was like before a hurricane, but there wasn't any music. No children. Men and women moved through the aisles, staring up and down the shelves, pulling items based on private calculations, stuffing them into bags.

"Here," Eddie said. "Let's get these."

She helped him load some jars of pickled peppers. He took Spanish olives, too, and a glass bottle of apple cider vinegar.

"It doesn't seem like it's been long enough for this," she said.

"People are just being cautious."

"Or they know something. We should have tried the radio."

"I tried the radio. There's not even static."

"We should keep it on anyway. They have that emergency-broadcast thing."

"It's dead, Laura. How are we going to get an emergency-broadcast thing?"

She looked at him crossly. "Just forget it," she said.

There were still a few green bottles of lemon juice and Eddie took one of those. Beneath the water filters, the shelves were empty where the bottles of water should have been.

"Let's split up," he said.

There was meat in plastic wrap in the back, but when Eddie reached for it, there was nothing cool coming out of the refrigerating vents, and he left it where it was. A cardboard box sat just in front of the plastic flaps that led into the stockroom. It looked like someone had forgotten about it there. Eddie pulled off the clear tape and counted eighteen red juices in plastic bottles molded to look like little barrels. They had foil caps. He knelt beside the box and placed them one by one into his pack, stacking them so they wouldn't burst.

Laura was in the freezer aisle. The doors were hanging open.

"You think these will keep?" She held up a couple of pizza boxes.

"Maybe," Eddie said. "For a little while, anyway."

She put them in her pack, and he followed her to where she took a box of cheese crackers.

He gave her a can of whole mushrooms and a couple cans of beans. "Here, put these in," he said. There was a woman standing just behind them, staring at the empty space in the shelf where the beans had been. She wore a long nylon trench coat, and held on to the handle of a metal cart—a low wire basket on wheels—to support herself. Eddie took one of the cans of beans from Laura's pack and extended it to her. He assumed she spoke no English. He made a *Go on* motion with his chin.

The woman shook her head, and Eddie put the beans back on the shelf. When the woman didn't move, Laura took them and put them back into her pack.

"I'm running out of room," she said.

"We've got enough. I'll take one more lap."

He walked toward the hardware aisle and stopped in front of an endcap of insect products. The cans of wasp poison read: SPRAYS UP TO 22 FT. The nozzles looked like little megaphones. A gray-haired man the shape of a bell dropped four of them—one at a time—down his shirtfront. His midsection bulged in geometric shapes from all his shopping.

"What do you need all those for?" Eddie asked, but the man only stared at him, spooked, and scurried away.

Eddie put a can in each of the water bottle pouches at the side of his pack.

At the registers, Laura was leafing through a *Cosmo*. When she saw Eddie, she put it back in the rack.

"So, we're just taking all of this," she said.

"There's no one here to pay."

"They must have insurance."

"Everyone has insurance."

Outside, people walked across the lines in the parking lot. There were only a few cars and they looked abandoned.

Eddie took a bag of charcoal briquettes that had been stacked in a pile on top of a wooden pallet. He held it in both arms across his chest.

"To cook the pizzas," he said.

"We're going to feel ridiculous with all this junk when the power comes back on."

"It's not ridiculous to be prepared," Eddie said.

They crossed an empty street and walked along the sidewalk.

"You're limping," Laura said.

"I twisted my knee a little."

A couple rode a tandem bicycle down the center lane without their helmets on. The woman's blond hair streamed back behind her.

"Like they're on vacation," Laura said.

In their neighborhood, the sky was eggy-white and the heat was rising. Eddie saw a man standing down the hill, arms akimbo. He was tall in the way Bill Peters had been tall.

"Let's go this way," he said to Laura. He nudged her with the bag of briquettes and they made a left onto a side street. It was a longer way to go.

"Why?"

Thinking of the cyclists, Eddie said, "It's nice out, anyway."

THEY WERE IN front of the Davises' when Eddie saw the boy. He was stumbling through the street like a drunk, as gray as an early shadow. Eddie put the charcoal down.

It was like remembering a dream so clearly, it turned real.

"Who's this now?" Laura said.

Eddie flinched. He looked hard at Laura to see what she was seeing. That the boy *was* real. That he was standing right in front of them.

She went to him and Eddie followed. The boy's chest and shoulders were stained with ash. Laura touched his arm and then removed her fingers quickly, rubbing them together. The boy's hair looked spiky, Eddie saw, but it wasn't. It was singed.

"What are you doing out here, sweetheart?" Laura asked.

The boy looked at Eddie.

"Was there a fire?" Laura said.

The boy nodded his head.

"Where was it?"

"Laura—" Eddie said.

She turned to him so that the boy couldn't see her lips and whispered, "What are we going to do with him?"

"What do you mean?"

"We can't let him wander."

"He didn't get here without knowing his way back home. Were you playing in the woods by yourself?" Eddie said, sternly. "You need to stay with adults. Listen when they call you."

Laura kept her back to the boy, her face hard with concern. She said, "We can't just let him go."

Behind them, Mike Jr. came out and stood mutely against the end post of the Davises' chain-link fence. His little round face was white, and he stared at the boy as if into a tinted mirror. Mike Jr. was six. He held on to a five iron like it was a walking stick.

Eddie nodded at him. "You look after this guy for a minute," he said. "Teach him your golf swing."

Mike Jr. continued his vacant staring, and Eddie pulled Laura up their steps.

"What are we going to *do*?" she asked.

"Laura. He *belongs* to someone. We can't take him inside our house. We'll put the groceries away, and then I'll come out and help him find his parents."

"And what if his parents aren't back?" She set her jaw in a way that suggested the horrible consequences of Eddie's nearsightedness.

"What else can we do?" he said. "I'll walk him around the neighborhood."

"Turn around," she said, rummaging in his backpack. She pulled out one of the plastic barrels of juice and peeled the aluminum circle off the top, going back down to the sidewalk.

"Here," she said, handing it to the boy. "Drink this. It's okay. I'm not a stranger."

The boy took it in both hands and tipped it to his mouth. When he let up and breathed, his lip was red and the ash there was muddy.

They went inside and put the backpacks down on the kitchen table. Laura started putting things away.

Eddie reached to help, but she caught his wrist.

"I'll go around with him," she said.

"It's okay," he said. "I want to."

But when he went outside, the boy was gone.

Mike Jr. was still standing at the edge of the fence.

"What happened?" Eddie said.

"What?"

"You were supposed to be watching him."

"Who?"

"The other boy." In his mind, the other boy was Wemmick—his dimensions unknowable by anything but the most impenetrable vaults of his imagination—but, no, the boy had been standing right there. Laura had seen him, too. "Which way did he go?"

Mike Jr. pointed down the street, holding his hand outstretched, and Eddie went in that direction. The day was still quiet—the streets in the neighborhood bright and wide. He was halfway down the block before he turned around and hurried back.

"Mike Jr.," he said. "Let me borrow that."

Mike Jr. scowled and wrapped his arms around the golf club. "It's mine," he said.

"I'll bring it back. Promise."

Eddie grabbed the sticky black grip and struggled to tug it from the child's grasp. When he did, Mike Jr. said, "*Hey!*"

"I'll bring it back, all right?" he said. "Just be cool. Okay? Sit tight."

He walked and held the club by his side like a weapon, hot blood beating in his ears. He'd have been no less discreet dangling a shotgun.

The neighborhood was empty, and Eddie's mind was addled by the silence, the aloneness of the streets. It was useless. He wasn't looking for the boy, he realized. He was waiting for Bill Peters.

Hedges guarded yards from the street and threw long shadows. Even in this sun, there were blind corners. It wouldn't be hard for Bill Peters to conceal himself. Eddie could imagine him squatting with his jug, and gripped the golf club tighter.

Down another street, he saw a man standing behind a car with the hatchback open. He was making room inside the trunk.

Eddie rested the club on his shoulder like a Sunday morning golfer, and went to the man as if he'd been called, catching his attention. The man stood up straight.

He was loading camping equipment: a frame pack and a sleeping bag cinched tightly with webbing.

"You got power?" Eddie asked.

The man slammed the trunk, and when he turned back around, there was a Buck knife in his hand.

Eddie laid the club on the street and backed away from it. He held up his hands. "I was just walking by," he said. "I'm going."

"No," the man said. "No—ha—it's not for that." He rolled the knife over in his hand and considered the blade. "I've got knives I haven't opened in years. They're rusty. I'm just checking." He had a gray mustache and the kind of fat muscles developed with protein shakes. He folded the knife and pressed it behind him into his back pocket.

"No power, then?" Eddie said.

"No power here or anywhere. I came up from the city. That's where all the crews are." His face began to exert itself a little around the edges. "It's hell down there already," he said.

"I imagine they'll be up here soon."

"You hear any sirens? Let me know if you do. They're all in the city. People here are in a state of emergency, too—trust me—but what do we get? Nothing. They leave all the good folks out here to rot. What kind of America is this where you buy a house and pay your taxes and no one comes to help?"

"I heard a helicopter."

"Yeah? Which way was it heading?"

"South."

"Into the city."

"They'll come back," Eddie said. "The electric people will be here soon."

"Shit they will."

"Where are you going?"

"My brother lives up in Shepherdstown."

"You won't make it north," Eddie said. "The roads are blocked."

"I'll hike it if I have to," he said. "I'm not waiting around."

"He's got power up there, you think?"

"He's got a bunker. He's prepared. I'm too damn stupid to have one myself."

"But you were here in oh-eight? I heard it was out six days. It'll come back on."

"In oh-eight nothing blew up. We had water."

Eddie felt the quiver in the man's face enter his own lips and arms and knees. "What blew up?" he said.

The man smiled in a patronizing way. "Nothing, kid," he said. "Just wait here for everything to be okay."

"I saw the stream," Eddie said. "That's what you mean, right? There was a fire."

"Where were you?" the man asked, his mouth tightening.

"Right up the street. At the spillway. And underneath the Beltway bridge."

"That makes sense." He folded his arms behind his back and Eddie flinched. But the knife stayed in his pocket. "I got a call from my brother right before we lost the signal. He's got his pilot's license; he calls me from the plane. He saw the whole Potomac do it, the whole river go up." He smiled again, relaying this news.

"It isn't funny," Eddie said, keeping his voice under control.

"No. It's not."

"Did you see it in the city?"

"What?"

"The water burn."

"I didn't see it there, no."

"Then you don't know what really happened."

"*You* saw it. *You* saw beneath the bridge. Just pack a bag and get out. Don't you know anyone?"

"The electric people will come here when they're finished in the city."

The man closed the trunk of his car, locked it, and turned to go back inside his house. "If you say so," he said.

"Did you see a little boy?" Eddie asked. "All burned up? I mean like all . . . ashy?" He rubbed his thumbs across his fingers as if the ash was on them. "He was down by the stream, I think."

"What was he, fishing? There must be a real fish fry down there," he said, smiling again. "I don't like mine blackened, though." Then, more soberly, he said, "No, I didn't see any boy."

He went up the walk and into his house and left Eddie to the silence of the street again. Eddie picked the golf club back up.

When he returned home, Mike Jr. had gone inside. Eddie leaned the club against the chain-link fence.

He heard voices coming from the back.

Mike Sr. was talking to Laura there.

Eddie liked Mike Sr. He owned a landscaping business and sometimes brought ornamental plants home for Eddie and Laura to plant in their yard. They had a miniature Japanese maple next to the walk that had already doubled in size. He saw it there now. It looked the same as it had the day before. The man with the Buck knife hadn't witnessed anything. People would believe anything when they were scared.

"You got him home?" Laura asked as Eddie came around. She was talking about the boy, but Eddie looked at Mike Sr. instead of answering her.

"Welcome back!" Eddie said.

"Yeah, yeah, I made it," Mike Sr. said. "I had to leave my truck in Virginia, though."

Laura stepped closer to Eddie.

"You got him home?" she whispered.

He nodded.

"Really?"

"Yeah." Eddie squeezed her hand because of the way she was staring.

To Mike Sr., he said, "It's blocked all the way down in Virginia? That's why it's taking them so long. What a mess."

"Or because they're incompetent shits," he said. "We were out for six days in two thousand eight. They just aren't prepared, is what it is."

"Do you have supplies?" Laura said. "We just got some things."

"Oh, you were out there looting with the rest of them?" Mike Sr. laughed.

Eddie could feel the heat of Laura's blush. "There's no one working," she said. "I'm making a list of what we took."

"I'm kidding. Ed, can you give me a quick hand with something? I might be able to solve some of our problems."

He followed Mike Sr. into his basement stairwell. Inside, it was dark and full of junk, but there was fresh lumber framing the walls, and the junk was stacked up in an orderly way.

Eddie said, "I just met one of these survivalist types. He lives right up the street."

"What, he's got a year's worth of canned peas? I'd rather die."

"Maybe it's smart."

"Living in a hole in the ground? No. This is smart. Get over here." Sometimes he spoke to Eddie as though Eddie were a child. There was a workbench at the other end of the basement, and he bent down beneath it and took out a black case the size of a lunch box.

"If stuff gets crazy, you two are welcome to stay with us." He thumbed the numbers on the lock and popped the clasps open. There was a silver handgun in a foam cutout. "Just a burglar alarm," he said. "One that really goes boom."

"What'd you see out there?" Eddie said.

"It's bad. I'm not going to let on in front of your wife or mine, but I can be straight with you. It'll settle down, but it's bad right now."

"I saw some stuff, too," Eddie said.

"Let's just say I'm glad it was *me* who got stuck that far away. I don't know what I woulda done if Patty and Mike Jr. had been along."

"Laura had to walk home on the Beltway. I was really worried."

"Here," Mike Sr. said. "Let's take this up." He pinched a tarp off a pile in the corner. There was a generator underneath. Eddie took the black bar on one side, and Mike Sr. picked up the other, and together, they humped it up the steps. When they had it next to the house, Laura was still standing there. She'd reached across her chest to grab her elbow. It wasn't like her to stand around. Mike Sr. unscrewed the gas cap and said,

"Yep." Then he ripped the cord a few times. It whined, but only weakly. He ripped it again. Then a few times more. "Shit on it," he said. "I *thought* maybe it was busted."

"We're about to cook some pizza on our grill," Laura said. "You're all invited."

Eddie went back around the fence and poured in the briquettes. He had some lighter fluid in a dented can, and sprayed it on before throwing in a match. In the rush of flame, the pleasantness of summer returned to him, and when the coals were hot and low, he put the pizzas on the grate. Mike Jr. came outside with a Wiffle ball and a plastic bat. Seeing him there with his smudged face, he could forget that the other boy had come by.

"You're gonna hit the ball with me?" Mike Jr. said.

He stood on the sidewalk with the bat cocked over his shoulder, and Eddie walked down and threw the ball to him. When he made contact, it went knuckling into the street. He *was* a good little athlete.

"You get it now," Mike Jr. said.

"*I* get it? You're the one who hit it."

"Yeah, but. *You.*"

Mike Sr. cracked a beer. He was sitting on his porch stairs watching them. "You better go on and get that ball," he said to his son, and Mike Jr. scampered into the street.

When the pizzas were ready, Eddie brought out the cutting board and sliced them into wedges. He took five of the barrel-shaped juices from his backpack. Mike Sr. and Patty had some patio furniture, and they sat outside and ate. The evening cooled a little, and a couple of the stroller-moms passed by on the sidewalk.

"I might take a walk up the street later and check on some of the neighbors," Mike Sr. said. "If you want to join me."

"Okay," Eddie said.

When they were finished with the pizza, Patty brought out ice cream and poured it into bowls. They slurped it up like soup.

EDDIE AND LAURA sat on their sofa as the sun faded outside. He thought of Mrs. Kasolos—that jug of water she had in the basement.

She was a tough old bird, he thought. He wouldn't be able to live alone at her age. Just getting the pots from the stove to the sink. It took a certain kind of person to last that long.

She certainly didn't need another five-gallon jug of water just sitting in her basement. Eddie would go to her if the water didn't come back on soon.

Laura was reading a copy of *Field & Stream* that had been sent to their house as a promotion.

"Why are you reading that?" he said.

She didn't move her eyes from the pages. "There's an article about gophers."

If Eddie held on to the jug for Mrs. Kasolos, it would be safer, and he could move it around, for one thing. No way she was lifting forty pounds up those stairs. She wasn't *that* tough.

"Mrs. Kasolos has more than enough to drink over there," he said. "I think I'll find a jar or something and have her fill it."

"We should be the ones helping *her*," she said. "Please don't take anything from that old woman."

"Okay," he said. "But she has extra she doesn't need."

Laura went back to reading, but the image of the jug floated in Eddie's mind. The more he pushed it down, the more it bobbed back up to the surface.

If he wasn't the one to get it, it would be somebody else. In his mind, that person had no form. But then he saw it was a man. It was Bill Peters. Eddie could see him doing it. He could see him pushing his way in, babbling on about his son.

"I'm going to take that walk with Mike Sr.," Eddie said.

"Okay."

"It'll be good to know what's going on."

She moved on the sofa in a way that suggested she was coming with him, but Eddie put his hand on her shoulder to keep her there.

"I think he wants it to be just me and him. You know how Mike Sr. can be."

"That's silly," she said, but slid back to a comfortable spot.

"I don't want you to worry. You've got Patty right there if you need anything."

"I'm not worried," she said.

He went to the basement and took the flashlight off the workbench. Then he went to the shelf and held Laura's silver pom-pom to his face. He breathed it in again, as if he could find traces of her there. Still, there was nothing. Then he squeezed it in both of his fists and pulled until some of the strands strained and disconnected. It was a strange feeling. He held the severed strands between his thumb and forefinger, examining them as though they were a memento of her having once been young. He put them in his pocket.

"I'll be back soon," he said at the door. "Don't worry about me."

No one was out next door and he walked past the Davises' with his breath held in.

At Mrs. Kasolos's there was no response, and he went around knocking on the windows. When he got to the backyard, he heard her voice through the wall. "What in the hell?" she said.

"I'll go to the front!" he hollered.

She was wearing a thin nightgown, the kind that Eddie's own mother had worn, and she spoke very loudly—as though she'd never seen him before: "I don't know what to tell you! I don't have anything for you!"

"It's Laura Gardner's husband," Eddie said. He made his voice as loud as hers. "I'm Eddie Gardner. Remember? I checked on you before?"

"I'm waiting for my daughter," she said.

"Did you eat?"

"What the hell do you care?"

"I'm going to help you move that water upstairs. You said you had water in the basement? From the watercooler people?"

"I need it for my daughter."

"I'm going to bring it up the steps for you in case you need it," he said. "Can I come in?"

"Come in, don't come in. I don't care."

It was hard to see inside; the walls and furniture were the same brown color.

"Down here?" he said, tapping on the door at the other side of the living room.

"That's my basement down there."

She shuffled past him into the kitchen, and Eddie opened the basement door. He clicked on his flashlight. The stairs creaked beneath his weight with a wooden springiness that threatened to launch him forward into the dim space below. He wondered when she'd been down there last. If she were to try it now, she'd fall to her death. The uneasiness he'd felt at being in her home had settled into resolve. It was important to help old people, however set they were in their ways.

When his eyes adjusted, he saw the pale blue jug sitting by itself on the cement floor. He hefted it to his chest and made his way back up the stairs again, setting it down against the wall beside the watercooler.

"Mrs. Kasolos?" he said. He walked through the kitchen and stood in front of the bathroom door. He heard the clink of something hard on porcelain. "You okay in there?"

She was moving around. He could hear that much.

In the living room, he examined the jug already installed in the cooler, no more depleted than it had been earlier in the day.

"Mrs. Kasolos?" he called.

Even if her daughter came, they wouldn't need ten gallons of water. A woman her age—she probably didn't need more than a couple cups a day.

He lifted the jug from the floor and shouldered it, walking outside and down the steps. By then it was dark and the shadows were as thick as curtains beneath the trees, but he kept the flashlight in his pocket. He sat the jug by the side of the house among the bushes. Then he walked around in both directions to make sure he was alone. He was sweating and thirsty, and thought of going back inside and taking a coffee mug right out of the kitchen cabinet and filling it at the cooler . . . but what was in the cooler was hers, he thought—there was enough in there to keep her safe, and he would leave what was left alone.

He stood there in Mrs. Kasolos's dark yard. Laura would expect him back soon, but she wouldn't start worrying if he was gone a little longer. She wouldn't allow the jug in their house, no matter how much he explained. That much he knew. She'd make him give it back.

He hoisted it back onto his shoulder and walked, following the sidewalks until he saw that they revealed themselves too brightly in the moonlight. He walked on the dead grass of the lawns instead. The bubble in the jug slid back and forth in the corner of his vision as it leveled and unleveled with his progress.

He'd go into the woods and hide it in the park. It would be safe there, and when the water came back on it wouldn't matter. No one would know he'd even taken it. The park was less than a quarter mile away, but his shoulder ached beneath the jug, and when he reached the aluminum rails that marked the entrance, he was relieved to set it on the ground. It didn't feel as though he were down the street from his house. It felt as if he'd been on a journey—as if he'd left Laura behind long ago. He stuck a hand into his pocket and squeezed the plastic strands of her pom-pom. All he had to do was hide the jug. Then he could walk back up the hill and he'd be home again.

He set the jug back on his shoulder and clicked the flashlight on, walking slowly to keep from tripping over the roots and stones along the path. Still, his ankles gave way and pinched, and he teetered and had to grab hold of trees with his free hand. He tried to concentrate to keep from slipping, but his head buzzed. Only when he reached the bank of the stream, where the trees were charred and the ash was getting into his shoes, was he thinking clearly again.

This was the stream that flowed over the spillway, and he crossed the sand of the bed and climbed the bank on the opposite shore. From his pocket, he pulled three of the silver strands, affixing them in the crust of a burnt tree trunk. He swung the flashlight quickly in front of him. At the edge of the flashlight's arc, the strands glinted silver and white where they'd crimped. He would be able to find them again if he walked along the bank and shone his light. The woods were big and deep here and already he had to remind himself of the way he'd come.

He climbed up the slope and walked back among boulders larger than himself, finding three trees so close together they made a kind of fence. Behind it was a hollow place full of ash and sand, and he placed the jug down and tore at the ground with his fingers until he'd unearthed a deep enough trench. He laid the jug in and buried it, and then crossed the streambed and tucked three more silver strands beneath a low rock there.

He walked back to the street and stretched his shoulders, looking up into the night sky. It was not hard to imagine that he was lost between the reflection of the stars and the concrete beneath his feet—though whether he'd projected himself into space, or it had cast itself down on him, was not as clear. He stooped and rubbed his hands in the grass of one of the yards to get the ash from between his fingers.

IT WAS NOT yet late when they went to bed, and Eddie touched the inside of Laura's thigh.

"I feel too grimy," she said, but she relented. He held on tightly to both of her shoulders, their backs to the window, and when he was done, she said, "If it's all the way in Virginia, my parents' power could be out, too."

"That's the other direction," he said.

"We don't know how far it goes."

"There's a bridge between us and them."

"So what does that mean?" she said.

Through the window, they could hear people talking on the street. Eddie felt his heart quicken. He couldn't make out the words and didn't recognize the voices. He swung out of bed and pulled on some boxers. He moved quietly to the office, standing still in the middle of the room, listening for sounds in the backyard. But there were no sounds coming from there.

"What are you doing?" Laura called.

"Give me a second."

If Bill Peters was in the yard, Eddie would be able to hear him. There wasn't much insulation in the walls—in the daytime, he could hear the squirrels jumping branches.

"I'm going outside," he said.

He had a wooden bat that he kept in the corner of the office that he'd joked with Laura was for "protection."

"What are you going to do out there?" she asked, but he didn't answer.

He took the flashlight and went down the back steps very softly. He didn't turn the flashlight on.

On the grass of the back lawn, he smelled the overripe honeysuckle on the Davises' bush. The ground was soft enough beneath his flip-flops that his knee didn't hurt. The yard was empty, though he could still hear the chatter down the street.

Something snapped behind him, and he knew it was a man.

He spun and fumbled with the flashlight and felt the nearness of the footfalls as they passed him, the heat of a body, and the wind it stirred up. Tools crashed at the side of the house, and the beam illuminated the fabric of a shirt.

"Hey!" Eddie shouted, but he stood planted where he was. His heart was doing something strange to the gravity in his chest.

He hurried inside and took Laura's wrist to pull her out of bed. He didn't want to leave her alone in there.

"What?" she said. "What?"

They walked down the street in their nightclothes, Laura in a T-shirt and boxer shorts. They could hear the voices before they saw the group of people. It was just a block away. Patty was there. Eddie could see her outlines even in the dark.

"Someone was just in my yard," he said. The words came out too loudly and stopped the neighbors' chatter.

He was lucky Patty was there. "High school kids," she said, in a way that made it clear she knew him, that he hadn't been accusing *them* of being in his yard. "It happened in oh-eight, too. They ran a little wild. They broke into my car and took the change out of the console. I had CDs in there, but they didn't touch those."

"They didn't like your music!" someone quipped.

Patty laughed until it turned into a smoker's cough. "Ah, screw you," she said.

"Any of you have water yet?" Eddie said.

"No,"one of them said.

"Did anyone try the police?"

The cluster of bodies was just a darker patch on the street.

"The power must have done something at the pumping station."

"That didn't happen before?" Laura's shoulder was close enough to rub against him. Their hands brushed.

"No, and I been here twenty years," said a man whose voice was pitched as if by nose plugs. "Anybody fill their bathtub?"

"Did *you?* Who saw this coming?"

In the darkness, their conversation floated untethered around Eddie.

"I'm just worried about Mrs. Kasolos. She's eighty-five now."

"I'll check on her," one of them said.

"My husband already did," Laura said. "She's okay."

"She has a watercooler," Eddie said. "It's almost full."

There was a silence as they contemplated Mrs. Kasolos's cooler.

"You know what the cops told me after those robberies on Keswick?" Patty said. "Don't do anything stupid like leave your doors unlocked. Well, duh."

"But the cops aren't around now," Eddie said.

"I've been here twenty years and I've never called the cops once," the nasal voice said. "So what's your point? This is a good neighborhood. Go to sleep, and when you wake up everything'll be back to normal. They got crews for this sorta thing. They learned their lessons in oh-eight."

"I just think we should protect ourselves, is all," Eddie said. "People act differently when they're desperate."

"Who's desperate? You've got a roof over your head. Trust me. This is not desperate."

Patty turned her shadow to address Eddie and Laura for the benefit of the others. Even in the dark, he could tell that she was smiling. "You two can bunk with me and the Mikes if you want."

Someone said, "Oh, now it's an open invitation?"

"I didn't say *you*, Paul," Patty said, and the mood was light again.

Back in their yard, Eddie took Laura around and waved the flashlight over the grass. Having her with him settled his nerves. When the beam passed over the side of the house, he saw that his shovel and rake had been toppled. He didn't say anything, and she hadn't asked him what he'd meant when he told the group that someone had been in their yard.

"The guy was right," she said. "Let's just go to bed. We're exhausted. *I'm* exhausted. Let them do their work."

"Who?"

"The electric people. The water people."

He walked ahead of her up the stairs. "What did you see after you left your car?" he asked.

"What?" she said, and then added, "Nothing. People walking. Why? What did *you* see?"

"That's all you saw? People walking?"

She gripped the rail, and he saw the strength in her arm. *She* was built like a track star. "Why?" she said. "If you saw something, you can tell me."

"I didn't see anything. You said you saw a fight."

"Just the one lady who got mad at that kid."

"That's it?"

"Yeah."

"I guess a lot of people were walking into the city," he said. "Their tempers got the best of them."

"Yeah," she said.

They went inside and got back into bed.

Laura said, "It's okay to leave the window open. I'm hot already."

"We *usually* leave the window open."

"I just mean . . . if you're nervous about anything."

"I'm not nervous. It'd be hard to break in through that window. We're right here."

"I know."

But it made him think about the window in the back door, the one he'd broken with the rock. He'd never patched it up. Whoever had been in the yard could have doubled back.

"Hold on," he said to Laura. He took the flashlight and walked into the basement, poking the beam around where they stored their boxes. He kicked at the base of one to see if anything made a sound, but it was just the sound of a box being kicked. They kept an old mattress leaned against the wall, and he lifted it away. There were some plastic bags behind it and some dust bunnies.

He tore a cardboard flap off one of the boxes and went back upstairs to the kitchen and ripped a length of duct tape. He pressed the piece of cardboard up against the busted pane.

When he went back into the bedroom, she'd lit a tea candle and placed it on the dresser. Eddie told her about the window. He was ashamed of himself for breaking it.

"I saw that it was broken," she said. "I mean . . . I knew. When did you do it?"

Eddie thought about that. "When I first got back. When was that?"

"Yesterday."

"You weren't here and I left my keys in the car, I think."

"It's okay."

"You didn't say anything about it," he said.

"No," she said.

"What did Mike Sr. say to you? When he first got back?"

"He didn't say anything to me."

He thought about that. "How's your head?" he said.

"My head is fine."

"You don't have a headache? Not even a dull one?"

"No."

He went into the kitchen and took one of the juices in the plastic barrels off the counter.

"Here," he said, peeling back the foil for her. "Drink this."

"I'm okay."

"You're dehydrated."

"What about you?"

"I'll have some, too."

Eddie's head was pounding.

Laura drank half of it down and handed it back to him. It left a red crescent on her upper lip. Eddie took a bottle of ibuprofen out of his nightstand and drank down three of the pills.

"Okay?" she said.

"Yeah."

She blew out the candle and joined him lying down in bed. Eddie could still hear the neighbors talking in the street.

"A meeting of the minds down there," he said.

"Don't get mad."

After a while, she said, "I remember when Hurricane Andrew hit Florida. I was driving in the car with my dad, and we were listening to the forecast. They were saying how terrible it was going to be and my dad said, 'There's going to be a lot of destruction and people are going to die, but it's also going to be a little exciting.' He told me it was okay if I got excited."

"They're keeping everybody awake, though."

"Everybody but us is out there."

Eddie tried to hear past the side of the house into the backyard. But all he heard were the voices in the street. It wasn't long before Laura was breathing deeply. He could feel the ash on his body where he hadn't been able to wipe it away. When he ran a fingernail across his eyelid, it was filmy. He was falling asleep, too, and sleep came softly and soundlessly.

The ash had filled his ears. He was walking through it in the cold. Snow had piled up, and in the spreading landscape of it, he saw the flash of Bill Peters's shirt. He swung a flashlight and it illuminated the white of Bill Peters's face. It was Bill Peters rushing toward him.

He woke and couldn't breathe, not knowing whether to suck in or push out. He sat up, coughing. Laura was silent next to him.

When he touched her side, his breath came back. "Hey," he said, and she groaned a little.

He took the flashlight and quietly got out of bed. He went to the basement and looked behind the boxes again. Then he looked behind the mattress and shone the beam around the furnace, too. There were some old pieces of plywood in the furnace room, and he took a short piece and some screws and his drill. When he tested the drill, it whirred, but not convincingly. Upstairs, there was just enough juice to screw it over the broken pane, but the screws didn't go all the way in. There was a space, too, where he could still see a strip of the cardboard taped beneath.

He found his phone on the table by the front door. If he could get the police, he'd tell them a man named Bill Peters had tried to force himself into his house. His phone was dead, though. He picked up Laura's. It was alive, but the screen had an uninterrupted photo of the two of them at Broadkill Beach: no bars of service or the AT&T insignia cutting through them. He dialed 911 and hit SEND, but it never even went to CALLING.

He took another juice and swallowed a few more ibuprofen pills. There were ten juices left.

In the bedroom, he shook Laura's shoulder. "Hey," he said. "I'm lighting up the candle."

He dragged his thumb over the lighter, and she sat up in the shadows that it made. She was frowning. Pieces of hair were plastered to her cheek.

"Drink the rest of this," he said.

She closed her eyes and made a sour face.

"Come on," he said. "You've barely had anything."

"I had one with dinner, too."

"That's not enough."

"I'm going back to sleep." She slid down and tucked her head beneath the pillow.

"Fine," he said. "Make sure you have one in the morning."

He tipped the juice to his mouth and drank the rest of it. It was sweet syrup, only a few big mouthfuls' worth, meant for children's picnics. It nauseated him a bit.

IN THE MORNING, he went to the shower and tried the handle for hot water. Then he set all his dumb hopes on cold.

"*Fuck*," he said, hoping that she'd hear. He banged the sink handle up and down, up and down.

They ate dry cereal and each drank a juice.

"If I have another of these, I'm going to be sick," Laura said. She opened and closed her mouth dramatically, letting her tongue make a sticking sound.

"What are our options? You'd rather have that lemon juice in the fridge? We've got a bottle of it."

There was a knock at the door, and when Eddie flinched, his chair legs squeaked against the kitchen floor. He held up both his hands, palms facing the floor, as if to say, *Quiet. Stay put.*

Laura sat where she was, and Eddie went to the office for the bat, deciding how he'd hold it. He stood in front of the door, and then leaned the bat against the wall. He'd only have to bend down a little if he needed it.

Outside were two men. The one standing at the door had a face pink from shaving. Behind him, a second man was supporting the arms of a wheelbarrow. It had half a gallon of orange juice and a blue-tinted water bottle with liquid at the bottom. There were five or so bottles of water with the seals unbroken, too.

"Hello, there," said the pink-faced man. Eddie could smell the bathroom chemicals on his gleaming cheeks. "We're making the rounds, collecting whatever people can give for the elderly families on the block. The Cartwrights, for example."

"The Cartwrights?"

"They were there last night. We had a conversation? I'm Paul?" the man said. "We met you on the street."

"Right," Eddie said.

Laura stood beside him. "And you're collecting these for who, exactly?"

"We've got elderly people all over this neighborhood. A lot of them don't have family nearby, not that they could even get here anyway. Some of us who've lived here a long time just want to make sure they're okay."

"And people are giving you things to drink?" Laura said.

"If they have it."

"And what are *they* drinking?"

"If you're young and you've got your health, you're lucky. You'll be okay until they get this stuff worked out. I'm not saying to give me everything you have."

The man behind him spoke up. Eddie had thought he'd stooped to hold the wheelbarrow, but now he saw he'd let it go—that his back was hunched. He wore suspenders. Whatever Paul projected, this second man balanced out. His cheeks were loose and stubbly. "Shouldn't be more than a few hours till everything's back and running," he said. "Until then, we just want to make sure our neighbors are okay."

"How about *I* take it to them?" Laura said to him. "I mean, what I have to give."

"Sure," Paul said. "You can just follow us there."

"Why don't I just take it to them directly? The Cartwrights? I think I know where they are."

Eddie put his hand on her arm, as if to keep her from making good on the idea right then. "It doesn't make sense for you to go," he said. "They have the barrow."

To Paul, he said, "We'd help if we could. I guess we didn't plan very well."

"No one planned for this," Paul said, still smiling.

"It's okay," Laura said. She went back to the kitchen and brought back four of the juices. Eddie met her a few feet in front of the door and tried to hedge her back. "We don't have any to give," he said.

"We do," she said. She held up the juices by their lids, two in each hand. "These."

She walked past him, down the walk, and put them in the wheelbarrow. The hunched man reorganized his feet and grunted.

"We'll let you know if you can be of more assistance," Paul said. The other man hoisted the wheelbarrow and the two of them walked next door to the Davises' house.

"No way Mike Sr. gives them anything," Eddie said.

"Eddie, it's for our neighbors. They're old. What's the big deal?"

"Have the Cartwrights ever said hello to you on the street? Would they recognize you if you knocked on their door?"

"It's our responsibility to help *them*, not the other way around."

"You sound like such a saint."

"It's done, okay? Just drop it."

The house was heating up, and his headache hadn't gone away. When he went into the bathroom, he pissed an amber color.

The last beer in the fridge was almost cool. He poured it into two whiskey glasses. Laura was lying on the couch, reading the *Field & Stream*, and Eddie put one of the glasses down on the table in front of her.

"That doesn't seem like a good idea," she said.

"It's cool, at least."

They drank their half a beer. Eddie sat across from her in a reclining chair. He closed his eyes, but his thinking wasn't clear. He balanced there between wakefulness and sleep. It was difficult—as difficult as real balancing—and it only tired him further. When he slept, he was at the edge of the embankment, beside the highway. The snow was so thick between the trees that he had to hold them to keep from sinking. There were voices behind him, in the woods. "Don't tell," they said. "There's a reward." Eddie took deep steps through the snow. He tried not to sweat. If he started to sweat, he knew he would freeze.

"Come on," said the man in the flannel shirts. He had no face, no hair. Just a mouth, though Eddie couldn't really see what kind of mouth it was. "*Wemmick*," Eddie said to him. Wemmick held out his hand and Eddie took it.

"I thought you were dead," Wemmick said.

When he opened his eyes, he saw that Laura had fallen

asleep, too. She was spread out on the couch with the magazine on her chest.

"Maybe I should check on the cars," he said.

"No," she said without opening her eyes. "What good would that do?"

"Maybe mine's cleared out."

"Maybe."

"I should go."

"Do you have the energy for that?"

"It's my *car*, Laur."

She rocked her head back and looked up, as if she were exasperated with the ceiling. "I understand that. But getting home was hell. I can't imagine doing it two more times. There and back if it's still stuck."

"I thought you said you didn't see anything. What do you mean it was hell?"

"The only thing bad I saw was you throwing someone down the steps. That's all I saw."

"What are you talking about? I didn't throw him down the steps. I was trying to get him out of our house. If you force someone down the steps, it looks like throwing."

"Fine," Laura said. "What would you take with you on this journey to get your car? We'd need to bring supplies."

"You just gave our supplies away."

She flipped her legs around and sat up on the couch. "It'll be easier once they fix the power."

They ate uncooked hot dogs with mustard for lunch. Laura didn't think you could eat them raw, but Eddie said you could. They each drank a juice. Through the kitchen window, they could see Mike Jr. with the golf club. He was hacking at the grass in the manner of someone splitting wood. Eddie knocked on the glass.

"Now you've done it," Laura said.

Mike Jr. spun around, looking for the source of the knocking.

Eddie opened the window. "Over here, bonehead," he said.

Mike Jr. squinted at them. "Eddie!" he said. In a moment, they could hear him coming up the steps, and Eddie opened the back door.

"What do *you* want?" Eddie said.

"Ah," said Mike Jr., catching on to the ribbing. He was smiling with his mouth wide-open. There was brown sauce on his face.

"I bet I can guess what you had for lunch," Laura said.

"Barbecue," Mike Jr. said.

"Why are you beating up the ground with that golf club?" Eddie said.

"I dunno."

"C'mere. Let me show you how."

He led him back outside and picked the club up off the grass. "First, you've got to hold it right," he said. He took Mike Jr.'s hand and put it around the club with his index finger pointing down the shaft. He put his other hand so that it gripped the finger.

"Now, you've gotta swing through," Eddie instructed, standing beside him and making the gesture. "Wait!" he said, anticipating Mike Jr.'s backswing. "Let me get out of the way."

He stepped back and a fatigue enveloped him. Something cinched down hard on his lungs. He couldn't breathe. He had to bend and put his hands on his knees.

Mike Jr. swung and hit the ground. The club shivered out of his hands, end over end.

Eddie looked up. The air was coming in again.

Mike Jr. ran to retrieve the club.

"Good," Eddie said, standing up straight, regaining himself. "Let's do it again." He helped him with the grip. He was breathing fine. The air was close, but he was okay. He found the Wiffle ball lying at the base of some ornamental grasses. "Now try it with this." The grasses were brown, but maybe they were supposed to be. Eddie couldn't remember what they'd looked like before. He set up the ball and backed off beneath a mulberry tree at the edge of the yard. The branches drooped low, and Eddie grabbed one between his fingers. The leaves were as loose as dead skin. The light green undersides had curled up and around, making them look inside out. The same thing was happening to the leaves on the oak. Mike Jr. swung and clicked the Wiffle ball in a miraculous arc that landed in the street. He put a hand to his forehead, gazing into the distance the way Mike Sr. must have taught him.

"Yeah, yeah," Eddie said. "Beginner's luck."

Across the street, a group of teenagers was walking through the front yards of his neighbors as if the sidewalk went straight through their lawns. They stepped on flower beds and broke through bushes. They held on to one another. Two girls laughed and doubled over in the way Eddie had seen girls laugh and double over when leaving bars in college. Something flashed in the sun. One of the boys held a knife—a long silver triangle.

"Get over here," Eddie said. He walked Mike Jr. up the

Davises' front porch and knocked on the door. Patty answered and cradled Mike Jr. to her side by palming his head. "He making trouble?"

"No. Just playing golf."

"Hotter than hell out here," she said.

"Everything's wilting," Eddie said.

She looked down at Mike Jr. "You gotta stay inside where it's cool, little man."

"Is it cool in there?"

"Cooler than out here. Not really, though. I'm sweating like a hog."

"Did you give those guys anything when they came with the wheelbarrow?"

"We've got Mike Jr. to think about," she said, and when he heard his name, Mike Jr. maneuvered his head from under her hand and smiled up at his mother. "They'll be okay. Can't be much longer now. The power company must have gotten a thousand complaints."

Eddie went back inside his house and took the knife block off the kitchen counter, placing it on the floor beside the bookcase. It was inconspicuous there. Laura was in the bedroom.

"Let's go to the stream," she said. She stood with one arm up the doorjamb and canted her hips in a saucy way.

"Why?" Eddie said.

"We'll take a dip. It's roasting."

"You know how dirty that water is?"

"How?"

"That trail follows sewage pipes. Whenever they leak, guess where it goes. Not to mention the runoff from all of this." He twirled a finger at the ceiling to indicate the network of suburban streets.

"We can go down and see what's there, at least."

"If you can't swim in it, you don't want to drink it. I think that's a rule."

"Just for the walk, then."

"You can go. I was just out there. It's a million degrees."

"Fine," she said. "I can't sit around here all day."

She went into the bedroom, and when she came back she was wearing shorts and a brown bikini top. Eddie thought of the burnt streak in the sand at the bottom of the stream and how the ash had piled in the spillway.

"Don't," he said. He held her and could feel the delicate bones interlocking in her shoulder. Her skin was smooth and warm. "Please. It feels like we should just sit tight."

"What makes it feel like that?"

"There were kids outside. Just now."

"So what?"

"High school kids or something. I think they were drunk. They go down to the stream to drink. I've seen their empties there. One of them had a knife."

"You think they're going to mess with me? Don't worry, Eddie. I'll defend the family honor."

"Why look for trouble?"

"Eddie, this is ridiculous."

"It's ridiculous? Really? You want to go take a dip in our local cesspool."

"People fish in it."

"They don't eat what they catch."

There was a scuff of footsteps on the front walk, and Eddie

waited for a knock to follow. The air in the room seemed to suspend them where they were. When the knock came, Eddie let his breath go out.

Paul was standing on their doorstep. His face was dour and he'd clasped his hands behind his back. The second man with the wheelbarrow wasn't with him. Bill Peters was with him. He stood down on the sidewalk, looking up at Eddie. He wore a head bandage like a Civil War casualty—gauze wrapped around his ears.

Paul said, "Did you assault this man?" His eye contact was severe.

Eddie let a short laugh escape him. "No," he said. "I didn't assault him."

"He says you did."

"Paul," Eddie said. "What are you doing here?"

"Did you *assault* this man?" he said again, more slowly.

"I just gave you juice to give to old ladies. I'm your neighbor. I was playing with the little kid next door. What are you accusing me of?"

Down on the sidewalk, Bill Peters shook his bandaged head. "He did it," he called.

"Do you know who he is?" Eddie asked Paul.

"He's a man trying to take care of his family. He says he's got an unhealthy child."

"He was in my yard last night." Eddie shifted his gaze and met Bill Peters's. "I know you were here," he said.

Bill Peters shook his head again.

"Look," said Paul. "I don't want to make this difficult. But for now I'm going to make a citizen's arrest."

"A citizen's arrest."

"The cops aren't here yet. But they will be."

"Paul, do you know what a citizen's arrest is?"

"Just come sit on my porch. As long as I know where you are, it won't be a problem."

"A citizen's arrest."

"You assaulted this man."

"Go home, Paul."

Bill Peters called up from the sidewalk. "They'll lock you up when this is over. I'm pressing charges to the full extent of the law."

Paul turned to Bill Peters for the first time, and lifted up his hand for quiet. "Bill," he said. "Please."

Laura came into the doorway, and Eddie saw both men keep themselves from looking. She was showing a lot of skin in that bikini top. "I witnessed it," she said. "He was threatening my husband. All Eddie did was ask him to leave."

"You're a liar!" called Bill Peters.

Paul bobbed his head judiciously. "Well, that confuses things," he said.

"It's pretty straightforward, actually," Laura said. "Now you can get off our lawn. I don't know you."

"Ma'am, I—" Paul said.

"I'll citizen's arrest *you*," Laura said.

She closed the door, and they looked out the living room window as Paul and Bill Peters confabulated on the sidewalk. Bill Peters pointed to his head. When they walked away, he lifted his middle finger up behind him again.

Laura gasped.

"No, screw *you*," she shouted out the window.

THEY'D FINISHED THE last of the juice. Eddie's knee was swollen and purplish below the kneecap, but he could bend it and walk without much pain. Laura had convinced him not to go for the car, but Eddie couldn't see another way around it. The Davises had been out in Patty's minivan, and Mike Sr. thought that maybe things were clearing out on 29, though he couldn't say for sure. "You can ride up and down University, but the Beltway's the same," Patty told him. They'd brought Eddie and Laura back a twenty-ounce soda. "That's what we could find. Twenty bucks. It's just guys who set up in front of that convenience store on Carroll. They've got a couple of coolers."

Laura gave her a twenty, the last of their cash.

Eddie said to her, "I'll ask Mike Sr. to take me up."

"Then we'll both go," she said.

WHEN THEY ASKED, he said something about gas, but then agreed, and they got into the minivan.

"*My* car has gas," Eddie said, but it was after the fact.

They were alone on the road, and as they passed the empty spillway, Eddie tapped on the window opposite it to keep her from turning her head.

"What?" Laura asked, looking where Eddie pointed.

The spillway was on the southbound side, sheltered by the ravine, and the heat blurred the daylight so that the black trees at its edges seemed to disappear into the woods. A little farther on, they saw a cop car parked in a driveway. Eddie didn't remember seeing it before. He leaned forward into the front, hovering near her headrest.

"Look!" Laura said, pointing at the cop car.

"He probably lives there," Mike Sr. said.

"Still," Eddie said.

As they came to the bridge, Mike Sr. stopped the minivan, and held his foot down on the brake. Debris was spread across the road.

"I'll get a flat tire."

Eddie got out and used the inside of his foot to scrape as much of the broken glass and plastic as he could to the center of the road. It pinched his knee, and he switched to the other foot. By the time he was done, he was limping again.

"There," he said.

With the way the cars were positioned, there was a little channel they could navigate through. It looked like they'd been moved. Mike Sr. went slowly, almost scraping against the safety wall.

When they'd gotten through, he stopped the van again. "Hold on," he said. "We should check the cars."

"I think we should just keep going," Laura said.

"There's nobody in them," Eddie said.

"I'm talking about checking the cup holders and stuff," Mike Sr. said.

He parked right where he was and the three of them walked back down to the wrecks. Some of the doors were so bashed in they couldn't get them open, and some of the doors were open already. On one of the dashboards was a spill that looked like syrup.

"Gross," Laura said.

In another car, they found a blue sports drink, two-thirds full. It was as hot as broth, but they took turns sipping. Heat rose from the asphalt.

"I drink worse than this on the job sometimes," Mike Sr. said, "when my workers leave the thermos out."

Eddie turned and looked down the highway, the way they'd come. Though he couldn't see it, there was a pull-off just down the road, a little gravel lot with a grassy patch and a picnic table, and he remembered stopping there the summer before, coming back from visiting his college roommate Jason's family. Laura had looked ill at ease, jutting forward in her seat like she had a stomachache. He'd thought it would do her good getting out right then, and they'd sat at the little table in the fresh air and listened to the cicadas in the woods. There'd been shade and the trickle of a creek below.

He remembered it so clearly—the way she'd stared down into the grain of the picnic table. Eddie was godfather to Jason's little girl, Ellie, and they'd spent the afternoon in the yard of their town house. They'd eaten corn on the cob and grilled burgers, and he'd gotten Ellie to eat some spinach by joking with her. "You'll be the strongest girl in school!"

he'd trumpeted, and she'd smiled greenly, fragments of the leaves stuck between her tiny teeth. Yet Laura had been so glum.

He wondered what that pull-off looked like now, scorched and barren.

She stood with Mike Sr., the two of them leaning out over the safety wall. Mike Sr.'s voice was slow and full of reverence. "What. The. Fuck?" he said.

Laura gripped the wall with both her palms.

"Look at this," he said.

Down below, the riverbed was empty, just sand. A scar through the middle was pocked and rust colored, just as it had been below the Beltway. Often, when Eddie drove across this bridge on his way home from work, he'd watch the sun glisten above the water as it set—the view spanning five seconds of drive time that engulfed him as if, rather than being suspended above it, he'd driven into the water's depths. He would look out and feel it all around him, the river coming up to the base of the trees, curving back into what looked like wilderness. It had been like that just two days before.

And now the water was gone. It must have been gone when he ran through the wrecks on the bridge to get home, but he'd been too furious with horn noise to notice.

"The trees!" Laura exclaimed as if she were pointing out a rainbow.

"Must have been a fire," Mike Sr. said. "A big one. They must have drained it since."

"Can they drain a river?" she asked.

"This is a reservoir," he said. "You were wondering where our water went? Here's your answer. It's been diverted. That means some other place in the city has it." He thought on that a moment.

"Goddamn," he said.

Eddie watched Laura's face for signs of panic. "You're not an expert," he said to Mike Sr., but his voice was weak, almost a whisper, and Mike Sr. didn't hear.

"Look how far it goes." Mike Sr. waved his hand into the distance where the band of charred trees stretched along the path of the river.

"What could cause that?" Laura asked. There was a strange excitement in her voice. Eddie backed away from the wall.

"Must be chemicals," Mike Sr. said. "I've never seen anything like it. A chemical leak or something. Something flammable that could travel on water."

"Fuel?" Eddie suggested. "I think that happened once in Cleveland."

"Fuel, maybe. Yeah. If it's gone that far, it could have messed with the power grid."

Laura said, "You think it could have traveled to the Bay?"

"Doubt it."

"That's where her parents live," Eddie explained.

Mike Sr. was leaning dangerously far over the safety wall. His hands were pressed on the outside of it. When he stepped back, his palms were black.

"Look at this!" he said, holding them up. "The flames came up this high."

Laura looked at Mike Sr.'s blackened palms. Then she looked at Eddie. "Where's your car?"

"It's up a ways. There was a wreck here. It backed everything up."

"Your car wasn't near the wreck?"

Eddie shook his head. "Uh-uh," he said.

"So which way did you run?"

"This way," he said.

"Through all of this?"

"Yeah."

"Were people hurt?"

"What?"

"Were people hurt when you got here?"

"No," he said.

"How do you know that?"

"There was no one doing anything—I looked. No one was hurt. There weren't even any emergency workers."

"That doesn't mean no one was hurt."

She began walking through the cars, opening the doors to peer inside. The sound of each door she closed echoed across the bridge.

"So, you just left," she called back to him.

"I was worried about *you*," he said.

"Why?" she asked. "I wasn't anywhere near here."

He watched her poking her head inside, one car after another. Mike Sr. looked at him with a blank expression.

"There were already people helping," Eddie said. "Lots of them. They didn't need me getting in the way."

Mike Sr. looked down at the broken plastic in front of his shoes. When he looked up at Eddie, he said, "Wives," and smiled benignly.

She could be impossible sometimes. On that drive coming home from Jason's, he'd pulled over to lighten her mood, to cheer her up with the last of a summer day. He'd slid down the slope to the creek below and tried to get her interested in skipping rocks. He'd wanted to be joyous, even childish with her. It was okay to be playful sometimes. Just to breathe in the fragrant air. Just to run.

Now he went over to a little Honda. It was against the safety wall, right at the halfway point of the bridge. On the leather console between the seats was a brown film. Eddie saw that it was skin. There was still hair at the edges. His stomach rose up and he knelt onto the pavement, putting his head down until it touched the hard surface.

"Look!" Mike Sr. called. He was holding a hatchet. "Found it in one of the trunks."

"What are you going to do with it?" Laura asked.

Mike Sr. eyed the space beyond the bridge. "See how far it can fly."

Eddie stood and moved quickly from the car. He bit down on his voice to keep it from coming out.

"Should we report any of this?" he said softly.

"Report it to who?" Mike Sr. said.

"What about that cop car we saw? You think he's really there?"

Mike Sr. held the hatchet with both hands above his head. He took a step and chucked it, end over end, off the bridge.

"Geroni-*mo*," he yelled.

As Laura walked toward him, Eddie positioned himself between her and the Honda, boxing her toward the minivan.

"What did you find?" he asked her.

"Nothing."

They got back in and drove a little ways up until they couldn't get through. The cars were too thick where they'd been abandoned. Eddie got out and found his car where he'd left it. The key was still in the ignition, but when he turned it, the car was dead.

"Let's go," he said. "I'm still penned in. I can't get out."

"Where's the fire department?" Laura said. "Shouldn't they have been here cleaning this up?"

"Yeah," Mike Sr. said. "Where are they? That's the million-dollar question."

He made a five-point turn with his palm resting on the bottom of the steering wheel. His face was serene. He said, "Let's not tell Patty about all this. No need for her to worry about something we don't know anything about. She's got to deal with Mike Jr."

"Okay," Laura said.

"This could be something simple," he said. "They've got the water company around here working for us. A lot goes on that we don't see."

"But you've never seen anything like this."

"I'm in landscaping, sweetie. I'm no engineer."

"They can shut off Niagara Falls," Eddie said. "Did you know that?"

"If they can shut off Niagara Falls," Mike Sr. said, "they can do anything."

SHE PUT CANDLES around the living room and they sat in the heat of the flickering darkness.

"What color is your pee?" Eddie asked.

"I don't know. It's too dark in there. It just goes down the hole."

"We should be peeing in jars."

"How will that help?"

"It's good to know what color it is."

"I'll start tomorrow."

"What did you drink today?"

"That blue stuff with Mike Sr."

"Did we finish off the juice today or yesterday?"

"Today. This morning."

"What else do we have?"

"We have the rest of that soda."

Eddie went into the kitchen. The soda existed only in four puddles—one in each of the plastic nubs that served as the container's base. It was a sip's worth. He brought it to Laura.

"Here," he said. "Drink."

"What about you?"

"I had some already."

"I think we should go to my parents'," she said. "We could walk."

"How?"

"We walked back *here*."

"Your parents are thirty miles away."

"We could do it, though, if we had to. We'd just keep walking. We could walk over the Bay Bridge."

"And what would we drink on the way?" he said. "It must have been a hundred degrees today. We'd die out there."

"We could bring supplies."

"If we had supplies to bring, this wouldn't be an issue."

"Try the phone again," she said.

"The phone isn't working."

"Just try."

He picked up the phone. The battery was dead. "Look," he said.

The candles sent dim golden light to the edge of where she was. He could see her spread out on the sofa, lying on her back.

"We have to stay where we are right now," he said.

When she didn't answer, he thought maybe she was thinking about what he'd said.

"Your dad's the most competent guy I know," he said. "They're on well water. He can get down into it if he needs to. And they keep all that bottled stuff in the garage. They never run out of bottled water."

"That's why we should go. Going there could save us."

"Jesus, Laura." He squeezed the phone and stood over her. "We don't need to be saved. You heard what they said about oh-eight. They didn't have power for six days."

"But they had water."

"Yeah."

"Yeah, what?"

He thought of Mrs. Kasolos's jug, buried in the woods. There was no reason for them to be arguing like this.

"This is stupid," he said.

He took the flashlight off the kitchen table.

"Where are you going?"

"Just stay here," he said. "Please? I'm just going out for a while."

"You can't," she said. "You can't just go out anymore. Not when everything's like this."

But Eddie left anyway. He waited on the sidewalk, thinking that she'd follow, but she didn't. Through the picture window, he saw her shadow against the candle's flickering light.

He walked, and at the base of the hill, he could smell wood smoke. His shoes beat against the ground too loudly for him to hear anything else. But when he stopped, the beating carried on. It was his blood pumping in his ears.

Near the aluminum rail, a deserted campfire released a dim gray cloud into the air. There were cans on the ground, a dozen of them, and he bent and picked up each, but they were empty. A white bra was in a pile. He took a stick and raised it by its strap.

In the woods, he tried to be silent. Even in the shadow of the trail, there were darker shadows, and he hid himself in them.

When he came to the place along the streambed where he thought he should cross, he held his fingers over the front of the flashlight before he clicked it on so that the beam was divided and weak. He swung it back and forth but saw none of the glint from the silver threads, and so he kept on walking. In the dark, it was easy to get confused. He kept the flashlight on, pointed at the ground. The threads would reflect with a quick flash—he could see it in his mind, and his mind projected out onto the ground so that he had to stop several times to swing the beam again and again to prove that what he thought he'd seen wasn't really there.

Finally, he saw it, but it was small, and he pressed in closer with the light. There was only one silver strand. He crossed the streambed and shone the beam over the sand on the opposite side. He walked ahead and saw another gash of silver in the ground when the light caught it. The cluster had been moved.

Someone had scattered it.

Eddie crouched and ran his fingers through his hair. He made a fist of it and pulled.

Whoever it was must have been watching him as he walked from Mrs. Kasolos's with the jug on his shoulder. They'd either taken it for themselves or disturbed his landmarks to keep it hidden where it was.

Another pom-pom strand was in the rocks. He followed it up the slope where there were trees close together, but none of them were as close as the trees where he'd buried the jug. The rocks were too low, none of them larger than a soccer ball. He picked his way between them, going back along the opposite bank. Whoever it had been could have taken the strands and strewn them a hundred yards down just to confuse him.

Farther up, the bank sloped higher and was soft beneath the rocks, but there were still no boulders. The ash on the trees was only on the sides that faced the stream.

He looked around to get his bearings, but he'd gone either too far ahead or too far back. He waved the flashlight beam over the ground but found no more silver strands. There was a smooth rock at his feet and he sat there and rested his head in his hands, feeling his fingers dry and soft with ash.

Bill Peters.

It must have been him. He could still see him walking away down the street, Laura opening the window to shout after him. Eddie should have followed. Bill Peters was the kind of canker-ous man to fester in a neighborhood. He could have been just around the corner from Mrs. Kasolos's, hiding in a bush. He must have watched Eddie carry the jug into the park, following at a distance.

The story about his sick kid was a lie; Eddie was sure of it now. He no longer believed Bill Peters had a kid at all. He was a con man, and Eddie was his patsy. He'd scattered the threads and taken the jug and hidden it somewhere.

The water would be back soon, and when things were normal, Eddie would walk the neighborhood streets and find him. He wouldn't threaten his life or punch him—he'd simply walk to his house in the shadows and put a brick through the windshield of his car. Or spray-paint THIEF on his front door. Something to let him know that *Eddie* knew. Something to keep him looking over his shoulder. Eddie would let a few weeks pass after that and then go back and do it again.

He stood up and crossed the streambed and found the trail.

He walked a long time in one direction. He was waiting for the place where the path widened and there were many small rocks and roots, where the runoff from the streets had cut a gully. That would lead to the aluminum railing along the entrance. But he walked so long that he knew he must have been walking in the wrong direction, and so he turned until he'd redoubled his steps and then some but still found nothing. He thought he might just sit down and rest until the sun came up. His legs had lost their strength and he imagined he could see the pulsing cloud of energy as it left him. He walked farther still, and then the trail opened up and he saw the gully. He passed the aluminum rail and stumbled up the hill into the neighborhood streets, and made it home.

Laura was asleep in the bedroom, but she was only sleeping lightly, and when Eddie came in, she stirred.

"Where were you?" she asked, but he didn't answer.

And then she was asleep again.

IN THE MIDDLE of the night, he woke. He'd been dreaming he was walking in the cold. He'd had a sled full of tools, and when the grade steepened, he'd stepped awkwardly, and the sled tipped over.

There was a clatter in the kitchen, but he couldn't tell if it was real, or simply an echo from his dream. He walked through the house with the bat raised to his shoulder. The plywood he'd screwed into the window panel was knocked out, but the door was closed and locked.

In the basement, the drill was out of power. He found some nails, but they were short, and when he hammered the piece back in, they only just bit through. Anyone who tapped on it would knock it out again.

"You're making too much noise," Laura said. She'd come up behind him with a flashlight.

"I'm not happy with this door. Someone could get in."

"You can get into any door if you kick hard enough."

"Yeah, but this one's easier than that. The panel's no good."
He touched the piece of wood. "Help me move the sofa."

They got one of the sofas on its side to fit it through the opening to the kitchen. It slid easier on the linoleum and the armrest met just below the knob.

"Let me test it," Eddie said. He unlocked the door.

"Why did you unlock it?"

"In case *they* unlock it."

"Who's *they*?"

"Whoever. There is no they. This is just in case."

He went out the front door and around to the side of the house. The grass was crisp beneath his feet. He'd forgotten to bring the bat, and he stayed close to the brick wall, ducking low when he walked up the driveway. Though it was dark, the sky was filled with starlight. At the back porch he turned the knob and pushed on the door. Even without leaning his shoulder into it, it opened far enough for him to squeeze through. The sofa wasn't enough weight. "Shit," he said, coming all the way in.

"It's not the end of the world," Laura said.

He rummaged in the utensil drawer to find the can opener. The cans of beans were in the cupboard, and he opened one and poured its contents into a Tupperware container. Then he placed the empty can on the knob and tried to balance it where it was. With a little piece of tape, he kept it up, but it wouldn't stay if the knob was turned. If the knob was turned, the can would fall and clatter.

"Alarm system," he said, pleased with his bit of engineering.

"I don't like this," Laura told him. "I don't like the way you're thinking."

Setting up the can had steeled him, though. "Only a coward breaks into a house," he said. "That's why alarms work in the first place. The noise scares them off. If they think we're here, they'll run."

"So why put the couch there?"

"Why not be *over*cautious?"

She smiled at that, but not in the kindest way.

There was a roll of duct tape in the basement, and he found it and brought it up.

"You need to sleep," he said to Laura.

"For what?"

"The more you move around, the more you dehydrate."

"So, I go to sleep while you set the booby traps?"

"It's just a roll of tape."

When she was gone, he took the chef's knife out of the block and held the handle flush with the barrel of the bat. He wound the tape around and around—maybe twenty times—until the blade no longer wobbled when he pressed it with his thumb.

To avoid the couch and the can alarm, he went out the front door, holding the bat under his arm, with the knife tip pointing forward like a bayonet.

He wanted to stand out there for a while, to stare into the darkness. There might be men out there, yes, but he was a man, too. If they were dangerous, so was he.

The starlight made his vision two-dimensional. His head still ached, but it was a dull ache, and he could forget about it. The shadows weren't as crisp as they should have been; it was possible that the noises he'd heard had been imagined. For instance, right then he thought he heard Mike Sr. and Patty sitting on their porch furniture, and he walked up their steps and put a hand on each patio chair to confirm that it was empty. He didn't know what time it was, but it was late, and the Davises were probably sleeping.

He crouched beside his own porch, laying the bat on the ground beside him. He put his fingers into the latticework to keep his balance.

Then he forced himself to become very still. He even held his breath.

He could feel someone in the yard. It was similar to the sensation of being watched, but not the same. Though he saw nothing, it was as if they were staring at each other. Going up on the Davises' deck had exposed him. That had been a blunder, but there was no undoing it now. Staying low, he took the bat and crept to the back of the house. The air around him was as taut as the skin of a balloon, and it made his breathing shallow.

At once, the feeling changed. The ground beat from the corner of the yard—footfalls coming quickly. Eddie turned and thrust the tip of the bat in front of him, and a great weight met it there and knocked him down and backward. A man stood above him. It was Bill Peters. The bat shook from where it stuck into his chest. The tape around the knife had loosened enough to let it wobble back and forth.

"*Yaah*," Bill Peters yelled like a victory whoop. He pulled at the handle of the bat, but couldn't get it out. The knife had gone through two of his ribs like a key. He struggled and loosened the tape, and the bat flopped like a fish.

Eddie pressed himself against the back of the house.

Bill Peters sat down on his knees, his feet behind him. His head was still bandaged.

"*Whuff,*" he said. It was a wheeze, and Eddie thought for a moment he was joking, that his friend Paul would step out from behind the shrubbery and laugh at him about the citizen's arrest.

"*Wuh wuh,*" Bill Peters said. Thick blood obscured his mouth and chin.

Eddie stood and tried to find his voice. "Where is it?" he said, finally. "Where'd you hide it?"

Bill Peters stared somewhere past him. His eyes weren't working.

"You idiot," Eddie said. "You bastard. It didn't belong to me. It belonged to that old woman. You couldn't get it from her, so you stole it from me. Tell me where it is, you bastard." He had to stop talking because a sob was clogging his throat.

When his voice came back, it was desperate.

"Tell me," he said. He pushed Bill Peters's shoulder back, and it stayed where it was, askew. "I'll find your kid," Eddie pleaded. "If you tell me, I'll help him."

The top half of Bill Peters fell backward and stilled, though his legs continued twitching.

Eddie was talking, but only softly, as if to himself. "It was hers," he said. "You stole it."

He sat in the grass and swallowed hard, but whatever was lodged in his throat wouldn't go away. It was a dry, painful swallow.

The whole great universe of night screamed around him. He could hear it.

What had he done? What had happened here?

He loosened the tape around the knife handle and jiggled until the bat came free. Bill Peters's eyes shone dimly, but his face was a mess of shadow. Eddie flopped his arms above his head and tugged on them to pivot the body. Then he dragged him to the corner of the property where he'd made a pile of yard waste earlier in the summer. The pile was thick with clippings that had begun to rot. Beneath dried daylily stalks were branches from a dogwood he'd pruned, and when he pulled at one, it was connected to everything else. He left Bill Peters and found a shovel, and used the tip of it to try to hollow it out. It was hard work, and he was sweating. He got under Bill Peters's arms and staggered to get him up and on top of the pile, but the hole he'd made wasn't deep enough. Eddie covered him with the dirt from around the edges and pulled out a tarp from the side of the house to drape over him. He put stones on the tarp to keep it in place.

Inside, he used the disinfectant wipes to clean the dirt and blood from his arms and neck and face. His mouth was thick and rough, and his head was rhythmic with pain. He was still sweating. There was a panic in his lungs.

"Eddie?"

Laura was in the bedroom. The door was closed.

He tried to clear his throat. He tried to ignore the jolt that he still felt in his arms—the jolt of Bill Peters's body slamming into the tip of the bat.

"I'll be there in a sec," he said.

In the kitchen, he opened a jar of pickled peppers and brought the lip of the glass to his own. The vinegar made the sides of his tongue curl, and he tried not to gag, tipping the jar until the peppers bumped against his nose. When he'd drunk it all, he poured half the peppers into his hand and chewed them.

He got into bed and pulled the sheet up to his chin. "Why do you smell like that?" Laura asked.

"I ate some peppers."

"What were you doing outside?"

"Just checking."

He lay there and tried to concentrate on keeping his head from throbbing. Before a race in college, he would sit and envision the blood in his body swirling to his arms and legs. It would calm him. He couldn't get his blood to move down from his temples, though.

"You're holding your head," Laura said.

"It hurts a little."

He tried to sleep, but couldn't. Laura was still watching him.

"There's another jar of peppers," he said. "You can drink the juice. It's not that bad."

"That's what you did? Yuck."

"It'll help your head."

"Mine's not bad. It doesn't hurt when I'm asleep."

"You were asleep?"

"Yeah. Until you came back inside."

He could close his eyes and see the night. He could feel the jolt in his arms. "Yeah," he said. "I was outside."

He slept, and in his dream it was deeply cold—the type of fiercely bright cold that brought an unwavering knowledge of his body, that he wouldn't last there long, dressed as thinly as he was in his dream. The beauty of the landscape was a solitude that enveloped him. He began to run, and as he did, the sweat started coming. He could feel it beneath his arms and on his upper lip. He could feel it at his temples.

But he couldn't stop—couldn't even slow himself down. If he stopped, the sweat would freeze, and he would die. The only thing to do was run faster. He was pulling a sled. On the sled was Bill Peters's body. There were sirens in the woods.

Laura shook him awake.

"Eddie," she said.

"What?"

"You're tossing."

"Am I sweating?" he asked.

She put her hand on his forehead. "You're dry."

Eddie ran a hand through his hair. She was right. He touched the collar of his shirt. His neck was dry, too.

"I feel it," he said.

"What?"

"I'm out of breath."

"Stay still," she told him.

"The water's got to come back soon," he said. He got up and stood beside the bed. "Don't they plan for this? Isn't this why we pay taxes? Why we elect people?"

"There's a cop right up the road," she said.

"No," he said, the word escaping him before he had a chance to pen it back.

"The cop we passed with Mike."

"So what?"

"So, we're safe. There are people around, is all I'm saying."

"Yeah," he said.

When she was asleep, he went very quietly out the front door again. Around back, he took the tarp off Bill Peters's body, tugging on his arms until his legs dropped from the pile.

With small backward steps, he pulled him across the grass.

The body was heavy, and it strained his back and knee. On the sidewalk, he stopped, even though it was open and clear for anyone to see. His eyes burned, and maybe he was crying. He checked with his fingers, but his fingers were numb. If he left the body right there on the sidewalk, it would be found by the time the sun was up. He would be questioned, but there was nothing he couldn't deny. Why would he leave a body in front of his own house? He'd been in bed with his wife. Laura would say that that was true.

The knife handle stuck out from Bill Peters's chest, and Eddie used the corner of his shirt to wipe it down.

What else had he touched? Bill Peters's skin? He didn't know if fingerprints could be left on skin.

A couple of houses down, there was an abandoned house. It looked just like Eddie's, except there were county papers taped to the door and the lawn was in poor repair. It had been empty since they'd moved there, five years ago.

He dragged the body down the sidewalk and around the back of the abandoned house. There was a hedge that divided the yard from the neighbor's. It was six feet tall and full of long waxy leaves. Eddie pushed Bill Peters's body beneath it, and then he lifted each leg, rolling it over so that the body flipped onto its stomach and then onto its back again deeper into the hedge. He was in there pretty good. No one ever came around this side of the house.

On his way back, there was motion on the sidewalk. It was two people, a man and a woman. They had backpacks on and a little girl between them. She had a pack on of her own.

As they approached, Eddie stopped. They hadn't noticed him yet and he looked down at his body to see if he was visible.

"Where are you going?" he said, as calmly as if had he been saying hello.

As they passed, the father pulled his daughter close in against his hip. They didn't look at Eddie. They used each step to put themselves between the world and the little girl.

"Stay with us," Eddie heard the father say sharply.

EDDIE AWOKE WHEN the sun was high and hot in the bedroom window. Laura was already up. She was in the kitchen, squinting into the light, but it wasn't from being groggy.

"My head hurts more now," she said. "Maybe we can find that guy with the wheelbarrow. Maybe he has extra."

"Drink the juice from the peppers first."

"That's not for drinking."

"Here." He took the second pepper jar and held his fingers over the opening so that only the juice drained into a glass. It made about half a cup.

"Pinch your nose," he said.

"We can go down to the stream and get water. We can boil it first."

"Forget about the stream."

"Why?"

Eddie hesitated. Laura knowing about the dry streambed

seemed worse than the dry streambed itself. "There's barely any water in it," he said.

"What are you talking about? Some is enough."

"Listen to me. I don't want to do it. There's nothing down there for us."

"Then *I'm* going this time," she said.

He caught her wrist and squeezed.

"Ow," she said. "Okay."

"It's dangerous," Eddie said. "Even when there's not an outage. There are homeless people down there. They'll be desperate."

"I'm not an idiot, Eddie. People walk their dogs there."

"You're not an idiot."

"If you say so." She rubbed her wrist as if it were cold. "I'm going to have a mark here. So thanks for that."

She went around by the stove where he couldn't see her.

"My parents are going to wonder why we didn't try to come," she said.

"No they won't," he said. "That's absurd."

He heard her clinking dishes.

"You're putting those away?" he called, not moving.

"Well, they're *dry*."

She began to sing. She had a low, somber voice, and when she used it with any seriousness, it could make Eddie weak. Her previous life apart from him was still so mysterious—a childhood he could never really know, textures he could only touch the surface of. The singing brought it out of her somehow.

It took him a moment to recognize the song, she was singing. "Idiot Wind." It was a dig at him, he knew, but he loved that song. And she knew he loved it. He'd played it for her—had introduced her to the album, in fact—that first year that they'd met. It was the deepness of her voice, though, not the words, that touched him. The words were nothing. He knew this about the way he loved her—that there were times when it was the vessel, not what shifting matter it contained, he needed most.

She stopped as he walked up behind her. She was standing over the counter and the dishes were put away and she was staring down into the drying rack. He laid his palm on the flat of her back.

"I have something we can boil," he said.

She didn't turn around. "What?" she said.

"Just hold on."

He took the two water bottles from the closet downstairs and pressed them to his chest.

"Where did you get those?"

"From the top part of the toilet. It's clean in that part. It hasn't been used."

"It's okay to drink?"

"I'm going to boil it anyway."

Outside, the leaves on the trees were as shriveled as prunes. He touched one and it crumbled between his fingers. There was only a third of the bag of charcoal briquettes left, but he got them going hot. He poured the water into a pot and put the pot on the grill. It was over a hundred degrees out there and standing next to the flames was impossible.

So he walked away, toward the corner of the yard. When he saw the tarp on the ground it shocked him as immediately as if had it been moving. The sound of Bill Peters's death wail flooded him afresh. He couldn't breathe. The air was as thick as rubber.

"Hey, neighbor."

It was Patty. She'd come up to the fence in front of him. Her voice pierced the seal on his breathing and the air came back again.

"Yeah," he said.

"I hate to ask this, but do you have anything left?"

"Anything to drink?"

"Mike Jr.'s not feeling good."

"He's got a headache?"

"Bad, I think. Poor guy. All he wants to do is lie on the floor."

"I'm just waiting for this to boil."

"From the toilet?"

"Yeah."

"We boiled ours yesterday. I learned my lesson: always stay stocked up."

"You couldn't have known, though. Nobody did."

It took a long time for the water to boil. Patty leaned against the fence and didn't say anything. After a while, she went back inside and brought out her own pot. When the water boiled, she came around to his side of the fence. Eddie held the pot handle with both hands, and they poured the water back and forth between the pots to cool it. On the last round, Eddie poured half of the water into her pot. Maybe more than half.

"Thanks," she said. "I was actually worried last night. The power's one thing, but the water's something else. They can't let us go without for too much longer. I guess they just have to get the trucks through all those cars on the highway. Mike

Sr. told me they're all abandoned. If they can't get the trucks through, they can't fix the water. They'll have to start towing and that can take forever."

"They'll bring water trucks around, though," Eddie said.

"I expect they will. They just need to hurry. We've got a lot of old people around here. And kids."

"We took up a collection for the old people," Eddie said. "I'm not worried about them. You tell Mike Jr. to start feeling better." He raised his pot in a salute.

LAURA WAS SITTING at the table.

"I want you to drink all of this," he said.

He tipped the water in the pot into a tall glass, filling it.

Laura drank from the glass. "I just want to lie down," she told him. "Will you come lie down with me?"

"Yes," he said.

But they didn't lie down. They sat there at the table.

"If we had water, we could help people in the neighborhood," she said. "We could bring whole buckets."

"What are you talking about?"

"If we could get water from somewhere. We could boil it."

"I just used the last of our charcoal."

"Anything can burn, Eddie. We could boil it and strain it with a coffee filters. We could bring it all over."

It sounded like the half-dreamt pillow talk she'd murmur after a long day, and Eddie squeezed her hand to keep her awake.

"It's Mike Jr. you should worry about," he said.

"What's wrong?" she said. Her eyes shifted suddenly, and it was that, more than the fear in her voice, that startled him.

"He's just thirsty. Just like the rest of us. He's dehydrated, is all."

"If we got water from the stream . . ." she said.

"No," Eddie said. "You're staying here. You're staying right where you are."

"Eddie, please. If I want to go, I'll go."

"We're trying to conserve our strength. And you're talking about going for a hike in the woods."

"I'm talking about walking a few blocks."

"Let me tell you what you're talking about. You're talking about going down to a muddy little stream to bring back water that will make you sick. They'll be here to fix it soon. Everyone knows it's out. They'll helicopter in water bottles if they have to. I heard helicopters out there before. But it's not going to come to that."

"There's no water in the stream, is there?"

"I'm sure there's water in the stream."

"Have you been down there, Eddie? Did you see that it was empty? It's like beneath the bridge, isn't it?"

"No. I haven't been down there. There's water in the stream."

"Oh, God."

"There's water in the stream, Laura."

"What's happening?"

"Go lie down. I will, too. We just need to rest. They'll be here soon. There's too many people for them not to come."

Eddie put his hands on her hips and guided her to the bedroom. She was trembling.

"Easy," he said.

The more she shook, the more steadily he walked with her.

"Tell me," she said. "You've been thinking about it. Even if you're not sure. Just tell me what you think."

"It's nothing. Something at the reservoir. Something with the power."

"I saw those burned-up trees."

"Then maybe there was something in the water that was flammable. The other water's probably fine."

"My parents."

"It's different water. That's what I'm saying. We're on reservoir water. That means it's all connected to one spot. It's like dominoes, but ours are on a different table from your parents'. Right? The dominoes aren't going to jump to another table."

"They'll fix it, though."

"Fixing it is their job. The engineers or whoever. The people who can dig a highway underneath a river to get to New York City. Can you even imagine that? It's all magic to people like us, but they can do it. They fix things like this."

"You have faith in them."

"I do."

"Then I do, too."

"Just rest now," he said.

OUTSIDE, THE SKY was white and the sun was buried somewhere in it. Eddie walked down the sidewalk, past the abandoned house, on to the end of the block. Then he walked back past it again.

From the front of the house, the backyard was hidden. He looked up and down the street. At the north end, he could see the tops of the hedges, but that was all. From the south end of the sidewalk, he could see a strip of fence along the property line and, if he craned his neck, the edge of the back porch. He'd never seen anyone stop where he was standing, though. There was no reason to stop there.

When the power came back he would think of something. He was almost certain you couldn't leave fingerprints on skin. There'd been no struggle, no DNA beneath his fingernails. He would simply call it in—say he found a body in the neighborhood.

He'd be questioned, but he'd say he'd been with Laura. She could verify that—and the Davises had seen him.

Eddie turned around and saw Mike Sr. standing behind him in the street.

"What are you doing?" Mike Sr. asked.

"Nothing."

"Come with me, then. They're having a meeting across the street."

"What kind of meeting?"

"Like a council-of-elders-type thing. To decide our fate." He stared hard at Eddie and then smiled. "I don't know," he said. "Just a bunch of these jerk-offs talking."

They walked together up the street to a house Eddie had never before considered. The door was open, and inside, a group of people stood around a living room. A few of them shook Mike Sr.'s hand.

Paul was there, near the bay window, with the man in the suspenders. He looked at Eddie and then quickly at the carpet in front of him. Eddie looked away, too. Mike Sr. squeezed them into the middle of the room, in front of two large men. One of the men crossed his arms against a chest so barreled it seemed it would take a dolly to move him. The other had his hands balled deep in his pockets. He rolled back and forth on his heels and grunted at Mike Sr.

"How 'bout all this?" he said.

"Yeah," Mike Sr. agreed. "How 'bout it?"

"I told Sid here what the problem is. Just busted pipes."

Eddie turned his head to listen. Sid continued to look ahead with his arms folded, the buttons of his shirt straining against his chest. "Pipes," he said, shaking his head. "It's more than just pipes."

"Then you tell me."

"An aquifer thing."

"We're not on an aquifer."

"A different one," he said. "They go dry and create a suction. It's the physics of it. You don't know."

"Trust me," the first one said. "It's pipes." He took a hand from his pocket to wipe beneath his nose. Then he rocked on his heels some more.

"*All* of our pipes?" the other man scoffed.

Mike Sr.'s forehead strained from clenching his teeth. He shook his head in a very small way.

At the other end of the room, a man who might have been the owner of the house stood facing them. He had thick gray hair that curled down his sideburns into a beard, and he wore the bulbous glasses of an earlier epoch. A general whispering had begun. The man in front was talking intently to the women closest to him, and he raised his voice as if something had been decided between them.

"If people can leave for the city, they should," he announced, continuing his thought. "And it would be best to go in groups of at least three." He spoke like an inveterate coordinator of volunteers. "We'll draft some sign-up sheets," he said.

"Why the city?" someone in the back called over Eddie's head. He turned to see a woman in a flowered dress with enormous stains beneath the armpits. "Won't the city be more dangerous if that's where people are running to? There was crime in the city before all this. Now it'll be worse."

"Mrs. Ramos told us," said the man up front, "that they have stations set up there. Cooling stations and water stations.

The benefit of going in groups is that we can pool our resources for the walk, and we can look out for one another. We all know each other here, and that's to our advantage. Not everyone down there will have the advantage of a group."

"Where did she hear that?" Mike Sr. asked, his voice rising. People turned to look, and Eddie felt himself flush. Mike Sr. was scowling. "About the cooling stations and all?"

"You'll have to ask Mrs. Ramos that."

"Where is she? She's not here?"

"It doesn't matter where she is," the man said. "This is the time for evacuation."

Mike Sr. looked over his shoulder at Eddie.

"More like ejaculation," he mumbled.

"That's where all the resources are right now? In the city?" someone called out.

"It's a rumor," Mike Sr. said. All the bodies in the room had made it hotter still, and his face was glowing red. "One lady says it's true. So what? Where did she hear it? Did she see these cooling stations? Does her TV work right now? Because I'll go over there and watch the news with her."

"What are the alternatives?" said someone else.

"If you could all give me your names," said the man up front.

The woman with the pit stains strained forward on her toes to make her voice carry. "There will be emergency workers down there, at least. Paramedics. Police."

Eddie had turned to look at her, but instead noticed the woman beside her. She was wearing a blue top with little white flowers across the front, and her gray hair was back in a bun. Her eyes were closed, and she was doing something strange with her lips—moving them quickly. "Isaiah fifty," she whispered, opening her eyes.

"What, dear?" her friend with the pit stains asked. She stroked the woman's shoulder. "We'll be okay now. Strength in numbers."

"'By My rebuke I dry up the sea,'" the woman recited, her eyes widening, "'and turn rivers into deserts. The fish rot and die of thirst.'"

She began to shake her shoulders up and down as if she were holding back sobs, but her eyes were clear. She turned to her friend. "Pray with me," she said. She clasped her hands together in front of her waist.

"Pray," she said again, this time loud enough so that other people turned. "We need to pray together!"

"Now, Doris," the man up front said, "we're being practical about this."

"It's *hell*," the woman said. "This is hell *right here*. We're in it already. Don't you see that?" She began to shout. "Pray! Pray to God with me!"

"*Sid*," the man in front said sternly, "can you get— Can you and John escort her out of here, please?"

The two men behind Eddie stepped on either side of her and held her arms where they were. "Settle down," said the barrel-chested one.

The woman with the stained dress tried to pry them off, but it was like trying to pry cement. She had a frenzied look. "What are you doing?" she cried. "You can't take her."

"Just outside," the other one said. "We're just taking her right outside."

The woman between them closed her eyes and let her mouth

hang open. Her legs went limp and she fell halfway down before the two men caught her by the shoulders and lifted her so that her feet dragged on the floor.

"It's too late," she began to whisper. "Too late."

The woman's friend followed them outside.

There was a muttering among the group, but no one moved to stop them. It was as if the woman was a regular fainter at meetings.

Eddie looked at Paul again, who was staring out the window at whatever was happening outside. The man beside him cleared the phlegm from his throat and bowed his head as if to heed the woman's admonition.

Mike Sr., though, was unfazed by the removal of the limp-legged woman. "We don't need to go to the city," he said. "We'll get crews up here, too. They just haven't come around yet."

"They would have been here by now," the man up front insisted.

"How about for people who can't go?" Mike Sr. asked. "You want us to just leave them here? I've got a kid. You want me to abandon my kid?"

"It's only nine miles," the man up front said. "A child can walk nine miles."

"Maybe your child," Mike Sr. said.

"My boys are grown," he said.

"Come on, Ed," Mike Sr. said, loud enough to address the group as a whole. "Let's get the hell out of here."

Eddie followed him out into the startling sunlight, back across the street. There was no sign of the group with the praying woman. "What do you make of it?" he asked.

"All that talk? Right. Mrs. Ramos heard they're handing out icy pops in the city. Sure thing. Let's all go to the city for icy pops."

"It'll be a mess down there," Eddie said. "I don't trust emergency workers in this kind of emergency."

"You're right," Mike Sr. said. "You're absolutely right. Power goes to their heads. You remember Katrina."

"You need to stay here for Mike Jr., anyway."

"He'll be okay. Little man's tough like his mom."

"Yeah," Eddie said.

They stood in front of the Davises' house, and Eddie watched Mike Sr. cross his yard and go up the steps of his deck, past the patio furniture that had seemed, just the evening before, to pulse with his presence.

Eddie felt foolish—foolish for having been scared by anything on this block, scared by anyone in this whole neighborhood. They were a bunch of terrified old-timers. He was strong and young, and if anything, he should be helping. Bill Peters was gone. He needed to forget about Bill Peters.

He walked across the street to the Mathiases' door. The curtains were drawn, and after he'd knocked, Mr. Mathias answered, shirtless, his belly moist with sweat. He had small buttons of black hair on his chest.

"Please," he said to Eddie. "Just leave us alone." He didn't seem to recognize him. The interior of the house was almost black, and Eddie could see beyond him that they'd affixed blankets over the curtains.

"I'm your neighbor," Eddie said. "Ed Gardner. From right over there. I just want to see how you are. I'm checking on you."

"Oh," he said. "Yes. You."

"There's going to be an evacuation," Eddie said.

"Who?"

"People are leaving in groups. I thought I'd tell you."

"You're going?"

"No, I think we'll stay. It'll all come back on soon. We're okay."

"Right," he said.

"You're okay, then?"

"All right as we can be," he said, and then added, "Too hot to leave this door open," and he closed it.

Eddie went back and stood on the Davises' porch. He looked into a window. If they saw him looking, he would wave them out. They weren't in the kitchen or the den, as far as he could tell. They were probably somewhere dealing with Mike Jr.

From up there on their porch, he could see into his own yard—the tarp along the back fence had the half-pitched quality of a complicated tent. Something welled behind his heart and rose into his throat. He turned and retched over the railing into the flower bed. It was hardly anything, thin and yellow, but he had to put his hands on his knees and gasp for breath.

IN THE LATE afternoon, Eddie and Laura stood in their doorway and watched a group of their neighbors set off from across the street. They were outfitted as if for an expedition, with packs and visors and hiking shoes. An hour later, another group gathered, but this one was smaller, only three. Eddie thought he recognized the man with the beard who'd organized the evacuation.

"How many signed up?" he called from the doorway. Two of the evacuees were bent over, pressing clothes into unzipped packs; the organizer was doing some final stretches. He whipped his head around, trying to place the origin of Eddie's voice. He held his hand up to shade his eyes.

"Are you coming?" he called. "Is that what you're asking me?"

"No," Eddie said. He laughed one short, derisive laugh. "I think we're going to stay right here."

"There are more groups leaving later. If you want to join

them, of course, you can. They're prepared to pick up others from the neighborhood. They think it's best to travel at night. I disagreed, but they insisted. There are pros and cons."

"Well, break a leg, then," Eddie said.

"Ha!" he exclaimed. "A dramaturge."

They looked like a sorry lot, walking down the street turtled beneath their bulbous packs, their naked calves flexing with the weight. The packs were ill-fitting and rattled at each step, making them look like a derelict Boy Scout troop.

When they were gone, the street was silent. The neighborhood looked cleared out and deserted.

In the evening, Eddie took the mattress from where it leaned against the basement wall and laid it on a section of the floor that was bare cement. It was maybe a degree or two cooler there. Lying down, he could almost feel a current of air flow just above the floor.

"You're okay with this?" he said to Laura.

"With what?"

"Staying."

"Well, I don't want to go with them."

"But you do want to go?"

"What do you think?" she said.

"I don't want to overreact accidentally."

"But what's a reaction and what's an overreaction? We won't be able to tell until this is over."

"At least we know who we can trust here. When this is over, I want to be around people who know our reputation."

"What are you talking about?"

"I mean," he explained, "we can all vouch for each other. People here know us."

"Who?" she said. "Who are you talking about besides the Davises?"

"Whoever," he said. "All of our neighbors."

"Our neighbors are the ones who're leaving."

"Not all of them," Eddie said, but he felt it, too. The weight of being left behind.

IN THE MIDDLE of the night, she stirred and sat up cross-legged at the edge of the mattress. She clicked on the flashlight.

"Nothing's going to make it any different," she said. "I can say it all day and it doesn't matter." Her words came out with almost no space between them—a stream of syllables—and she swung the beam of the flashlight against the walls. "Tell *me* I can't press charges? Tell *me*? I'll get the courts here thirty years later."

"Laura," Eddie said.

"I'll get them. He's going to *jail*."

He shook her shoulder and the flashlight fell to the floor and rolled against the mattress so that there was only a small disk of light glowing.

She lay back down, but crooked, her legs up where her head had been. Her forehead was sticky and hot and her hair was plastered there.

Eddie went upstairs and fumbled through the cabinet, pulling the handle of the faucet up and down without even looking. When he opened the refrigerator door, the air was as warm as the air in the room. He poured the bottle of lemon juice into a glass and took a gulp that made him shudder.

There was still a can of mushrooms and the can of black beans, and he opened them and held a colander over a glass. The liquid poured through like syrup, and in the darkness, the glass was almost invisible. He stirred it and brought it down to her, kneeling on her side of the mattress.

"Laur," he said, shaking her shoulder. "Come on, Laura."

"Oh," she said.

He put the light down against the mattress so that there would only be the slightest glow.

"Eddie. I feel bad."

"What hurts?"

"My hands are tingling."

"Give me," he said, and he took her hands in his and massaged down her knuckles with his thumb.

"Drink this," he said, lifting the glass from the floor.

"What is it?"

"Just drink. It's okay."

He held her head up and took the glass to her lips.

"*Uhn*," she said, and wrinkled her face.

"You have to," Eddie said. "You've got to get it down."

He could feel her heat against his skin, slightly hotter than the heat in the room.

She drank and Eddie watched her feet flex. She got through half of it.

Then he lay still on the mattress, listening to her breathing.

It was steady, but every so often, she rasped. When she coughed, Eddie's stomach tightened.

Upstairs, her phone was turned off, and when he tried to press it on, nothing happened. The moon lit up the street through the picture window. He heard voices coming from the Mathiases' and looked across into their yard.

It was kids again. He'd watched Mr. Mathias before—large and stiff-necked—silence the innocuous street chatter of stroller-moms by merely opening his door. Now these kids were in his yard and his door remained closed. Eddie checked the lock. The can on the back door knob was balanced where it was—the sofa beneath it, unmoved.

When the voices died out, he went downstairs and felt Laura's forehead. It had cooled, but the commotion he'd made hadn't roused her.

SHE WAS STILL asleep when the light turned gray. There was one stippled window at ground level, and the light that came through made the liquid in her glass look like thin dark milk. She was breathing okay. Eddie tipped the glass to his mouth and held it there until he could muster the courage to swallow. He felt clammy all over, but his skin was dry. Laura's was, too.

While she slept, he walked down the street to the abandoned house. It was still early, but he checked the perimeter of the yard and looked for anyone across the street. The big sycamores, he saw, were as bare as in winter. A spray of leaves had collected on the eastern side of the house, where before it had been overgrown in weeds. The stalkier growth was as limp as rope on the ground. He could still see the top of the hedge around back, but it had wilted. The leaves hung like flags on a windless day.

Nothing was moving across the street. The air was quiet.

In the backyard, Bill Peters's arm had flopped out from the bush, and it rested on the burnt grass. Eddie felt the nausea again, but controlled it from coming up. The hand was grotesque—the fingers as pink and swollen as Vienna sausages. Eddie walked to him quickly, not looking at his face. With the toe of his shoe, he tried flipping the arm back up over the body, but it only fell back where it was. He had to stoop down and grab it and fold it over onto Bill Peters's chest. Even then, whatever it had bloated with made the arm difficult to place. It slid slowly back out away from the body.

Eddie whined to himself softly through gritted teeth. "What can I do? What can I do?" he said. He squeezed his fingernails into his palms and looked over his shoulder at the empty yard.

By the back of the house were chunks of cinder block, and he took a piece and weighted the arm back on the outside of the elbow. It stayed where it was. Some of the trees had been shedding branches, and Eddie collected them and propped them against Bill Peters's side in camouflage.

Eddie looked back into the yard. If someone had seen him, at any point, they would have moved the body. People would have been here already. The cops would have come.

He stood in front yard and called "Hey!" over toward the evacuation leader's house.

There was only silence in response.

"Hello!" he called again. The street was as empty as a canyon. How many of them had cleared out in the night? How many had tottered off with backpacks and flashlights and street maps held in front of their faces?

He left the body and stood on the sidewalk. He looked up and down the street.

The sound of Mike Sr. banging down the steps of his deck

roused him. Mike Sr.'s face was red and his hair as dry as the yellow grass. He got into the minivan and Eddie watched his shoulder twitch as he turned the key. He watched him pound the steering wheel with his fist.

By the time Eddie reached him, he was standing in front of the gas flap.

"Look at this," he said, though he'd not yet acknowledged Eddie was there. "They drained it. What kind of animals do a thing like this?"

Eddie looked. The gas cap was gone. He backed up and stepped on it in the driveway.

"Here," he said, handing it back to him.

Mike Sr. screwed the cap in place. "I need to get to a doctor," he said. His voice was close to breaking.

"He's that bad?"

"I can't get him cool. He's in pain. It's something serious, I can tell."

"What's he drinking?"

"What are any of us drinking? Nothing."

"There might still be people evacuating."

"Don't start with that. A nine-mile walk in this heat? Those idiots. It would kill him. And how do you think Patty would handle it? Where're the fucking power people, is what I want to know."

He banged his fist hard into the hood of the car. Then he banged again and again. His fist was heavy and finally left a dent.

"Hold on," Eddie said. "I have something."

He went back into his house and soaked a washcloth in apple cider vinegar. Mike Sr. had gone back inside, and Eddie had to knock when he returned.

Patty opened up, but didn't speak.

"Here," Eddie said, holding up the washcloth.

She walked through the kitchen, and Eddie followed her down the basement stairs. With each step down, she pulled the railing, until Eddie thought she'd wrench it free.

They had Mike Jr. lying down in an old bathtub liner, a pillow under his head. His naked body was pink.

"Look who's here," Patty said. Mike Sr. stood above the boy, gently fanning with a towel.

Mike Jr. looked at Eddie and managed a smile. "Eddie," he said.

"Yeah," said Mike Sr.

"Here you go, slugger," Eddie said. He laid the washcloth on his forehead and Mike Jr. let it rest there.

After a while, he said, "It stings."

Patty reached down and folded the washcloth over once so that it wasn't so close to his eyes. "Probably the fumes," she said. "Vinegar?"

Eddie nodded.

"We've got some wine somewhere upstairs. I'll use that next. We sure as shit ain't drinking it," Patty said.

"Alcohol. No way," said Mike Sr.

"You'll be celebrating with it soon," Eddie said. "I bet the work crews are here this afternoon."

"They have to be," Patty said. "There was just a rate hike. They're all crooks down there."

"Look, Eddie, we've been talking," Mike Sr. said. "That wheelbarrow full of goodies that Paul was rolling around . . . it couldn't have gone very far."

"You know Paul?" Eddie said.

"Yeah, I know Paul. He's lived here for years. He's a royal pain in the ass. Probably out on the highway now trying not to melt."

"You know the man he was with?"

"Who was he with?"

"Another guy."

"I didn't see another guy."

Mike Jr. whined in a way that otherwise would have brought a scolding. It was the whine of a spoiled child, but equally, Eddie realized, of pain.

Mike Sr. looked at Eddie and said nothing about his son. Instead, he said, "I know where he would've taken it. Down to Mrs. Kasolos. He treats that woman like his mother."

Eddie couldn't keep the heat from spreading up his neck, and he covered it with his hand. It was too late, though. He was hot all the way up to his ears.

"Which one is she?" he said.

"Little old lady at the end of the street."

"That's who they were collecting water for," Patty said.

"They probably gave it out to people all over," Eddie said.

Mike Sr. touched his thumb to the side of his nose. "And some of it to her," he said.

"You want to ask her for it?"

"Nope," Mike Sr. said "Tried that already. They must've gotten her outta town. She's not answering her door. I want to go in there and take it."

"Who would have taken her out of town?" Eddie said.

"She's got family nearby. A daughter up in Burtonsville."

"So, you want to break in. What happens when the cops show up?"

"There aren't any cops. If they show up, then we saved the neighborhood. Second, I'm not going to break in." He held Eddie with the sharpness of his gaze. "You are."

Eddie felt a further weakness travel up his legs. "I don't know," he said.

"I'm too big. I need your skinny ass. You go in, check the fridge, come out. I need to get some liquids in my son. It's as simple as that right now."

"I'm not breaking into her house," Eddie said, flatly. "That's like looting. I'm not starting in on that."

"Looting," Mike Sr. said. "Listen to yourself. My son is sick. There could be water a block away that no one's drinking. You're my neighbor, Ed. I shouldn't have to even ask you like this. You should have already volunteered."

Eddie had never seen Mike Sr. angry, but it was coming now. He was a big man with the thick arms of his trade. His breath was making little huffing noises in his nostrils.

"Okay," Eddie said.

"Okay," Mike Sr. repeated. "Okay. Let's go there, then."

They walked up from the basement and back out onto the street. Mrs. Kasolos had bushes with leaves as dry as pencil shavings. Eddie knocked on the door while Mike Sr. waited on the walk with his arms crossed. When she didn't answer, they went to the side of the house and Mike Sr. took a knee so that Eddie could stand on it and reach up to the window. He leaned both his palms into the screen and pushed. The window behind it was unlocked, and it budged.

"I've got to break the screen," Eddie said.

"Break it, then."

He dragged his fingernails across the corner of the screen

and pressed until it tore. Then he got a hold under the window and pushed up to open it. Mike Sr. laced his fingers into a stirrup and Eddie stepped into it. When he said, "Okay," Mike Sr. hoisted him up and Eddie bent his body over the sill until he could touch the floor inside with his fingertips. The blood rushed to his face, and he fell and banged his knee across the sill as he went over. He lay on the floor in a heap.

"Mrs. Kasolos!" he called, not yet getting up. He was afraid he'd faint. "It's Ed Gardner. Don't be alarmed. I'm just checking up on you."

He lay there and listened to the silence.

"You okay in there?" Mike Sr. called.

Eddie stood up and steadied himself. The room had blurred a little.

"Hold on," he called, and was surprised by the rasp in his voice. He swallowed and got a little saliva in his mouth. He held on to the edge of the wooden breakfront, the plate with the two Bush presidents staring him in the face. On the table, the bunch of bananas had gone black. Against the wall, the watercooler was headless; only the white plastic stand with its triangular spigot remained upright. The jug was on the floor—on its side. Eddie could see the stain where it had spilled onto the hardwood.

He turned and saw Mrs. Kasolos sitting behind him in an armchair by the door. Her face was as wide across as a pumpkin. Purple veins piped through the insides of her elbows.

He stumbled forward and grabbed for the doorknob, not looking over at her. When he opened it to the hot air outside, it was as if he'd broken through a surface of water and could breathe again.

"She's in here," he said, gasping.

Mike Sr. walked past him. In a few minutes, he came out and said, "She's gone." He had a brown cylinder of prune juice in his hand that he held by the plastic lid. He jiggled it to demonstrate the slosh of liquid.

"A little left," he said.

"What are we gonna do?"

"Got any bright ideas? I'm not digging a grave. Not in this heat."

"She's swollen."

Mike Sr. pulled the door shut behind him. "She was old, Ed. Don't get too worked up."

"I know."

"Old people die when the power goes out."

Eddie had trouble moving. The air seemed to have congealed around him.

"We'll call it in when the power's back," Mike Sr. said.

They walked back to their yards, and Eddie went inside his house. He took a steak knife from out of the block. He held it very still and very close to his side. Whatever death gasses were inside Mrs. Kasolos were expanding. It was their nature to expand.

He walked down the street holding the knife very still.

Bill Peters's arm had moved the piece of cinder block a little, but it hadn't gotten free. His wrist had swollen like a baby's, and his shirt strained against his chest and belly. Eddie let his gaze travel up: the cheeks, ballooned, a bee-stung forehead. His eyes were lost in it.

Eddie placed the tip of the knife just below the sternum, and looked away. Then he leaned into it. The knife hit something hard—maybe bone—and he pulled it back and aimed a few inches lower into a softer spot. There was a faint sound, almost the rumble of indigestion. Eddie's arms were weak, and when he flexed his hands into fists, he couldn't squeeze them hard. He walked to the opposite side of the yard and held on to the chain-link fence. With his eyes closed, he could imagine that he was dreaming.

IN HIS KITCHEN, he soaked another washcloth with the rest of the vinegar and brought it down to Laura. She was still lying down with her eyes closed. The washcloth was almost cool. When it touched her forehead, she squeezed her eyes tighter.

"It's a breeze," she said.

"Just a washcloth."

"It feels good, though, Eddie. Thanks."

"It's daytime."

"I have a really bad headache."

"I know."

"You have one, too?"

"Yeah," he said, and then wished he hadn't told her. She would worry about his headache on top of suffering from her own.

"What else can we drink? Let's really think about it."

"What else? Can you think of anything? Our own pee, I guess."

"Yeah. That's what we should do."

"I think we're a long way off from that."

"How long do we wait?"

"It'll come back on soon."

"What were you doing outside?"

"I was helping out at the Davises'. Mike Jr.'s still not feeling good."

"Are you hungry? Everything we eat has water in it. We should be eating. You should tell the Davises to eat. No. I'll do it."

She pressed up to her elbow and took the washcloth in her hand, blinking her eyes as if the lights had just come on.

"You stay here," Eddie said. "Rest."

"I'm feeling better. That washcloth did the trick. It was smart of you to think of that."

"There are still some hot dogs in the fridge."

"I'll give them to the Davises."

"The Davises probably have their own hot dogs."

"I'll check, then."

"It's hotter out there than it is down here. A lot hotter."

She stood up and Eddie watched her climb the stairs very slowly. Then he lay down and stared up at the drop ceiling. The house was silent. If he could fall asleep, even for a few minutes, he might escape the pain in his head. But he couldn't fall asleep.

Bill Peters's bloated face filled the space behind his eyes. It was too thick to push away. He stared at the ceiling again, but even there, he could see it.

The handrail creaked on its screws where Laura leaned into it. He thought it was the sound of her leaving, but she was already coming back.

Her skin was pale—Eddie could tell even in the bad light. The thirst had changed her summer tan. She'd taken two hamburger buns and spread mustard on them and put a slice of American cheese on top of each.

"Eat this," she said.

"You saw Mike Jr.?"

"I gave them the rest of our hot dogs. Patty says they're still okay."

"Laur . . ."

"It was only two of them."

"You need to eat, too."

"We have this. Okay?" she said. "Eat it." She looked at him kindly, and he took the hamburger bun and ate it. It stuck in his mouth and he had to chew for a long time to get it to go down.

They rested on the mattress, and with Laura there beside him, Eddie could fall asleep. It was a shallow, crackling sleep, though, and his dreams stung and spat at him like drops of water in a hot oiled pan.

When he woke, his breath was shallow. Laura was awake and sitting above him.

"I want to tell you something important," she said.

"What?" The word tore through the smoke in his mind like a rock, leaving a patch of clarity. He saw her eyes; they were only panels. Behind them was a sadness.

"When I was fifteen," she said, "I was really wild."

"I know," he said. "You told me. The drugs and stuff."

"But it's more than you know. I shouldn't have kept it from you."

"What?"

"I was pregnant."

He could feel her breath on his face—yes—he could reach out and squeeze her wrist, her arm, her thigh—but it was as if she existed, truly, at a greater distance and had left her body behind to fool him.

He tried to feel her breath again, but it wasn't there, and he reached to touch her arm, tightening his fingers on her skin. It seemed impossible that she'd lived a life that could contain all this—to have once been wild and fifteen, and now be sitting in this basement here with him.

"Like a teen-pregnancy kind of thing?" he asked.

"It didn't feel like that to me. I was pregnant like anybody else."

"You got an abortion?" he said.

"I had her."

He tried very hard to concentrate—to keep his mind from wandering. He could see her standing over Bill Peters's body. She was carrying a child.

"I was ashamed to tell you."

He waited for his voice to come. But it was like waiting for someone else to speak, and so all that came was silence.

"I wasn't ashamed of having her," she said. "I was ashamed of something else."

"What's her name?" The words left bluntly, loudly—beyond his control.

"Her name was Sophie. She's not alive anymore."

He wanted to say *I'm sorry*, but he wasn't sorry for this life of hers he knew nothing about. He was interested. And then he was sad. He was sad that this was happening now. His thirst only deepened the sadness.

"How did she die?" he asked.

"It was when we lived in Philadelphia. My parents were raising her. She was going to be like my little sister. That's what we agreed on. I was just a kid, too. She was two and a half already, and she was out in the garden. I was babysitting. I was supposed to be watching her, but I was inside watching the end of a TV show."

"Who was the dad?"

"A boyfriend."

"Who was he?"

"He was nobody. A kid in my class."

"You were having sex already. You were fifteen?"

"Eddie . . ." He heard her crying, and it welled up inside him, too, but he experienced the tears as joy. That they could cry. That they were still in this together.

"She was in the garden?" he said.

"My dad used to try to teach her how to find purslane. It's a weed you can eat. It was on the edges of the driveway. She didn't really eat it, though. He'd hand it to her, and she'd put it in her mouth and chew, and the leaves would get stuck between her teeth and stick to her lips. She'd make these faces."

She stopped talking and looked at the ceiling.

"I guess there was some on the sidewalk, too," she said. "And across the street. I should have been watching her. The car never stopped."

Eddie could see the car. He could see the fragile bones and all the precious life contained around them.

"I'm crying," he said.

"It happened a long time ago."

"I'm sad for your family—for everything."

"She was an angel. That's what my parents say."

"You kept it a secret. Your life."

"But it doesn't feel like my life, anymore. This is my life. You and me."

"Was it on the news?" he asked.

She turned away from him. "Let's pretend I'm two different people. Okay? Can you pretend you never knew about it? I needed to tell you, but now it's done."

Eddie sat very still. "Why are you telling me, then?"

She was quiet for a while. Then she laid her head down on the mattress.

"Because . . ." she said. Her cheek was pressed so that it scrunched up against her mouth. She opened and closed her eyes. "I think I am again."

"What?" he asked.

"Pregnant." She kept her eyes closed as she said the word.

"What?" he said, again.

"I took a test."

"A test."

"A couple of days ago."

"But you didn't tell me."

She was quiet again.

She whispered something he couldn't hear.

"That's fine," he said. "It's okay. This is *good*. God, Laura. We'll be okay." He took her hand and squeezed it.

"I'm sorry," she said. She rolled onto her back and hugged her belly. "I don't know if I still am," she said, shaking her head. "I don't know."

When she looked up, her eyes were red. It brought color to

the rest of her face. She nuzzled her head into his thigh and shook like she was crying.

Eddie watched the back of her head—how with the gentlest movement, strands of her hair would collapse to the side of her face.

"You don't know," he said. "Only a doctor would know if you've lost it."

She shook her head and pushed herself flat out on the mattress.

"Everything is just slowing down," he said, "because we're tired. We're dehydrated. It's natural."

He felt he had to go somewhere—to get someone to help her.

"Stay here," he said. "Don't do anything."

He walked upstairs with a spike of pain in his head, and when he opened the door, the heat draped around him like a blanket. The street was empty, and he ran to the end of it. Then he ran back in the other direction. He ran on past the bigger homes, closer to Route 29—the homes of lawyers and doctors, maybe. He went up walkways and pounded on doors, which no one answered.

Finally, a woman opened up. She blinked at the light. Her hair was unbrushed and twisted.

"I need a doctor," Eddie said. "It's for my wife."

She lifted her hands to express their emptiness. She said, "The phones are still no good."

"Who lives here who could help?"

"There aren't any doctors here."

"In this whole neighborhood?"

"Snyder on the corner's a podiatrist."

"What number?"

"What's wrong with your wife?"

"She needs medical attention."

"I have some supplies."

"She's pregnant."

"Oh," the woman said. "How far along?"

"I don't know," he said. "Not very."

"She's uncomfortable?"

"Yeah."

"Try to keep her comfortable. She's resilient. You'd be surprised. The human body is amazing. Especially a woman's."

"Have you heard anything?"

"From who?"

"From the power people."

"I'm just waiting like everyone else. It can't go on forever. People live here."

Eddie went to the podiatrist's address and knocked. Then he pressed through the dead bushes and held his face up to a window. He kicked at a basement door until he had to sit on the concrete steps to keep his head from spinning. His arms and legs felt numb. He couldn't make a fist anymore, and when he tried to stand up, the ground beneath him pitched.

His vision was acting funny; he could see his fingers in a way that made his fingers seem to be the only part of his body that remained. There was writing on his palm. He breathed in and out slowly and a vision eclipsed the world around him. He was working, sitting in his office, and it was spring. He knew it was spring because the sky outside his window was as clear as a glass of water. From his office window, there was no horizon; there was nothing, until maybe, once a day, a plane would plunge through it. The sun lit up the room in bright white squares.

He held his hand out into one of those illuminated patches, and looked again at the writing on his palm. It was faint and smudged from where he'd tried to wash it off that morning, and still too indelible to erase the memory of the night before. He and Laura had discovered a website enumerating the benefits of writing out an argument before allowing it to explode. *Like passing notes in high school,* the site had said. *This defuses the building tension.* But the previous night, he hadn't been able to find a scrap of paper. He could still make out the word *Who?* underlined just below his thumb. He'd held it up to Laura like proof of his commitment to communicate the obviousness of it with her. But by then, it was too late. They'd already had their blowup.

It had been a Thursday night, and she'd been on him again about going out.

"We have work in the morning," he'd told her. "I have zero interest in slogging through a day on no sleep."

"Going out is how we'll meet people," she'd said.

"What people?" He'd widened his eyes and raised his hands in exasperation. They'd had this argument before, and still, this fundamental counterpoint remained unanswered. "Who are they? Who is it that you want to meet?"

"Anyone."

"That's nice."

"It's just the two of us, Eddie."

"Isn't that the point?" he'd asked.

"Where are all our friends? We used to have friends."

"We grew up, I guess. We don't need friends anymore—we have each other. Look at your parents."

"Eddie . . ."

"*You're* my friend. We don't need anyone else."

"We do, though. It can't just be us. It's like we're floating."

Eddie sat in his office, staring at his palm and remembering it. He closed his eyes, but the brightness of the day turned his vision red against his eyelids. When he opened them, Scott from fund-raising was leaning on his door.

"Some hot chick here to see you," Scott said.

"What?"

"Says she's your wife, but no way that's true."

Eddie walked through the cubicles at the center of the office and felt the eyes of his coworkers on him. Some of them smiled openly. Laura was standing by reception, holding a brown paper bag. She was in her work clothes: a blue skirt and black top. She wore a necklace with a wooden pendant that Eddie had bought her for their anniversary.

"Hey, there," she said, trying to be playful as she did when she was trying to apologize. She leaned against the reception-ist's desk. "Jenny says you won't mind being hijacked. She says you're never busy anyway." She looked at Jenny in a way that allowed her to be part of the ribbing.

Eddie's voice was sharper than he intended. "What are you doing here?" he said.

Jenny dropped her head down to her papers, and Laura looked at him with hurt in her eyes.

He reached around her waist to guide her through the heavy door into the stairwell. He didn't want her apology. He didn't want her martyring herself so close to his lunch hour.

"Why aren't you at work?" he whispered.

"I wanted to surprise you."

"I'm surprised."

"Well, good," she said. "That was the point."

Her voice echoed thinly against the cement walls of the stairwell.

"What'd you bring?" he said.

"Do you actually want to know?"

"Yeah. Of course I do."

"Forget it."

"Sorry, Laur. I do."

"You embarrassed me out there. I was doing something nice."

"I know . . . I was being stupid."

"Cheesecake," she said. "Not enough for everyone, though. I thought we could eat it in your office."

"It will be strange if you go back there with me."

She shook her head and smiled, but it wasn't a happy smile. "Do you realize I don't know any of the people you work with?"

"They're just people."

"Are they nice? Are they your friends?"

"They're nice."

"I don't get it, then."

Eddie brushed the edge of her cheek the way he might a delicate fabric.

He said, "Maybe we should have a baby."

Laura flinched, as if startled by a loud noise outside, though the stairwell was soundproof.

"Are you ready?" he asked. "I think I'm ready."

"What does that have to do with anything?"

"It would be another person."

"That's not the solution. That's a different problem."

"It's a problem?"

"That's not what I meant." She put her hand on her forehead as if to judge the temperature the discussion had taken her to. "I have to sit down," she said.

She sat on the step, her skirt hugging up and exposing the tight skin at the bend of her knee. The stairs were lipped with crosshatched edgings that looked like graphite. Something about it made him sad—that brutal edge so close to Laura's knee. There was nothing in either one of their bodies as permanent as those emergency stairs.

When he looked down into her face, it was gone.

It was Wemmick's face, instead.

Eddie stared, overcome.

His hair! His shirt! His post-office mouth! He could see every bit of it.

"Wemmick," he said.

Wemmick squinted at him, his arms behind his back, as if holding a surprise. His mouth remained rectangular as he spoke.

"Hey, pal," Wemmick said.

But the voice was coming from somewhere else.

Eddie was kneeling on the cement walkway. It took him a moment. He saw the dead shrubs at his sides. It was the podiatrist's house. His face was six inches from the front door. He was staring at the mail slot.

"You locked out?" the voice said.

"Who are you?" Eddie asked.

"Station Sixteen, what's left of us."

Eddie raised his face into the sun. It was a man in a tight blue T-shirt with a firehouse insignia on the breast. Two other men stood behind him.

"You have water?" Eddie said.

"You're okay," the man said. "Get inside. This your place?"

"No."

"Go back to your place, then. It's too hot to be outside."

One of them leaned over and held out a long plastic nozzle that reached to the pack on his back. Eddie put it between his teeth and sucked. The water stung his tongue and tore at the skin down his throat.

"My wife . . ." he said.

"We're coming back. Don't worry. There's all kinds of madness in the city. It's safe up here. You're lucky to be in the burbs."

"What should we do?"

"We'll be back."

"The stream back there is burnt."

"It's everywhere. They told us the reflecting pool was in flames. The Anacostia, too."

"The Potomac is what we heard," said another.

"Just part of it," said the third.

"It jumped, then," said the first. "It must have jumped."

"We'll get reserves from out of state," the man with the water told Eddie. "We're prepared for it. Won't be long."

"Have you heard from them?" Eddie asked.

"Heard from who?"

"Out of state."

"No. Power's down."

"Then how do you know?"

"*They* know."

"*Who* knows?"

"Out of state." The fireman reached down and squeezed

Eddie's shoulder. "Listen. Conserve your strength. That's the name of the game."

Eddie looked up at him, though the sun curling around his body burned his eyes.

"The cops are coming?" he asked.

"Why?" said the first. "You got a complaint?"

"No."

"Then just sit tight. Go back to your home. You're lucky. Trust me."

"Are they arresting people?" Eddie said.

"Leave it to the crime fighters," one of them said, and they went off down the street. Eddie watched the backs of their blue shirts grow fainter in the sunlight.

He tried to get up. He could feel the sip of water in his stomach. His legs were weak, but he could stand. Soon, he could walk, and he let his legs take him down the hill, like following a stream, back home.

LAURA WAS STILL on her back, her legs crooked as if she'd been dropped there from above. The sheet was bunched on the floor.

"Where'd you go?" she said.

He stood over her, not answering, as she gazed up at the ceiling.

"You're right," she said. "I don't know anything."

"You're going to be fine."

"Yeah," she said. "I haven't even been to the doctor. Like you said."

"The human body is amazing," Eddie said. He looked at her legs and wondered how she'd gotten them in that position, how they weren't hurting her, tucked beneath her as they were. "Did you hear me?"

"The human body is amazing," she repeated.

"I shouldn't have run," he said.

"You ran?"

"Up the street. It was stupid."

"Just be still now. We don't need anyone else."

"Okay," he said, and he lay down next to her.

"I met some firemen," he said, finally. "They're working in the city, but they're coming back for us. They said the city is a mess."

"Okay," she said. "It's good we didn't go with the rest of them."

"Yeah," he said. "They have water coming in from out of state."

"Good," she said. "That's good for us."

That night his dreams were a slurry. He reached for Laura but only felt flesh. When he shook her, she moaned but didn't wake. He waited for the gray of morning, as if only the gray of morning would tell him they'd survived the night.

But it seemed the gray light would never come. When he closed his eyes, he saw red. Opened, black spots swarmed. He rose to climb the stairs but had to sit and rest when he was only halfway up. He brought down two glasses from the kitchen.

"We have to do it now," he said. "I'll drink mine. You drink yours. You have to wake up for this. I can't make you drink mine."

He turned the flashlight on in the bathroom and balanced it on its blind end. There was a dome of light, and its circumference on the walls was brighter, like a watermark. He stood above the toilet holding the glass below himself, but it was a long time before anything came out. When it did, it was almost nothing, brown and cloudy as cider.

He got Laura up and took her into the bathroom and sat her down, holding her shoulders like she was a child. On his knees, he held the glass between her legs, his hand down in the toilet bowl. When she could, it dripped hot on his wrist and he adjusted his catch beneath her. It was only a few drops, coating the bottom of the glass.

"Don't think about it," he said.

They held the cups at their chins. There was no smell. He was preparing to say *Go* when Laura tipped hers back and swallowed. Eddie knocked his back like a shot but held it in his mouth too long and had to breathe deeply through his nose. The room started to spin and he concentrated hard to keep it still. He swallowed and sat down and rubbed his tongue and the inside of his lips with the edge of his shirt.

"You're going to keep it down?" he said.

"Yeah."

They lay back on the mattress, and Eddie closed his eyes until Laura shook him.

"You're talking," she said.

"My dreams are hot."

"Try to stop."

"It hurts to talk. It hurts my mouth."

It was dark enough that he couldn't see her face, but could feel her breath on his skin. He could smell it, but it smelled like nothing. He tried to smell *something* on it.

She was sleeping again, and her breath was even, and Eddie felt himself relax a little. It was the same breath he heard next to him every night, rasping just at the end of each exhalation. It was easy for Eddie to think that this was all a memory he was making his way through. It was a comfort to think like that, and he worked to rein his mind within the fantasy. That he'd have work in the morning, that it was late, but not so late he couldn't fall back into the milkiness of sleep. He squeezed the muscles in his mind, but saw the little girl. Sophie. That was her name, but it felt like something else entirely, as though in dying, it had disconnected from her body and now floated there in front of him. He saw the car, but couldn't see the car—heard the squeal of its tires without knowing the sound, only knowing it was there, that the sound had happened—and though he wanted it to be soft, it was hard—the strike—because beneath the skin was bone.

Laura continued her nighttime noises next to him, but it was no longer any comfort to him. She was not who she'd been the week before. She was his wife, yes, but she was also someone else, and Eddie was afraid—for the first time—that he was already alone.

WHEN THE GRAY came through the window, he was able to gather his strength. Laura got up with him and they sat in the living room and looked out the picture window. A car drove by. Eddie banged on the window and Laura opened the door and shouted after it, but it was gone. Mike Sr. was coming up their walk. They watched him huff up the steps and take a break. He stared down at his stomach and took deep breaths that made his chest rise and fall.

They let him inside and he sat down on the sofa.

"We need to go out again," he said.

"Where?" Eddie said.

"Anywhere."

"It's best to rest," Laura said.

"We need to act on this right now. This is our window. Right now. What do you have left?"

"Nothing much," Laura said. "Some bread. Some beans. Ramen noodles."

"Nothing else in cans?"

"Nothing we haven't used."

"We've got one of tomatoes," Mike Sr. said. "That's it. Patty's trying to get it down Mike Jr. now. I'll bring you over some."

"You keep it," Eddie said, "for Mike Jr."

"Let's get out there, then," he said. "You and me, Ed."

"Eddie." Laura touched the back of his hand. "You'll be exhausted." She looked at Mike Sr. "You'll exhaust yourself, Mike."

"I'm exhausted already."

"It won't be much," Eddie said. "Just knocking on a few doors."

"Why would anyone want to give you anything now?" she said. "We're all in the same boat."

"Some people never got back home," Mike Sr. said.

"Break-ins, then," she said.

"It's an emergency."

"Eddie met some firemen."

"Where?"

"Down the road," Eddie said. "They're going to the city, but they'll be back, they said."

"Why didn't you get me?"

"They were gone already."

"Still," Mike Sr. said.

"They said the city's a wreck. We're better up here," he said. "We were smart to stay."

Outside, the sunlight filled the air around them like a pool.

Mike Sr. held on to Eddie's shoulder, and Eddie led the way. Both their shirts were dry; even around the collars there was no sweat.

"No one's left," Mike Sr. said. "Dammit. Where are we going, Ed?"

"I know a place. I was there before."

"What's it got?"

"I don't know yet."

They sat beneath a sphere of bare branches where once there had been leaves. The branches were thick and close together and gave a little shade.

The podiatrist's house was at the top of a slope, and Eddie counted his steps in his head and thought *one-two-three-hup*, moving each foot forward as he'd seen soldiers do in old war movies.

"I'm cooked," Mike Sr. said. He sat down on a lawn.

"You can't stay here."

"This was a bad idea," he said.

"It's not much farther."

Eddie got him up and going again, and soon they were at the podiatrist's house. There was no answer at the door, and Eddie looked for stones to break the windows.

"*Then* what?" Mike Sr. said. "Then you have to climb up through broken glass on your belly. You can't risk losing blood."

Eddie took him around to the basement windows and they kicked at them. Eddie threw stones, but they only bounced off. When Mike Sr. tried, one left a white nick in the glass.

"Too tough," he said.

"Look," Eddie said. In the backyard was a crab apple tree.

There were a few brown apples in the branches. "We need a ladder," Eddie said.

They found a big blue recycling bin and wheeled it around. It was sturdy. Mike Sr. held it and Eddie knelt on top. He stood slowly. It felt like he was a hundred feet up. "Keep holding!" he said. His breath buzzed inside his chest, and he held the trunk and reached out for an apple. Two of them were close and he got his hand on the nearest one. It was like squeezing a leather pouch. He had to lean down hard to disengage the stem. When he pulled the second one, the branch dipped. He felt the bin slide beneath him and hung on to the apple, thinking in that flash that it might keep him aloft. It broke from the branch and he fell and landed hard on his shoulder. The apple was in his hand.

"You okay?" Mike. Sr. said.

"I'm okay."

"Check yourself out."

He lifted up his shirt and peered over his nose to see a raspberry on his shoulder, blood just beneath the surface.

"It's not bad," Eddie said. He bit into the apple. Beneath the thick skin, the flesh was all but gone, but he worked it in his mouth and got some moisture out of it.

"Eat," he said to Mike Sr.

"I'm saving it," he said.

"You need fuel to get back."

"I'll make it back." He held the apple between his thumb and forefinger and tilted it back and forth in the way of someone showing off a medal. "Now I *know* I'll make it back."

On the way, they passed the house of the woman who'd opened up for him before. Eddie thought about knocking, but didn't.

"I spoke to a woman in that house," he said.

"Which house?"

Eddie pointed.

"What are you waiting for, then? Let's try it again."

Eddie thought of what to say. Mike Sr. had a strange look. It seemed to Eddie that all these houses had been abandoned. That everything was there for the taking. But he kept himself from thinking it.

"I already bothered her once," he said. "She couldn't help."

But Mike Sr. had walked up to the door already. He knocked a few times and waited. The woman opened with the safety chain secured. They could only see the right-hand side of her face. She looked older than Eddie remembered.

"Ma'am," Mike Sr. said. "My son is sick. Do you have anything at all that you could give me?"

"I'm sorry," she said. She looked at Eddie and he tried too late to look away.

"Are you a parent?" Mike Sr. asked. She tried to close the door, but as she did, he wedged his shoulder in. "Come on, Ed!" he said.

Mike Sr. ground his feet into the walk and leaned, and eventually the chain broke, the door swung open, and he went pitching headlong into a banister. The house was a split-level, and the woman retreated up the carpeted stairs into the kitchen.

"Get out!" she shrieked. "I don't have anything!"

"You have something. You're still alive," Mike Sr. said. He followed her up into the kitchen and she cowered by the sink. Mike Sr. found the knives and threw the block down the stairs as if for Eddie's safekeeping.

"Help me search the place," he called to him.

"How can you do this?" the woman cried. "We'll die."

"Ha!" Mike Sr. said. "If you have nothing, you'd have nothing to worry about. You'll die anyway."

"He has a kid," Eddie said to her. "That's the reason."

Mike Sr. found a glass jar of salsa in the fridge and a soggy bag of strawberries in the freezer. The bag had been resealed with a paper clip.

"Have you eaten these?" Mike Sr. said. "Will they make him sick?"

The woman shook her head.

"Let's look around. Check the back," Mike Sr. said.

"No!" the woman shrieked. She ran to Eddie and grabbed his shirt, pulling him down on the kitchen floor. "Don't do it. Please."

"What you got back there?" Mike Sr. said. He walked past them and placed his hand on top of the woman's head to keep her on the ground—or maybe to keep his balance.

"Stay where you are," he said.

"Why are you doing this?" she pleaded.

Eddie squatted beside the woman and touched her shoulder. She winced as though his fingers were sharp.

"Don't," she moaned. "Leave him alone."

Mike Sr. walked down the hall and opened a door back there. Eddie leaned on his heels to look. A bouquet of silk flowers, a white wall, an apparatus with handrails. He closed his eyes and felt he could stay there for a while.

"Mike," he called. "Let's go."

Mike Sr. had stopped in the doorway. Eddie got up and stood next to him, putting a hand on his hot, doughy shoulder.

Sitting up on the bed was a man with wisps of gray hair. His cheeks were hollow, his eyes as big as quarters. He worked his jaw. His lips had trouble separating. "*Mup*," he said, reaching a skeletal hand at them. The flesh on his arm was as loose as rotted canvas.

"We need to go," Eddie said.

"What's going on in here?" Mike Sr. said.

"We need to get out of here."

Mike Sr. nodded sternly at the salsa in his hand. "I'm keeping this," he said, but he put the strawberries back in the freezer.

The woman was still lying on the floor.

"You've killed him," she called as they left. "He'll be dead because of you."

Mike Sr. pulled the front door closed. They stood on the patio without speaking.

"Don't listen to her," he said after a while. "That guy was dying before we got there. I guess we're all dying now."

It took them a long time going back. Mike Sr. had to stop and sit and eventually Eddie did, too.

"You've got to eat just a little," Eddie told him.

But Mike Sr. refused. Even the color in his eyes had drained. They made it another block and rested on an elaborate wooden planter. The dirt inside was as weightless as perlite. Eddie ran his fingers over the surface and jostled the stalks of dead plants that were the same color as the dirt.

Mike Sr. unscrewed the salsa lid.

"Here," he said. "You're right. We should." He held the jar out to Eddie. "Take a little," he said.

Eddie scooped out a few chunks of tomato and onion with

his fingers and put the pieces into his mouth. He let them sit there, sucking the juices.

"Nothing's more important than my boy," Mike Sr. said.

Eddie looked at him. "I want to live, too."

"It's different being a father. You're still just thinking of you."

"Let's get back, then," Eddie said, "to your boy." As he said it, an ink stain spread across his vision. He lay back in the dirt and could feel his shoulder hanging off the planter. The air was soundless. A cough would have thundered through the neighborhood. Eddie reached over his head and felt past the corner of the planter. There was something soft there, and he let his fingers play on top of it. He thought of the stuffed dog he'd slept with as a boy—Louis—how he had worried its paws until the material felt as soft as this. His parents had let him name a stuffed dog Louis. It had probably been cute—that name in a child's mouth.

What a world. To get from there to this.

He could feel Mike Sr. grabbing at his wrists and lifting him.

"Easy, now," Mike Sr. said. "Don't go touching that."

On his feet, Eddie saw what the softness was. In the corner of the planter, a couple of squirrels had died. They were bunched up with their heads together, like they'd been trying to burrow.

"I thought it was something else," Eddie said.

"Easy, now," Mike Sr. said again.

Their houses weren't far, and they leaned on each other and took small, slow steps to make it back. Eddie went inside and called for Laura. Then he stretched out on the sofa.

He could see the old man with his enormous eyes, lifting himself up to stare at them. The woman had been right. That far gone, an effort like that would probably be the end of him.

"Laura," he called again.

Eddie thought that maybe he'd been sleeping, though how much time had passed, he couldn't tell.

The house was quiet, and panic shot through him.

"Laura!" he called.

She wasn't on the mattress in the basement. She wasn't in any of the basement rooms. It was dark down there, and he swung the flashlight over all the floors.

In the corner of the basement was a door they rarely used. He opened it and walked up from underground like he was climbing from the center of the earth. The sun was a terrible wall of light that made a froth of the line of empty houses and bushes down the sidewalk.

He was walking, though he thought he was standing still. It seemed the street was turning around the steady point that was his head.

He was at the abandoned house, through the yard, standing at the hedge. All the leaves were gone from it, and the turning stopped. The world was still again.

Through the sticks, though, he saw Bill Peters's dead, clay-like face.

He'd thought it would be Laura.

A strange hatred welled inside of him.

Bill Peters.

Bill Peters didn't have to face any of this. Eddie had to face it.

Back at the Davises, it took Mike Sr. a long time to answer the door.

"Have you seen Laura?" Eddie asked.

"She's with us."

When Eddie saw her, he said, "How could you do that to me?" She was sitting on the love seat. Patty was lying on the sofa, breathing heavily with her eyes closed. Mike Jr. was on a nest of blankets in the middle of the floor. All his clothes were off, his penis like a cork, gray and removable-looking.

"I came over to help. You were gone for a long time," Laura said.

"Were you helping?"

She stared at him fiercely. "Were you?"

"What are you talking about?"

Mike Sr. was leaning on the counter, and Laura turned to him when she spoke to Eddie. "You could have done something for those people on the bridge," she said. "I've been thinking about it, is all."

"You're on that now? Laura, I didn't even see them. There were other people standing around gawking already."

"They could have been hurt. You didn't know. You just ran past it all."

Eddie looked at Mike Sr., who stared into the space above Laura.

"Mike?" Eddie said.

Mike Sr. raised his eyebrows.

"You know about work crews and stuff. Tell her. You're supposed to wait for the paramedics."

"And what if there are no paramedics?" she said. "What then? You just ignore it?"

"Oh, shut up," Eddie said.

Mike Sr. said, "We just pray no one gets hurt when we're on a job."

Mike Jr.'s eyes were closed like his mom's, only his breath didn't seem to be coming.

"What can I do?" Eddie asked.

Mike Sr. went into the kitchen and started messing with a bowl. He brought it over and mashed the salsa with a spoon.

"You can help me get this down him," he said.

Eddie sat down next to Mike Jr., and Mike Sr. knelt across from them.

"Just make him comfortable," Mike Sr. said.

Eddie stroked Mike Jr.'s arm. It was dry and hot.

Mike Sr. took a spoonful of the red mash and put it onto Mike Jr.'s lips. It sat there on his face.

"Come on, Mikey," he said. He put a finger between his son's teeth and got his mouth to open. Then he pushed the mash in. It was clear from the way Mike Jr. lay there that the salsa was just inside his teeth, resting on his tongue. Mike Sr. ran his fingers up and down his son's throat, the way he'd get a cat to take a pill.

"Where are the cats?" Eddie said. The Davises had two Siamese he'd often seen pressing against the screens.

"Gone," said Patty. It was the first she'd spoken, and Eddie felt relieved that she was able to. "They were gone right off the bat."

"They're smart animals," Mike Sr. said. "If there's a way to survive, they'll find it."

Mike Jr. swallowed.

"Yes, buddy!" Mike Sr. said. He worked another fingerful into his son's mouth and rubbed his throat again. When he'd swallowed a second time, Mike Sr. brought four teacups from the kitchen and put a spoonful of the salsa into each. He handed one to Patty, and then one to Eddie and Laura.

"We can't," Laura said.

"Don't be a hero now."

"I just keep thinking about those cars on the bridge. I don't know why. What if there were people in them? People who died? I can't get it out of my head."

"She's punishing herself," Eddie said. He smiled, and the muscles in his cheeks tightened beyond his control. "She lost a daughter when she was young."

Mike Sr. looked over at her. "I'm real sorry to hear that," he said.

"Eddie," Laura warned. It was almost a whisper.

"But it's okay," he said. "She's pregnant again."

Laura stood from the love seat. "I need to go," she said, but her legs gave way and she crashed onto the carpet. She lay there making small sobbing noises.

"At least she *might* be pregnant," Eddie said.

Mike Sr. went to her and put the spoon of salsa close to her mouth. "Can you swallow?" he asked. "Don't think of anything else."

Eddie chewed his own spoonful, releasing the sharpness of the juice. He couldn't so much taste it as feel where the liquid touched his palate, where it settled between his teeth. He kept it forward with his tongue, letting it release slowly to the back of his throat.

The day felt inconsequential, like a lazy weekend. He moved over to where Laura was lying and went down next to her. The dreaminess had returned.

"No one holds it against you," he whispered. "You know Mike and Patty are nice people. They understand."

"But why would you say that?" she asked.

"I don't hold it against you, either. We're starting over. Both of us."

They sat there on the floor in silence, staring just beyond themselves as if sharing the quiet of a fire. Old cigarette smoke clung to the yellow walls, and it buzzed in Eddie's nostrils.

"How far along are you, sweetie?" Patty asked.

Laura didn't answer, and Eddie rubbed her back.

Then she said, "Just a couple weeks."

"It's not anything yet, then," Patty said. "You can't think of it as anything."

Mike Sr. said, "What about fracking?"

"What?" Patty said.

"Hydraulic fracturing. These gas companies pump all kinds of chemicals into the ground to break up where the gas is. It goes into the water and messes it up. You can light your tap on fire. I saw it on the news."

"That's up in Pennsylvania," Eddie said. "They're not doing it down here."

"Do you know that for sure?"

"That's what I heard."

"The ground is all connected, though," Mike Sr. said, "with plates."

"It's too big," Eddie said. "It couldn't happen all at once. You're wrong about that. You're just scaring them."

"It's an answer."

"I'm not scared," Laura said.

"It's the wrong answer," Eddie said. "So what does it matter?"

"What happened, then," Mike Sr. said, "if you know so much?"

"It's something deeper. Like, something wrong with the earth."

"You're not scaring me, Mike," Laura repeated. She spoke in the tender way she would to a child. "It's a start. It's just an idea of what it could be. We have to start with something, right?"

THEY SLEPT IN the Davises' living room.

Eddie curled up next to Laura on the carpet, but she turned and pushed him away with her leg.

"Laur," he whispered. "It was a dumb thing to tell them." Then he said, "I don't know why I said it. Come on, Laur."

"Now they know," she said into the carpet.

"You have to conserve your strength, though."

"So?"

"Being angry takes up energy." When she was silent, he said, "I need you to be strong. We have to forgive each other." He stroked her hair until she was breathing lightly again. "I'm sorry. Really. I didn't mean to.

"Laura," he whispered. "Laur . . ."

WHEN HE WOKE, it was dark and Patty was snoring on the sofa. Mike Jr. was near his feet in the nest of blankets. Eddie pushed at the boy's shoulder with the toe of his shoe. His own legs were wobbly. He had to hold on to the coffee table to stand. Mike Sr. wasn't there.

Eddie stood at the window facing the street. The dark inside the house was deeper than the dark outside, and it took a moment for his eyes to adjust. There were people moving out there. A big group of them. Some had backpacks— some pulled heavy-looking suitcases on wheels. He tried to speak, but his voice was splintery and stabbed his throat, making him cough. He grabbed for the wall but it was slick and he slid down and continued coughing on the floor. There was a pain deep in his side that felt like something tearing. He squeezed to keep it whole until the coughing fit had passed.

When he could stand, he opened the door, but the street had

emptied out. He walked out into the night. How long had he been on the floor? The sky had the whitish tint of dawn. It was hot out there, but maybe the house was hotter. Had he seen them? Those people in the street? The memory had sunk beneath the clarity of his vision like a coin to the bottom of a pool.

In the living room, Laura was sitting up. Mike Jr. was in her lap and she was bent over him as though he were a much smaller child. The way she cradled his head made him look like a corpse she'd lifted off the ground.

"Laura," he said.

She rocked Mike Jr. and his head lolled.

"Laura. Put him down."

Mike Jr.'s eyes flashed open, and Eddie caught his breath, stepping back.

"He's sick," Laura said.

"It's okay," Eddie said. "You can put him down."

"I have to take care of him. I'm responsible this time."

He saw that she was dreaming.

He touched her shoulder and she flinched.

"It's okay," he said.

She looked down at the boy in her arms. His eyes had the unhinged quality of blindness.

"How you doing, buddy?" Eddie asked.

Mike Jr. was silent and didn't redirect his gaze.

"I don't remember it," Laura got out. "Picking him up."

"You were concerned," Eddie said. "It's okay to be concerned about him."

He took Mike Jr. and placed him back down on the blankets on the floor.

"Lie down," he said to Laura. "Rest. It's night. We'll start over in the morning."

"Okay," she said, and when she was down, he knelt beside her and stroked her hair again. He bent to kiss her ear, and felt her hair at his mouth. It was still coarse and strong.

She slept, and he went back and stood at the window. There was no one in the street, but he watched as if he could produce the vision again. They'd been leaving the neighborhood, leaving their homes, and Eddie had not gone with them. When he shut his eyes he could feel the asphalt beneath his shoes, could feel himself running through the night—that old buoyant joy of sprinting through late-summer streets.

But they were gone.

He had missed them.

The salsa jar on the counter was empty except for a residue. He tipped it to his mouth and got out a few sour drops. When the retching came, he went to the sink. His stomach tightened and he spat out a brownish gob.

There was only baking soda in the fridge, and he got a spoonful of it and put it in his mouth. It stayed powdered until he worked it around. After a minute or so, it turned into a paste that he could swallow. It would settle his stomach, at least.

A flashlight was magnetized to the door of the freezer and he clicked it on. He expected to see Mike Sr. sleeping in the next room—a dining room with a polished wooden table— but the room was empty. The hallway was empty, too. There was a linen cupboard at the end of the hall, and on a top shelf, a box of bandages and ointments. A bottle of liquid cold medicine. Eddie unscrewed the cap and held it to his nose. He had to breathe in hard to smell the orangey syrup, children's strength.

In the living room, he pried Mike Jr.'s mouth open and pressed the plastic bottle against his teeth. When the liquid touched the back of his throat, he swallowed, and kept on swallowing. There was more in the bottle than Eddie had realized, but he continued to hold it to Mike Jr.'s mouth.

When the bottle was empty, he sat beside Mike Jr. and touched the boy's silken hair, letting it float electrically between his fingers. It took a long time for Eddie to check on the boy's breathing. He pressed in close, but Mike Jr.'s little chest didn't rise or fall. Eddie put a hand to the boy's mouth and felt nothing—nothing coming from his nostrils, either.

Laura had turned onto her stomach, her hands at her sides as if she was going to push herself up. Her eyes were open. She was looking at him.

"Is he okay?" she asked.

Eddie listened to the quiet in the room. "Yeah," he said. "He's comfortable now."

"Is he okay?" she repeated.

He tried to imagine their life together, what it had been—but he couldn't.

He felt the warmth in the boy's chest.

She lunged forward, reaching for Mike Jr., but she was too far away and only flopped down on the carpet.

"Please!" she sobbed.

She thrashed around there, but made no progress toward the two of them.

Eddie put his hand over her mouth, hushing her and squeezing her by the shoulder. "He's not yours," he said. He felt her tongue and teeth on his fingers. "He's not yours," he said again.

She rolled onto her back and looked up at the ceiling. Then she pressed her hands into her belly.

"Mine's gone."

"Don't say that."

He got her beneath her armpits and moved her toward the door.

"No," she said. "Let go."

"We shouldn't be here," Eddie said. "This is a family thing."

Outside, they sat on the Davises' deck. Eddie put his head down because it hurt to keep it lifted. The boards were hotter than the air, and pressed into his bones. His temple ached where it touched the wood. He needed to get onto the grass, but when he tugged on Laura's arm, she didn't budge.

"Leave me," she told him.

"We can't sleep here."

"I can."

"Come on, Laur."

She was lying down, too. He got his arm under hers again, and when he tried to stand, his weight moved her forward. She groaned a little. Her head was near the edge of the porch, but it wasn't hanging off.

"Okay," he said. "I'm here. I'll be right here."

He went down to the grass and lay on it. It was as sharp as splinters, but he pretended it was cooler than the deck. The basement would be cooler, softer, but he couldn't conceive making it back inside his own house. The basement might as well have been a mile away, ten miles away. His fingertips tingled, the insides of his elbows, too.

He looked up and saw Laura watching him from the porch. She was smiling. Maybe he'd done something funny. He was beneath the overpass, and he had fallen from high above. He'd covered himself up with ash again. The ash was warm and velvety on his skin.

IN THE LIGHT, he saw a man coming from the Mathiases' across the street.

He had a suitcase on wheels with the handle extended so that he didn't have to bend as he bumped it down the steps. He wore long pants that looked like suit pants and a shirt that wasn't tucked in.

Eddie lifted his face from the ground and felt where the grass had stuck into his cheek.

The man was coming up the driveway. Laura wasn't near the steps, and Eddie felt the panic of having left the knives inside. He sat up. The inside of his mouth was rough against his tongue and his tongue was fatter than it should have been. It felt more like a piece of meat. He didn't know if he could speak. He couldn't get to his feet.

"Hush, now," the man said as he approached. "I'm just a neighbor."

Eddie dropped to his side and used his elbow to drag himself along the ground, but didn't make it far. The man stood next to him. Eddie could feel the weight of the suitcase—its black rectangle blotting out the sun.

"I'm here to help," the man said. He unzipped the suitcase and took out a clear gallon jug. Eddie looked up beneath it and saw where the liquid in the bottom made a section of the sky dance like a swimming pool. The man tilted it over a coffee mug.

"Here," he said. "Drink."

The man got Eddie sitting against the base of the house, and put the cup to his lips. He couldn't swallow, but felt it going down. Whatever skin and muscle was in his throat was swollen and almost numb. He let his head drop and took deep breaths. Then he felt his head get lighter.

"Easy," the man said.

"Who are you?" Eddie managed.

"My name is Steve McCarthy." He knelt down next to Eddie and kept his eyes pressed closed. It was as if he were trying to keep them from floating off his face. There was stubble on his chin and his teeth were yellow. His shirt was stained coffee brown beneath the armpits. Eddie couldn't smell him, though. He couldn't smell anything. His nose was full.

"I have a wife," Eddie said.

The man nodded, but continued to hold his severe expression. Eddie pointed at the Davises' porch. "She was up there."

He looked at Eddie and then dropped his chin to his chest. When he lifted his face, his eyes were red-rimmed. "This is going to end. God sends everyone everywhere, so I guess he sent me here. I really believe that." He paused as if to double-check. "Do you?"

Eddie examined Steve McCarthy's face. "Yeah," he said.

"Your wife? She's living?"

"On the porch."

"That's good. Just rest now. Let the water do its work."

"How many have died?"

"I only minister to the live ones."

"Where did you get the water?"

"I have a supply."

Eddie tried to ask him *How?* and *Where?*, but his voice was stuck again.

"It doesn't matter now," Steve McCarthy said.

Eddie collected himself. He swallowed.

"My wife was on the porch," he said. "I could see her there last night."

He left Eddie sitting there and walked up the Davises' steps with the jug of water swinging in his hand. The sunlight played inside of it like golden ropes. On the porch, he bent down in the corner. Eddie couldn't see him from where he was.

"Is she there?" he said.

"Yes," Steve McCarthy called.

Eddie waited. "Is she okay?" he said.

"She's taking water."

He tried to stand but his legs still didn't work. He held on to the fence behind himself and used his arms to push himself up, but that, too, required strength he didn't have.

"It takes a little while," Steve McCarthy called. He was still bent down next to Laura; Eddie could see only the top of his head, the graying hair, the little curls at the base of his neck. "You'll get some strength, but you have to wait," he said.

"There are more in the house."

"How many?"

"Maybe two or three."

"You sit tight now," Steve McCarthy said, but he said it gently, only to Laura. He knocked at the Davises' door. While he waited, he stood with rigid arms, like a man uprighted in a coffin.

"They're in there," Eddie said.

"I can wait. For a while, at least."

"Eddie?" It was Laura's voice.

"I'm down here. Do what he says." He slumped back against the fence. He was feeling better, though. The blood was coming back into his legs.

Steve McCarthy knocked again. In the silence that followed, he took the slow deep breaths of a sickly fish.

"We're going to get out of here," Eddie said to him. "Then we'll come back and help. We'll do what you're doing."

"The roads are all blocked," Steve McCarthy said.

"Then we'll walk."

"Not in this heat. Your systems will shut down. And there are people who would rob you."

"Then how are you doing it?"

"I'm not going far. This is just my neighborhood. I move slow. See this? I breathe deeply. It helps."

"We'll take it slow, then."

"If you want to make it, take it slow."

"We need to get out of here," Eddie said.

"My advice? Stay where you are. Wait for it to end."

When the door opened, Mike Sr. leaned against the jamb. He twisted his face at Steve McCarthy. One arm was hidden behind the door, and when he raised it, it held a gun. Steve McCarthy backed away.

"He's got water!" Eddie cried.

"Water?" Mike Sr. asked. He was a full head taller than Steve McCarthy and had to point the gun down to level it at his face. "Where were you yesterday?" he shouted. His neck was wide with veins. His fury made him naked-looking.

Steve McCarthy held up his hands. It was as if Mike Sr. had said *Stick 'em up*. "I wasn't here yet," Steve McCarthy said. His voice had the calm of someone not afraid of death by bullets. "I was doing something else."

The gun shook in Mike Sr.'s hand, and he lowered his arm to his side. He closed his eyes, breathed, and held it up again.

"My son is gone. My *son*."

"Shooting me won't bring him back," Steve McCarthy said. He'd planted his feet at the end of the porch. "It won't answer any of your questions."

"You will, though. Tell me. Tell me why my son is dead."

"It's okay, Mike," Eddie soothed. Mike Sr. jerked his arm toward Eddie. He fired, and a moment later, the air was filled with the absence of the bang.

Eddie opened his mouth and exercised his jaw. He waited for pain, but the bullet had missed him by a mile. Mike Sr. slumped from the door to the railing of the porch. Laura was standing, steadying herself. Her mouth opened, but Eddie couldn't hear the words.

The water traveled up the sides of the jug as Steve McCarthy backed off the porch. Mike Sr. leaned forward on the top step but couldn't get his legs to follow. His big chest was a weight held too far out, and he pitched and fell, stumbling down to lie flat on his stomach in the driveway. The gun was still in his hand. When he looked up at Eddie, his nose leaked blood.

"Don't," Eddie said. The word was muffled, as if spoken underwater. He stood, but he couldn't walk yet. He looked down at the back of Mike Sr.'s head. "He's helping you."

"Helping me?" Mike Sr. said. "Why doesn't he help me bury my son? You bastard."

The door opened wider, and Laura had a hand under Patty's armpit to keep her standing up. Patty leaned her weight to one side and lifted up a foot. When it was down, she lifted up the other. In this way, she went forward, rocking back and forth.

"Mike," she croaked. "Drop it."

Mike Sr. was still splayed out on the asphalt, but he loosened his fingers off the grip.

Laura steadied herself against Patty and got her to the steps. They teetered on the edge. Laura's knees were shaking and then jutting forward, bending her in half. Patty reached out and caught the railing as Laura sat beside her in a heap.

"Sorry, Patty," she said.

"You're fine, hon." Patty set her jaw and stepped. Then she stepped again, her whole body rocking. She was like a piano being lowered.

"Come here," she said to Steve McCarthy, who backed over into Eddie and Laura's driveway.

"Ma'am," he said. "I don't mean any harm. I'm sorry that you've lost someone. I've lost somebody, too."

"I didn't lose someone." Patty stepped finally onto the flat asphalt. Her face pinched as she bent her knees and retrieved the gun from Mike Sr.'s hand. "I lost the only thing I had."

Eddie tried to take a step forward, and this time his legs held him up. "Patty," he said. "He has water. He's helping."

"When you lose your family, nothing else matters," she told Steve McCarthy.

They were standing as if in a duel: Patty with the gun at her side, and Steve McCarthy with the jug of water.

"You have your husband," he said.

"We're not a family. We're just two people. The family part's gone."

Steve McCarthy looked at the ground and closed his eyes again. "Not if you have them in your heart."

"Bullshit!" Patty croaked.

"There are people all over suffering," he said. "Some have lost everything."

"Put the gun down, Patty," Eddie said.

"*I* lost everything."

"Put the gun down." This time when Eddie said it, it served only to remind her she was holding something deadly. She raised it and pointed for the second time at Steve McCarthy.

"Drop it," she said.

He placed the jug of water by his shoe. "If I give it to you, you might as well just shoot me in the head."

"Step away. Go on. Get outta here."

"I'll die," he pleaded. "I was helping you."

"You say another word, another fucking word, and I'll pull the trigger. Answer my husband. I heard you. I heard what you said. Bullshit! Where were you yesterday? Where were you?"

Steve McCarthy bent down and touched the top of the jug; Patty took a step closer and stood at the edge of Eddie and Laura's driveway.

"Can you do what I'm doing with this?" he said. He picked

up the jug and hugged it to his chest. "Can you keep this from happening at every house? Do you believe you can?"

Patty fired into the air. "Run," she said, but Steve McCarthy froze. She fired again and his shoulder burst open. A flap of bloody fabric hung down. His hand went limp and the jug thumped onto the driveway. Eddie took two steps and fell on it like a fumble. He looked up to see Steve McCarthy running. It was freakish, the speed of his awkward stride; Eddie couldn't imagine ever running like that again.

Patty put the gun against the side of her head and fired, collapsing to the ground as though her bones had disappeared.

"No!" Mike Sr. shouted. He lifted his forehead from the ground and bashed it against the pavement. "Baby!" he cried, bashing. "Baby, baby, baby."

Eddie called for Laura. She pushed on the rail and stood, coming down the steps. Mike Sr. was bashing his head just below her, and she had to time her steps to make it over him.

She bent down and lifted Eddie by the arm. Eddie held on to the water.

"Oh, God," she said.

They went inside their house and fell onto the carpet.

"I have it," Eddie was saying. He was triumphant, stroking the plastic jug. "I have it, Laur. I got it for us."

IT WAS NIGHT, but they sat there by the door, leaning up against the side of the couch. Laura held the jug. Every hour or so, they took a little sip. It was like a tonic. Eddie felt bright and reflective. He felt that they would live. That they would leave here. There were maybe four cups of water left. It seemed enormous, but precious—the most precious thing.

"Just don't think about her," Eddie said. "Put it out of your mind."

"I see her when I close my eyes."

"Concentrate on something else. We need time to let this settle."

"It was so fast," she said. "I thought she was just going to walk back up her steps. I can see it with my eyes open, too. I was looking right at her when she did it."

"We'll leave," Eddie said. "We'll get away from here and come back when the power's back."

"Evacuate."

"Yeah, but not with the neighbors. Not into the city."

"We'll go to my parents' house," Laura said.

"Your dad will know what to do," Eddie agreed. "We can take the trail. That will keep us off the road for a few miles at least. We'll walk over the bridge."

"I've never done that."

"We'll leave tonight." He gathered himself as if to stand, but didn't.

"What about Mike Sr.?" she asked. "We're leaving him here?"

Eddie was silent. Then he said, "What are we supposed to do? It's up to him. We're not leaving him anywhere."

He watched Laura stand on shaky legs. She went into the kitchen and came back with an empty plastic water bottle. When she bent to take the jug from Eddie, he held on to it tightly.

"What are you doing?" he said.

She pressed down on the jug, locking her arms. She stared at him. "Don't be cruel," she said.

Eddie stared back. "There's no such thing as cruel right now. It's just us. The only people you can be cruel to is us."

"He won't make it."

"It's thirty miles to your parents' house. If we don't take all the water, we won't make it."

She nodded. "When the fire department comes, they'll help him."

"Right." Eddie looked at the black window. He couldn't imagine anything good coming from out there anymore.

"How fast can you walk right now?" he asked.

"I don't know."

"I'll get the tent, then. We'll need to camp out."

Downstairs, he found the tent in the furnace room, and stuffed it into his backpack.

"You're packing?" she said.

There was dry ramen in its plastic bricks in the back of the cupboard and Eddie took those, too. He packed the flashlight and a tarp and rolled a kitchen knife in newspaper so that it wouldn't cut the fabric. He took a raincoat. The pack was as tight as a beach ball when he zipped it, and the two canisters of wasp spray bulged from the side pockets.

"Let's go," he said. "It'll better to walk at night. We won't need as much water in the cooler air."

They stood there in the middle of the living room. The starlight didn't make it down to the ground outside their windows.

"We could stay till morning," she suggested, "and then go."

"The sooner we get there, the better."

"We'll go twice as fast in the morning," she said. "We'll get lost in the dark."

"I have the flashlight."

She sat down on the sofa and touched the spot beside her. "Rest," she said.

"Come on," he urged, but he sat down and she put her legs onto his lap. Eddie didn't mind that they were hot. After a little while, he squeezed her thigh and woke her up.

"We're going to be okay," she said.

"Yes," he said. He held the jug at his side. "This changes things."

"Yes."

Eddie looked at her. She'd lost the pleasant firmness in her features. Instead, her face was soft with daydream.

"When this is over," he said, "it won't even feel like part of our lives. It'll feel like a dream. Or a story we heard about someone somewhere else. What happened yesterday and the day before . . . I can barely remember it now. It's like I didn't do any of it, not me."

Laura remained silent.

"I've been in a fog," he said.

"Okay," she said. "But don't keep talking about it."

"None of this counts against us. Whatever you did when you were walking home from your car, whatever you saw . . ."

"It happened if you keep talking about it."

"Whatever happened to your little girl . . ."

She swung her legs out of his lap and sat up straight. He could barely see her face in the dark but he could tell something had changed inside her.

"It all happened," she insisted. "All of it. You can't turn it off. You can't start over. Can't you see that?"

"We'll get out of here. All that matters is right now."

"That's a lie," she said. "Don't fool yourself. I've been fooling myself for years. It all happened. Everything that happened happened. I'm different now."

"Just try. Just try to do this with me."

"I know what it feels like—like you're in a cloud, like your brain isn't working. I've felt that way for a long time. Like nothing I did mattered. But it does. I've felt that way since Philadelphia, but I wouldn't *let* myself feel it."

"You met me after Philadelphia," he said. "That's when we fell in love."

She looked at him, as if only then had he discovered the heart of it.

"Do you regret that?" he asked. "That you were like that when we met?"

"That part of me was clear."

"How can you know that for sure?"

"It's all so terrible, but I don't regret it. It's just my past. It all happened, but sometimes I can't believe it happened."

"Like us. We happened."

"You didn't know me when I was different. You didn't know who I was when I was young. This is who you fell in love with."

"But who will you be after all of this is over?"

"Who will you be?"

He thought about that question. "I don't know yet," he said. "It's impossible to tell."

"Just let it happen," she said. "Then we'll go from there."

SHE WAS STARING out the kitchen window. Somehow, it was dawn. They'd fallen asleep. He looked at Laura—the set of her jaw, the way she pinched her eyebrows. He felt sure she was watching Bill Peters walking up the driveway. A panic leapt inside his stomach.

"Mike Sr.'s out there digging," she said.

The jug was on the kitchen table. There was a glorious amount of it left. Eddie could see the pale waterline.

"Digging?"

"Graves, I think."

Eddie stood next to her. The panic was subsiding. Outside, the grass threw up a golden light. The sun seemed to be burning from below the horizon. Mike Sr. was pressed against a shovel. Digging wasn't the word for it. He was leaning. If the shovel wasn't there, he would have fallen.

"Did you look in the driveway?" Eddie asked.

"No."

"Don't," he told her.

They were quiet for a while, watching Mike Sr. lean on his shovel.

"It's not very big," Eddie said.

"What isn't very big?"

"The hole."

"It's not a hole. He's only scratching the ground a little."

"He has to decide how many holes to dig."

"I don't want to talk about this," she said.

Mike Sr. lifted the shovel tip from the ground. When he placed it back, he put his hand to his forehead.

"We could still help him," Laura said. "We're still here."

"We're going to your parents'."

"We could give him water."

"Look," Eddie said. He poked the jug so that the water rocked. "We talked about this last night. We need it. We're leaving."

"How do you feel now, though? You feel good, right? I feel pretty good. Not normal, but not as bad as yesterday."

"And how long will that last? Not long. Not in this heat. Maybe we can go ten miles today. That's three days it will take us. Look at this." He tapped the jug again. "That's not enough for three days."

"But right now we're feeling fresh."

"The fire department will be back soon," he said. "Remember? They'll help him. Like you said."

"You don't know that."

"They'll bring a water truck."

"Then where are they?"

"They're in the city now."

Laura looked back at Mike Sr. in the yard. "I'll help him, then," she said. "I'm feeling okay."

"No." He reached out and held her wrist. "We're going. Mike can take care of himself."

"You can't stop me from trying."

Anger squeezed through him like water through a crack in a dam—a dam he hadn't known existed, nor what it held at bay inside of him. His hand was in a fist.

"Stay here," he said. He made himself relax. "I'll do it if you stay."

The sofa was still buttressed against the back door, and the bean-can alarm balanced precariously on the knob. Eddie used the front door so as not to disturb it. The heat outside was ovenish and thick. The leaves on the azalea bush were gone. Blood from Patty's head had dried in a potato-shaped puddle. Eddie tried not to look as he passed her, but he looked. She'd already bloated a little.

"Mike," Eddie said.

Mike Sr. didn't turn around. He continued leaning on his shovel.

"Let me help," Eddie said.

He walked around to the patch of dirt that would become the grave for the Davis family. The earth wasn't broken; not even the pattern in the grass was broken. There was no strength in Mike Sr. to even scrape it away. The grass was yellow and dry. The shovel tip barely stuck in.

"Can you bring her back to life?"

The heat was already getting to Eddie. He was sweating. Mike Sr. wheezed.

"Why did she do it?" Mike Sr. said. He leaned more heavily

into the shovel, and his stomach hung. "We could have started over."

He pulled the shovel back, as if to rake the dirt away, but only combed the dead grass toward him. Eddie watched. Even burnt, the grass was elastic, erasing the path of the shovel tip. He looked at the creamy sky, the dead trees.

The shovel fell and struck the ground. Mike Sr. lunged, grabbing Eddie by the back of his neck, but there was no strength in his fingers. They peeled off when Eddie stepped away.

"Jesus, Mike," Eddie said.

Mike Sr. sat down on the grass. A wheezing persisted in his chest. Eddie rubbed his neck where he'd been touched.

"You have it," Mike Sr. said, looking at the parched ground.

"Have what?" Eddie said.

Mike Sr. ran his fingers through the grass. "The water," he said.

"No. He took it away."

"Don't lie." When he looked up, the skin around his eyes was iridescent with veins. "I saw you pick it up."

"I wasn't near it," Eddie said.

"You were there. You could have stopped her."

"I tried . . ."

"I'll go to the cops," he warned.

"I'm trying to help you, Mike."

"We'll see what they think," Mike Sr. said. "We'll see what happens when they investigate."

Eddie picked up the shovel and stuck it in the ground.

Mike Sr. said, "You give it to me, and I'll forget it. I won't tell them anything."

"There's nothing to tell." Eddie put his foot on the edge of the shovel and leaned on it. A little wedge of soil came up. Mike Sr. didn't move. He sat there looking in the other direction. Eddie dug a few more wedges out. He wasn't feeling well, and didn't hear Laura come out until she was right behind him, handing Mike Sr. a cup of water.

Mike Sr. was babbling. "Why did she?" he said. "Why'd she?"

Laura said, "It's what you do now that counts."

"Why did she do it?" The more he said it, the more it didn't sound like anything. "Why'd she doot. Wideshee."

Eddie walked past Patty in the driveway and tried again not to look. If he looked at her, he felt she might start talking—she might provide an answer for her husband.

Inside, he could see that the waterline in the jug was lower from when Laura had poured it for Mike Sr. He poured himself one, too. It was too much, maybe a third of a cup. He held it, and then put it on the table and looked out the window. Laura was standing over Mike Sr., who had his head between his arms, his fingers grabbing at his ears. Eddie picked up the glass and tried to take a sip, but couldn't stop himself from gulping it. When he was through, he poured another, and sipped from that one slowly. The first glass bubbled in his stomach. Outside, Laura was trying to dig. She was putting her back into it. Eddie was too tired even to call to her from the window. He could see her shoulder blades move beneath her shirt, but couldn't see the ground—whether it was becoming a hole or just a collection of more divots. After a few minutes, she came back inside, too.

Her shirt was damp beneath the armpits.

"That was stupid," Eddie said.

"You did it, too."

"It was stupid for both of us."

She didn't wait for Eddie to pour her a glass. She poured it herself, and drank it down fast, though not as fast as Eddie had.

"I can't leave yet," she said. "Now I'm tired."

"Is he still out there?"

"Yeah."

"He won't make it in the sun."

"I told him to go inside."

"Did you look in the driveway?" Eddie asked.

Laura closed her eyes in the way she might if stymied by an endless argument.

"No," she said.

"Where's the gun?" It struck him suddenly. "The gun that Patty had?"

"I don't know."

"Jesus, Laura. We can't let him have that gun."

He went out and stood in the driveway. Patty's head was crystallized like rock candy where the bullet had gone through. The creases at her shoulder and in her elbow were barely creases. The skin was too tight and full of gas to fold. She'd fallen on her arm, and her right hand was tucked beneath her body. Eddie went to the side of his house to get his shovel. When he returned, he pressed the metal tip beneath her belly to use it as a lever. He leaned down on the handle, but the curve in the head wasn't big enough, and the handle hit the asphalt before she budged. He had to get down on his knees and put his shoulder into her side and push back with his feet to get some daylight between her body and the driveway. He saw her hand under there—pink and meaty—but it didn't hold the gun.

"Get the hell off her."

Mike Sr. was standing at the fence. Eddie's chest tightened as he watched him stagger, his legs buckling. He fell hard into the grass and didn't move.

Eddie went back inside.

"Did you find it?" Laura said.

"No. It must have gotten lost."

"It can't be lost." She shook her head. "Mike Sr.'s got it."

Eddie leaned back on the sofa pillow. Laura brought him another glass of water.

"It's too much," he protested, but only weakly.

"Just a little bit of it, then."

He took a few sips. The water was warm and felt silky going down. The air in the house was hot, but not intolerably hot. Not like outside.

"If you're taking a nap," Laura said, "I'm taking one, too."

"I just need to rest," Eddie said. "Then we'll go."

Laura went into the bedroom.

He took another sip and then another, and then he lay back and thought about how they would do it. It would be slow going. He was right in thinking that they might have to travel at night, when it was cooler. At night, though, they'd have to walk on the highway, which he didn't want to do. He expected that if people were out, they'd be out on the highway. They wouldn't be safe with the jug of water there.

There were at least twelve miles of trail heading northeast through the park. Eddie had run that stretch when they'd first moved. It was soft and without much grade, and it followed the stream almost all the way. It connected with the big regional park to the north, and from there with another park, though he didn't know what it was called and had never been inside it. They'd have to cross along some roads then and cross Route 29, and then they'd be in the burned-up reservoir and could follow it east for a while. After that, they'd have to find the highway. There were woods alongside the highway, and if they stayed in the woods and kept the highway in sight, it would take them to the bridge and they could walk right over the Bay. Laura's parents were just eight miles on the other side. It seemed like a lot, but they could do it. He just needed to sleep for a couple of minutes to build his strength.

But he couldn't sleep.

Beneath his fatigue was an energy that made him tremble. *Mike Sr. with that gun.*

They were wasting time. The key was to get away from there, and yet they were sitting around, doing nothing. The truth was hardening all around him. The rest of the world wasn't coming. The fire department was gone. He'd have to muster the strength to do it now, to get out of the neighborhood.

His fingers tingled, but it wasn't like before. The map was mostly clear in his mind. He could run it, if he had to. He could put Laura on his back. He'd make bad time, but he would make it. He'd run that marathon without training. Once, he'd been a track star.

He went to her and could hear her soft breathing—a healthy breathing. Hadn't she said she was feeling better? When she stirred, he touched her thigh. It was warm, and he could feel the fluids straining beneath her skin. It was full of life! People had no idea what was happening inside of themselves. Eddie knew this. He rested a hand softly on her belly. Then he laid his forehead down on top of it.

"Eddie . . ."

He felt things. Tremors, currents—an incubating heat. It filled him up, just touching her like that. On the other side of this, they would be a family.

"You're crushing me," she said.

He crawled up close to her, so her ribs expanded against his own. The symmetry of their bodies brought him some relief.

"We have to go," he said.

"It's too much. I can't stop thinking about Patty."

"Try," he said.

"I don't think I'll ever get rid of that image."

"You will."

"How do you know?"

"Because everything fades."

She scooted to the edge of the bed and sat there. Eddie felt the cool place against his body where she'd removed herself.

"It's awful," she said.

"We're surviving," Eddie said. "We're saving ourselves."

"We're abandoning him."

"Mike Sr.?"

"He's got nothing left, and now we're leaving him."

"We can't save everybody. That's what you said."

"I don't want to save everybody. I want to save someone we know. Someone right there." She pointed at the wall in the direction of the yard.

"The fire department . . ." Eddie started.

She went into the living room, and when he came in, she'd curled up on floor and pressed her face into the carpet. "I'm no good at this," she moaned. "I can only keep myself alive."

"No," Eddie said. "You don't know what you're capable of."

"She's out there right now. His *wife*, Eddie. And his son is dead, too."

"You have to forget about them. When we go, you won't think about them."

"They're our friends."

"Our neighbors," Eddie corrected.

"If I could kill him now, I would," she said. "Just to put him out of his misery."

WHILE LAURA SLEPT, he tried to imagine the directions to her parents' house again, but his memory of the directions had begun to blur. Every turn led back to the sidewalk in front of the abandoned house. He needed to get outside to regain his bearings and see how the streets connected to one another. He looked out the window; Mike Sr. must have gone inside.

Eddie opened the door.

When he walked to the end of the block, he saw that his street intersected with Eisner, and that Eisner connected to Kerwin—and was relieved that the world possessed more dimensions than what his imagination had reduced it to. He could see the park in his mind again, how they would walk down the hill to get there.

They would be gone by the time Bill Peters's body was discovered. Eddie wasn't sure if Mike Sr. would corroborate his story, but they would think of something if he didn't. It was best to be far away. Bill Peters and the Davises were already casualties of this place, and there was no telling who else would be.

But Eddie needed to check one final time before they left.

He walked down the block and into the backyard of the abandoned house. All the leaves were off the hedge, making it a bouquet of tall sticks stuck in the ground.

From where he stood, he could see that something was wrong with Bill Peters's body.

There was something else on top of it.

Eddie was very still. The backyard was silent except for the sound of shallow breathing. Behind him was the outline of a flowerbed made up with paving stones. He gathered his strength and lifted one. It was a jagged rectangle the size of a quart of milk. He held it in both hands and walked across the grass.

The sound came again. It was the noise at the back of a throat. Eddie looked around; there was nothing to stand behind, nowhere to run but back to his door, through the open street. He listened, but the sound had stopped.

On top of Bill Peters was a man.

Eddie held the stone out in front of him. There was only the faintest whiff of putrescence in the air. He leaned in close to the man, and the branches of the hedge ran up along his chest and shoulders.

He was lying there, facedown. He wore a white shirt, stained dark brown at the shoulder. His hair was flat and matted, his ear as gray-green as mold.

Eddie bent down to take his pulse, but stopped before he was close enough. The shoulder rose and fell a little.

"Hello?" Eddie whispered.

The man turned his head to look up at him.

It was Steve McCarthy.

The branches had cut his nose and left scabs like raisins on his cheek.

"I'm all right," he said.

Eddie's heart pumped great jolts of blood into his ears. "What are you doing here?" he whispered.

Steve McCarthy moved his lips. "I found this man," he said. Eddie watched his eyes close and listened to his breathing.

When Steve McCarthy bolstered his strength, he said, "I was trying to help, but then I fell. I think this man is dead. He's not moving. I'm having trouble discerning how long I've been here." He rolled and lifted his hand. In it was the steak knife. "Look," he gasped. "He's been stabbed." Beneath him, Bill Peters's face bulged unrecognizably. Eddie saw where the collar of his shirt had turned his neck a dark blue from the pressure of the swelling.

"I need to report this," Steve McCarthy said. He was still for a moment. Then he said, "This used to be a good neighborhood."

Eddie's palms hurt. He looked down and saw he was still squeezing the stone.

"Violence," Steve McCarthy said, "all of it."

Eddie looked at his face. There was a clean spot at his temple—a stretch of skin between his hair and the stubble of a beard. The hard corners of the stone pressed into his hands. He still had the strength to do it, to lift it up over his head and bring it down. It would all be over quick.

"God gave me a gift late in life. That water . . ." Steve McCarthy began. He'd closed his eyes again. "But it's not too late. I can still use it. He's asking me to use it."

Eddie lifted the stone. He stepped forward to get his weight moving in the right direction.

"He gave me a supply to take to you people," Steve McCarthy continued. "His people."

Eddie held his breath. He looked at the spot of skin at Steve McCarthy's temple, and then lowered the stone to his belly. "A supply of what?" he asked.

Steve McCarthy opened his bloodshot eyes. "Water," he said. "There's more of it. I just need to get my strength."

Eddie put the stone down and knelt beside him. "Tell me where it is," he said. "I'll get it."

"No," he said. "I have to do it."

"I'll bring it back for you."

Eddie touched the shoulder of Steve McCarthy's shirt where the blood had dried. Beneath it the skin was as crisp as cellophane.

"I need to get my strength," he said.

"You're sick. Let me do it," Eddie said, but Steve McCarthy didn't respond. "Tell me where," Eddie said.

He got his arm between the two of them—between Steve McCarthy's belly and Bill Peters's chest. Steve McCarthy winced as he was lifted off the dead man's body. But Eddie got him to his knees. Then he laid him down in the yard.

"Can you stand?" Eddie asked. "Can you feel your legs?"

He bent again, pulling at the sides of Steve McCarthy's waist and raising him like a bag of heavy dirt. They staggered together, but once he was up, his legs straightened and held him. Eddie took him by the shoulders and guided him down the walk. The blood on his shirt was powdery. It brushed on Eddie's arm and cheek.

At the house, the door was locked. Laura must have gotten up. She must have been afraid that something had happened.

He knocked, and when she opened the door, he leaned Steve McCarthy against the brick wall beside it. He kept his hand pressed into the man's chest to keep him from pitching forward.

"He's alive," Eddie said.

Laura looked with horrified eyes.

"It's the guy who helped us," he said. "The guy with the water."

"We can't give it back to him, Eddie. We can't."

"Help me get him inside."

She got a sheet out of the closet and laid it out on the floor. She folded up a towel for his head.

"Put him here," she said.

"I think we have some gauze."

Eddie stepped back out onto the porch and surveyed the street. It was empty the way he'd come. When he looked in the other direction, Mike Sr. was standing in his driveway. Eddie nodded, but Mike Sr. only stared.

"Who you got in there?" Mike Sr. asked. His voice was hoarse.

Eddie stepped back inside and closed the door.

Laura was perched next to Steve McCarthy, wrapping gauze around his shoulder.

"Is it bad?" Eddie said.

"I don't know. We need some tape."

He got her the duct tape, and she filled the room with its wretched tearing sound as she pulled it from the roll. Then she wrapped it around the gauze on Steve McCarthy's shoulder.

"I don't know what this will do," she said.

"Is he breathing?"

She turned her face and put it down close to Steve McCarthy's mouth.

"A little," she said. "It smells really bad."

"We have to keep him alive."

Laura stood up fully and rested her hand on her hip as if examining Eddie's motives had returned her to a normal life.

"Why," she asked, a shrewdness in her eyes, "do we have to save him?"

"He was shot," Eddie said, "helping us."

He looked at Steve McCarthy's shoulder and his face full of scabs. His hair was too thin to cover the liver spots on his forehead. He was an old man, Eddie saw.

In the kitchen, he poured some of the water into a mug. Then he stood in the hallway holding it, looking at the two of them: Laura, and Steve McCarthy on the carpet.

"Eddie . . ." Laura said, looking at the mug.

He bent down and tipped it to Steve McCarthy's lips. At first, it bubbled back and poured out over his cheeks and onto the sheet beneath his neck, but when he tried again, he got it down. Eddie watched his Adam's apple move.

"Be careful," Laura said. "You're wasting it."

"It's okay," he said. "Maybe he can talk."

"Don't give him too much," she said. She stood above them, holding her hands together—one cupped beneath the other.

Then she said, "What are you doing?"

"Letting him drink."

"With your fingers."

Eddie hadn't noticed. He was touching Steve McCarthy's hair.

Laura stood there for a long time, frowning, as Eddie sat next to Steve McCarthy.

"Not too much," she said. Eddie tipped the cup up hard against Steve McCarthy's lips, and the water spilled out over his mouth again.

"Come on," Eddie whispered hotly. "Tell me where."

Laura went back into the kitchen. Eddie could hear the chair move when she sat down at the table.

After a while, Steve McCarthy's breathing came more steadily, and he opened his eyes. They were still red, but he was lucid.

"You're okay," Eddie said. "You can tell me where it is now."

"Don't let me die," Steve McCarthy whispered.

"You're better than you were."

"My throat hurts. It's dry."

"We'll help you. But you have to tell me where it is. The water," he whispered. "Just tell me."

"I need more," he said. "A little. Or I won't make it."

"You're okay."

"God gave it to me," he said.

"Laura," Eddie called.

When she came in, her eyes were pink and swollen.

"Pour me a little more," he said.

"We don't have much left."

"Just enough to wet his throat."

She went to the table and came back with the jug. "Look how much you used already," she said.

"It's important."

"We need enough for us. We're leaving. That's what you said."

"You wanted to help people. Let's help him."

He gave her the mug, and when she came back with it, he held it and looked inside. There was a thin layer of water at the bottom. He tipped it to Steve McCarthy's mouth, and Steve McCarthy closed his eyes as it went in.

"Go on," Steve McCarthy said. "Give me some."

"I just did."

Steve McCarthy looked at him. "There was nothing there."

"There was," Eddie said. "A little bit."

"Please," Steve McCarthy said. "I'm not your enemy. I helped you before. Didn't I help you?"

Eddie put his hand on Steve McCarthy's good shoulder and shook it against the floor of the living room. He said, "Tell me where it is, goddamn you."

"I was kind to you," Steve McCarthy said. He leaned his head back against the towel and parted his lips.

"Laura," Eddie called again.

He got up and went to the kitchen. She was sitting on a chair. "Don't," she said. "Don't let him do this to us."

"He's not doing anything."

"He's going to take everything," she said.

"He needs our help."

"Until you need help. Then what happens?"

"He's a Good Samaritan. This is the right thing to do." He poured a little more into the mug and took it back into the living room. Laura followed him in. Steve McCarthy had opened his eyes back up, but when he saw Eddie, he closed them.

"Did you see that?" Laura said. She stood up close to Eddie and spoke directly in his ear. She was excited. Eddie could feel her heartbeat. "His eyes were open. Did you see? He closed them for our benefit."

Steve McCarthy breathed through his nose in fits. "I have it," he said. "My strength is coming back."

"He's faking," Laura said. "He's putting us on."

"'Whoever has the world's goods,'" Steve McCarthy said, "'and beholds his brother in need and closes his heart against him . . . how does the love of God abide in him?'"

Laura knelt beside him and stared into his face. "What is that?" she asked. "What are you saying?"

"The word of God."

"Oh, Christ," she said. "What do you want from us?"

He closed his eyes again, and when he opened them he said, "Just a little more. That's all I need." He reached out and touched the rim of the mug with his finger. "It's helping me. I can feel it. I'm getting stronger."

Eddie took the handle of the cup, but Laura pushed his hand down, pinning it where it was on the carpet.

"It isn't right," she said. She was speaking loudly. "He's faking. Can't you see that? He lied to you the first time and now he's lying to you again. He threatened you."

"He didn't," Eddie said.

"You had to throw him down the steps."

Eddie sat up on his knees. "No," he said. "That was a different man."

"Eddie . . ." Laura said. "*Please* . . ." She stood with her hand clenched at her chin and walked back and forth between Eddie and the bedroom.

"I can get the rest," Steve McCarthy said.

"Where do you live?" Eddie said. "You can trust me."

"It's not at home," he said. "I can feel my legs. My legs are coming back."

"What's he saying?" Laura said.

"He's saying he has more."

Eddie took the mug into the kitchen, and Laura followed at his ear again.

"You can't," she whispered.

"You think that was all he had? One jug? For the whole neighborhood?"

"He'll say anything, Eddie. He's trying to live."

"So are we."

"He's desperate."

She held his shoulders and softened, so that for a moment he thought she might lean in and press her forehead against his.

"We need to save ourselves," she said. Her eyes weren't pink anymore. They were clear. "I was wrong. It's just us now. You were right about that. We have to go."

"He's giving us a chance," Eddie said. "If we get what he has, we have a chance."

"You're not thinking. Listen to me. He's taking advantage of you."

"I saved him out there. You didn't see him. He would have died."

In the living room, Steve McCarthy's breath was steady and Eddie bent down to look at his lips. The skin had splintered like old fiberglass. There was a moldy fragrance coming from his insides, but it wasn't as bad as Laura had said.

"We can get him better, at least," he said. "Then we'll see what he's making up. When he's better, it'll be easier to tell."

He pressed the mug to Steve McCarthy's mouth again, and it pushed his lip up and exposed his overlapping teeth. The water welled at the corners of his mouth before it sunk in.

"Stop it," Laura said. She was standing above him, her voice quaking. "Look what you're doing."

Eddie heard a boom outside, and Laura's body tensed.

The noise struck again.

It was someone knocking at the door.

"Who you got in there?" came a voice.

It was Mike Sr.

"Just be quiet," Eddie whispered to Laura. "Don't say anything. Don't move."

Eddie stared at the rise and fall of Steve McCarthy's chest.

"Who's in there?" Mike Sr. bellowed.

"It's just us, Mike," Laura called.

"Shhh . . ."

"Go back home," Laura called.

Mike Sr. knocked some more. Then he yelled, "I saw your husband take him. I'll kill him for it. I'll kill them both."

They could hear his footfalls down the steps.

"There are three of us and one of him," Eddie said.

"I know," she said.

They took little sips of water and stopped talking to save their strength. Steve McCarthy kept his eyes closed. The sun had dipped outside and made the lawn look fiery.

Eddie put his head between his knees and regarded the floor, watching its patterns shift. Laura's hand was on the back of his head, but it felt hot and he shook it off.

Something hit the kitchen window behind him and he sat up straight again. It sounded like the thump of a bird, but then he saw knuckles at the end of an arm.

A fist.

Mike Sr. was reaching up from the driveway.

They watched it. He pressed his fingers against the windowpane and the tips flattened and turned white. They sat very still, though the window was too high for him to see them. The hand retracted, but then came back and knocked again.

"God," Laura said. "Just give him to him."

"No," Eddie said. "Not until he tells us."

"Tells us what?" Laura cried.

He went into the living room and touched Steve McCarthy on the shoulder. His eyes didn't open, but Eddie could see he was awake.

"Tell me," he said. "I'll leave my wife here with you. She thinks you're lying. If you're lying, there's no point giving you any more."

Steve McCarthy whispered something.

"What?"

"In the woods."

Eddie looked over at Laura. She was staring out the window and hadn't heard.

"Where?" Eddie whispered.

Steve McCarthy smiled. "I hid it."

Eddie took hold of his wounded shoulder.

"Was it yours, or did you find it?" he said.

"What?" Steve McCarthy said.

Eddie squeezed his shoulder, and a light puff of powdered blood released above it.

"Did you find it there? Was it a jug? Like from a cooler?"

Steve McCarthy breathed in and out. If there was pain, his face showed no sign of it.

"A jug," he said.

Eddie banged the shoulder up and down on the carpet.

"Where? Where did you hide it?"

Steve McCarthy breathed out and moaned. "A little more," he said. He opened his mouth and touched his wrecked lips with his fingers. "I need a little more water to talk."

"Goddammit!" Laura yelled. She bent over Steve McCarthy and pointed a finger in his face. "You're lying! You don't have any more!"

Steve McCarthy put his hand back at his side. He was silent. The knocking on the window had stopped.

"Just give him a little more," Eddie said. "Then I'll make him tell us."

"Eddie." She held up her hands. "There's nothing for him to tell."

He went to the kitchen and poured more water into the mug.

"He's killing us!" Laura shouted.

"He knows where it is," Eddie insisted. "He'll tell me and then I'll go and find it."

He put the mug to Steve McCarthy's lips and he gulped the liquid greedily.

"Look," Eddie said, nodding toward the window. "It's dark already."

Laura slumped against the wall.

There was a shot outside and the kitchen window shattered. Glass sprinkled on the floor.

"Stay where you are," Eddie yelled to Laura.

He pressed his back into the wall and climbed over her to get to the kitchen, standing up slowly beside the window.

"Eddie . . ." Laura called.

"He can't get in here."

He turned and saw Laura with her hand at Steve McCarthy's hip. She was going through his pockets.

"He's got a knife!" she called.

"Hold on," Eddie said. "Just hold him there."

He could see Mike Sr. standing on his porch in the dusk. His arms were resting on the railing and the gun was in both fists, pointing at their window, but his head was hanging down. His belly sagged beneath him.

Eddie heard a thumping on the floor and turned to see Laura pressing the towel down on Steve McCarthy's face. The man's feet pulled frantically against the carpet. His hands grabbed at the air and flopped open on the floor.

"Laura!"

"Stay away!" she screamed. She pointed the knife at Eddie. It was the knife from between Bill Peters's ribs.

"Let him up!" he cried, circling around behind her. He took her shoulders and pulled back. When she was off him, he flung the towel away. Steve McCarthy's eyes were open, staring blankly at the ceiling. He didn't move. Eddie put his cheek to his mouth and felt nothing, smelled only the faintest trace of breath.

Laura sat with her back hunched and scratched at her palms, staring into them.

"It wasn't an accident," she said. "Nothing is."

"Oh, God," Eddie said.

"I saved you from him. I had to."

Eddie sat on the floor and watched her. Her hair was in her face. She was breathing hard.

"We can give him to Mike Sr. now," she said. "He'll have what he wants, and we can leave."

Eddie stared up at her. "He knew where it was," he said. "I can't get it for you now."

"I wasn't doing it for me."

THEY DRAGGED THE body to the front step and closed the door when they were back inside. They sat on the carpet and listened for the sound of the body being dragged away. Eddie had the backpack next to him. Once the body was gone, and they felt rested, they would leave.

But there was no sound.

They listened and listened, but heard nothing. Instead, they fell asleep. They were asleep when the door blew open. The gunshots in the air were trapped in Eddie's dream.

A black shape blotted out the starlight. It hadn't yet become the shape of Mike Sr.'s body.

"Eddie," Laura gasped.

There was a standing lamp next to the door, and it wobbled when Mike Sr. grabbed it.

"Give it to me," Mike Sr. said.

"Mike . . ." Laura pressed herself to sitting against the back of the sofa. "We left him outside."

Mike Sr. fell and the lamp crashed to the floor. "I know you have it," he said, not getting up. He wheezed airily, as if his chest were full of holes.

"He's dead," Laura said. "We left him out there for you."

"The water," Mike Sr. said.

"Just take it easy," Eddie said. "We'll give you some."

Mike Sr. sat up. He reached his arm out to them. "No," he said. "You'll give it all to me. I made all the sacrifices."

"We can't give it all," Laura said.

A shot cracked over Eddie's head, and he pressed himself into the carpet. He grabbed for the strap of the backpack in front of him.

There was a motion of shadows beside him as Laura scrambled to the kitchen.

"Stay down!" he yelled to her.

Another shot went off and shattered the clock off the wall behind him. Mike Sr. was aiming too high. Or maybe he was firing at random. Eddie brought the pack closer and reached inside for the knife. He felt something hard in the side pockets.

The canisters of wasp spray.

"I've made my sacrifices," Mike Sr. said weakly. "You haven't made any."

"Eddie?" Laura called.

"I'm okay."

"We'll help you, Mike," she said. "Just stop. Please stop."

"You could've helped before, but you didn't."

Eddie could see Mike Sr.'s shadow as it straightened upright and lurched toward him.

He put his thumb on top of the canister and flipped onto his back. Then he pressed the button and sprayed where Mike Sr.'s face would be, waving it back and forth. There was a hissing sound and Mike Sr. said, "What the . . . ?" and then began to scream. He fired shots around the room, and Eddie pressed himself harder against the carpet.

"Get behind the wall!" he yelled to Laura.

When the shots stopped Mike Sr. fell forward and hit the sofa. He grabbed Eddie's calf and Eddie bashed at his fingers with the can of spray. When he let go, Eddie took the backpack and stumbled to Laura in the kitchen. She had the water jug against her chest.

"*Go,*" Eddie said.

Mike Sr. moaned from the floor.

"Is he out of bullets?"

"He had a box of them. There might be more in his pockets."

They knocked the sofa away from the back door. When it opened, the can alarm fell to the linoleum and clattered.

Outside, they stood in the grass and looked back up into their window. Eddie had his arm through the backpack strap.

"We'll wait till he goes home," he said. "We can hide out here until he leaves."

"Why would he go home?"

Eddie thought. "We could stay at his house, then. I can break in if he didn't leave it open."

"He's got a gun. We're not safe in either house. Not as long as he's alive," she said.

"What, then?"

"We have to leave."

"We haven't rested."

"We have."

"Not enough, though."

"Do you know where you're going? Can you get there in the dark?"

Eddie could see the empty street, like a stream leading to the tributaries of the neighborhood. They'd follow it to the park, and then follow the trail in the park as far as it would take them. "Yeah," he said. "I can get us there."

At the end of the street, they took the intersection down the hill, just as he'd done before. There were voices in the dark, and he pulled Laura into the shadows of one of the yards. They knelt near the house's foundation and didn't move.

The sounds were coming from down the hill, near the entrance to the park.

"If Mike's dead we can go back and take his gun," he said.

"And if he's not dead?"

"I don't know."

"Then he's still a man with a gun," she said. "We can't go back and check. I'll go and see who's down there."

"No," he said, but she'd already started, and he had to run to catch up with her. They kept on the grass beside the sidewalk, and toward the bottom of the hill they stood inside a shadow-box fence.

There was a cluster of voices at the bottom of the hill. Eddie thought of the kids crashing through the Mathiases' yard. He couldn't hear what they were saying, but could tell that they were men.

"We can cut through ahead of the entrance," he said. "They won't see us. There are too many trees." Even leafless, the trees in the park amounted to a dark wall hemming in the street.

"Wait," Laura said. "What are they doing?"

"It doesn't matter."

"They're looking at something. Wait."

Eddie held her arm.

Beneath them was a dark line of shoulders and heads. When they stepped aside, he could see a glint of white, like they were circling a piece of marble.

"She's got her pants down," Laura said.

"What?"

Then he saw. It was the pale glow of skin.

"Let's keep going," he said.

"They must be drinking something. Or else they wouldn't be able to do it to her."

"There are a bunch of them."

"If they get me," she said, "you can run. I'll be a diversion."

"We have the jug," he pleaded. "That's enough."

"It's not enough. Not if you want to make it to my parents'."

"I want to make it together."

"Give me the raincoat," she said.

"What are you going to do?"

"I need to cover this up." She was wearing a yellow T-shirt. The raincoat was purple and black. When she put it on, she faded, even as close as she was.

"What should I do?" he asked.

"You're fine. I can barely see you."

He bent down and dug at the earth with his fingers, tearing up the grass and scooping handfuls of powdery soil. He wiped it on his face and arms, but it was too dry to stick.

He turned to tell her to be quiet, but she was already moving toward them, lifting the hood on the raincoat. Eddie didn't dare call out her name. She'd taken only a few steps, and he had to squint just to see her in the shadows.

When she came back, it was as if she were appearing from thin air. It sent a spiral of dizziness through his body.

"This is crazy," he whispered.

"I saw what they have. I'll show you."

"Let's keep going," he said.

"I was still far away. They couldn't see me."

"No." He grabbed both of her wrists and held on tightly.

"If we don't make it all the way," she said, "we won't make it at all. This is it. This is our last chance."

They crept beside the aluminum guardrail where the runoff had carved an empty rivulet next to the street. A thick dust covered their shoes. Eddie could feel it brushing up onto his calves.

When they were on line with the group of them, they crouched behind the guardrail. One of them was saying, "Come on, come on," but his heart wasn't in it. It was like he was taking tickets. The others had conversations in low, mumbled voices. They'd closed back up around whoever it was in the middle of them. As they moved, the dark outline of their shoulders jostled like water in a tank.

Laura pointed to a plastic grocery bag on the ground. It stood stiffly with whatever was inside.

Eddie pressed his mouth close to her ear. "It could be anything," he said.

When the circle broke apart, Eddie saw a naked shoulder, a screen of hair. A hand pulled back the bangs, and there emerged the flatness of a cheek, a dent of shadow resting there. A face. Her eyes were open, but drained of any light.

"I can get it," Laura said. "Whatever's in there, I can get for us."

Eddie watched her stare fiercely at the bag.

"We have enough," he said.

She flinched as if he'd raised his hand to strike her. "You don't know what enough is," she said.

The bag was several feet behind the group, maybe fifteen feet. Laura stepped out into the street and Eddie didn't stop her. He couldn't move. If he moved, they would see. She was almost invisible on her own. The air around him tightened like a rope being pulled. A shout was rising in his chest and made a pressure in his throat he could barely keep within.

In a few steps, she'd vanished; he watched the bag instead. He watched the stiffness of the handles. Finally, they were blotted out by the darkness of her sleeve. The bag lifted. Eddie's fingers clawed the earth without his knowing. It made his eyes hurt, to keep the pressure building up inside him from escaping. He followed the bag until it was right in front of him.

"I got it," she said.

She stood there like a miracle, floating in the night. Maybe she would save them.

"Look," she said. Inside the bag was a long plastic bottle. She shook it and it sloshed.

"Drink," she said.

"How do you know?"

"I tried some already."

He unscrewed the cap and put it to his lips and let it sit and coat the back of his throat. It tasted heavy—thick as paint— and he gagged before he swallowed.

"We need to go," she said. "They'll see it's gone."

She took the milk jug off the ground, and Eddie saw how light it was. There was almost nothing left. "Come on," she said.

The metal railing curved, leading to the opening of the trailhead. The woods were like a fresh and blacker night to step inside. The group of voices softened behind them. There were words, but they had no edges.

Then a scream split the words apart. A woman's voice, but pitched as high a girl's. The air drew toward it.

Laura stopped in front of him.

"Keep going," Eddie said.

"We have to try," she whispered.

"We *are* trying."

"We have to try to stop them." Her voice was breaking. "You don't know, Eddie. You haven't done what I've done."

Eddie reached for her, but she was gone, running back toward the scream. He could see the jug bobbing at her side like a lantern growing dimmer.

He ran after her, the backpack beating against his back. He'd lost the outlines of her body, but then he found them again. She was racing for the group, and then she disappeared, inside of it. Eddie ran harder, searching for her among the bodies.

He could see her hair being tossed around—her head loose and wild. He could feel it in his stomach; he could feel the sweat of their sex and bodies as he pushed his way through them. A pair of naked legs hung down from a chair, but whoever it was was facing the wrong direction, slumped forward against the back of it. Eddie reached further into the throng, and grabbed a hold of something plastic. It was the wheel of the chair. Arms and legs beat against him, not knowing who he was, and he followed their flex and spasm to where they'd taken hold of Laura. He grabbed for her as they pulled her back and forth.

"Close your eyes!" he yelled above their voices. He reached into the pack for the other can of wasp spray, and leaning back, he circled around her, spraying. There were shouts and the hands broke away. Bodies stumbled backward.

He took her hand and they ran hard to the entrance of the park. He couldn't see the trail but heard branches breaking all around them from the weight of the other bodies in the dark. A hand grabbed the back of his shirt, but he pulled away.

"Go!" he yelled, and stayed behind her, tripping through the underbrush. Something was wrapping around his legs— a tangle of branches—and Laura had gotten ahead of him. He yelled her name and wrenched his legs until they freed. Ahead, he saw the jug. It swung from her hand, and Eddie trained his eyes on it. The others were running all around him.

The jug stopped moving and trembled where it was. Laura was thrashing back and forth.

Someone had a hold of her.

Eddie plunged against her back, wrapping his arms around both Laura and her assailant, taking them to the ground. His feet tangled with theirs and he pushed her head aside and threw his fists into the head beneath. He felt a chin and teeth, and his hand was slick with blood. The jug had fallen next to them and Laura rolled away and picked it up.

"Go," he said. "*Go.*"

She pulled him up and they ran like that, together. There were puffs of voices—everything thumping. Then everything was clear. They'd found the trail again.

"We have to get off," Laura said. "They'll be here."

At the spillway, they stopped. The trail went down and crossed Route 29 and then spread out into a meadow. They could see it all from where they stood; the openness of it, like a puddle of wax. They'd have no cover there. Below them, a drop twenty feet down. It was a bowl of space from where the stream had pooled, silent and empty, full of shadow. The trees were nubs at the edge of the cliff. Eddie could see the shocked-out bottom of white sand, but the edges were blurry with ash where it had all come rolling down.

"If you don't hear my voice, keep running," he said.

He pushed off from the ledge and fell, the wind filling up his ears. When he hit, the ash went up to his waist, and as he breathed in the plume he'd made, he coughed and then tried to quiet his coughing.

"Jump!" he called out sharply.

A dull breath of air, and Laura penciled down. She landed closer to the base of the cliff wall.

He grabbed his left thigh and pulled it forward. Then his right, wading through the ash like it was thick, deep water.

"No, *no, no!*" she was yelling, and Eddie could see the cloud of ash as she shoveled it back up into her face with both her arms. "*No!*" she shrieked.

"Laura!" he pressed his voice out into a whisper. "Shh . . ." he hissed. "Quiet."

"I killed you!"

He saw a flutter of white. She was beating the jug against the air. The ash got deeper and he dragged himself to reach her.

"Eddie . . ."

He wrapped his arms around her.

"Eddie!"

"Quiet. *Quiet.*" He held his fingers over her mouth, but she bit down, and when he pulled them back, she wailed. He got his arms around her head and pulled her face into his chest.

"Shh . . . Be calm. Be quiet."

She slumped down his side, and he had to push her face into the ash to muffle her.

"I killed you, I killed you," he could hear her say.

"It's okay now. Shhh . . . hush, now."

She was shaking, but she wasn't shouting anymore. She lifted her face and wiped the ash from out of her eyes.

"It's all I can do," she said. "You were dead and I knew it. Because of me. You were dead as soon as I told you yes."

"Just stop it now. Come on, Laur. Stop talking . . ."

The silence of the woods opened like a theater to their voices.

She held up the plastic jug.

Eddie looked, and she shook her head. It was dented in and topless from where she'd landed on it. There was nothing left. Her face was pinched in ferocious sorrow.

"Shh . . ." he said. "Be quiet, now."

There were voices above them on the ledge. "Down there," he heard.

Eddie whispered, "Freeze."

The footsteps above them were soundless in the ash. It could have been two sets or all of them. "Down the hill," one of them said. "I saw them."

"The girl."

"This way."

When the voices came again, they were only noise—the words too far down the trail.

Eddie scooped the ash back with his hands. He was digging a hole for her, but the ash kept falling in.

"Come here," he said. "Get in here."

She sat in the hole and he covered her up so that only her shoulders and head were out.

"We have to stay like this. We'll get out of here in the morning."

"Where's the other bottle, Eddie?"

"Forget it," he said.

"Tell me. Tell me or I'll scream."

"I must have dropped it back there. It's my fault."

Laura collapsed back into the ash and put her face in her hands. Eddie leaned his back against the wall of the cliff. There was dirt there, roots—too steep to hold the ash. He put his hand on Laura's back. The sky was a trail of unmolested stars.

"We'll change our plans," he said. His head was aching again, and he had trouble keeping his eyes open. The knuckles on his right hand throbbed. When he touched his face, there was blood there, too.

"There's no plan now," she said.

"We'll make one," he said, letting his eyes close.

"Would you have agreed to ever meet me," she asked, "if you'd known that this was coming?"

"No one knew this was coming."

"I knew. I knew when I was fifteen."

"You didn't know."

"Everything dies for me. I loved you, Eddie. That's how selfish I am. I loved you but I let us be together."

"I'm glad of it."

"I let us go through with it, even though I knew that this would happen."

"You didn't know."

"When I lost her, I knew. You can't understand. I could see the rest of my life. Some people are good at it. Some people just make things die."

"I wouldn't be alive without you. What would I be living for?"

"You should have just lived for yourself."

After a while, she asked about the boy.

"Don't think about him," Eddie said. "He's at rest."

"Not Mike Jr.," she said. "The other one. The one who was all burned up. Remember? He was gray."

Eddie stared into the clarity of the sky as he would into a lake, looking for its bottom.

"He was at our house," Laura said. "Remember? He was standing right out front of our house at the beginning."

"I looked for him," Eddie said.

"But then what?"

"I don't know."

"What happened to him, Eddie? Tell me."

"He found his way back home."

The night had made her voice extremely soft. "I don't believe you," she said.

The truth was like a breath he'd been holding in.

"He was gone," he said finally. "I tried to find him, but I couldn't."

"You let him go."

"He was gone already."

"You can't just let a child go," she said. "Don't you know that?"

Eddie listened to her breath. It came in fits.

"At least we're okay," he said, and then was quiet while Laura made retching noises. His memories were smoky as they surrounded him. He could see the weeds in Laura's daughter's teeth.

No. It was the wet pieces of spinach stuck in his goddaughter's. Sleep was coming, unbidden. Eddie was saying, "You'll be the strongest girl in school," and he could see the fat thumbprints in the burgers on the grill, the corn on the cob. Her laughter, like water, filling the vessel of the world around them.

But he didn't let the dream come fully on. He made himself keep talking. "In the morning," he said, "we'll go to a bunch of houses. If there are people in them, then they're drinking something. We'll knock on doors. Someone will help us. We're right here in the middle of all these houses." He looked, for a moment, up beyond the bowl of the spillway. Where Route 29 passed, it was dim. On the other side of the road were more communities like their own.

"Why would anyone help us?" Laura said.

When he looked again, there was no sky, just the grassy spot in his dream. At the edge of the grass, the woods started and the land dropped off beyond them. It was a steep grade, and he could hear a stream down there.

"If they want to live," Laura continued, "they won't help us. Oh, please don't let them. I can't do it to anyone else."

The earth in his dream was soft. They were driving home from Jason's, having left Eddie's goddaughter laughing on the lawn. Eddie couldn't stop smiling. He said to Laura, "What a cutie," but Laura was silent. She sat rocking in the passenger's seat, looking ill. "Are you carsick?" he asked. "Do you want me to pull over?"

In his dream, he stood on the slope behind the pull-off and took a step, sliding, pressing his palm into the dead leaves on the ground to brace himself.

"Come on!" he called to her.

"What are you doing?"

She stood above him, looking into the sky beyond his shoulder.

"It's not that steep," he said, holding out his hand to her.

She took a step and slid, and soon she was down on top of him, hugging his neck.

They could see the water—silvery gold—and his mouth filled with the taste of it, how sweet it would be.

At the bottom was a gravel bed, and Eddie tried skipping a stone, but it hit the water and sank. He was out of practice, and the water was shallow. He found a few muddy ones and rinsed them off. He tried again, but the water only gulped as the stones disappeared.

Laura sat on the bank behind him, running her hand over the moss growing there. There were big roots where the soil had eroded from around the base of a tree.

"Look how it grows here," she said, stroking the moss between the roots. "It's perfect. Doesn't that drive you crazy? How everything is perfect?"

"What do you mean?" he asked. "It's just nature. You don't have to think about it."

"Everything is set up to fit inside everything else. It's just makes me so sad, sometimes, to see it."

Eddie looked at her.

"Come feel it," she said, petting the moss again. "It just grows here on its own. Nobody asked it to."

"I'm not going to feel it."

"It's perfect and it doesn't even try. Nothing else has to try."

In the breeze overhead, dark birds swirled like rags above the tree line.

EDDIE WOKE WHEN the sun was still behind the world, but the sky was almost gray.

Laura slept next to him, gray with ash, still mostly buried in it. The contents of the backpack were strewn out in front of her from when she'd rummaged through it: the tent, a couple of unfolded T-shirts, the packets of ramen. Eddie ran his hands over it all.

A sudden fear overtook him.

He hadn't packed the knife.

Laura's knees had poked through the ash—two islands of skin. Ash was in her hair. Her face was streaked with it. Eddie could see the dark spot in front of her arms where the water had released from the jug on impact.

Soon, it would be light enough for them to be seen from above.

The can of wasp spray was almost empty.

They had to move right away.

"Laura," he said.

When he touched her shoulder, she slumped to the side and her arms rolled out of the ash, which had clotted on her wrists.

Eddie's hands shook; his fingers refused to bend. He tried to touch her, but only bumped his hands against her shoulder. Beneath her, like an artifact, was the black handle of the knife.

It was covered in bloody smudges.

There were sounds. Low mewling noises. An animal in the woods, maybe. He would lie there and wait for it to come—he would wait to be ripped apart.

He heard the sounds again.

They were sounds that he was making.

He draped his body over hers, and her head moved sickeningly beneath his chest, her jawbone digging into his ribs. His face pressed into the ash beside her and he breathed it in. He could die this way, too, simply by breathing—he would drown himself in the ash.

But he couldn't do it. He lifted his face and scraped his tongue with his fingernails and spat.

He picked up the knife. The heaviness shocked him, the length of the blade, its sharpness. It seemed only an instrument of terrible violence, and it trembled in his hand.

His girl. Oh, God. His wife.

Beneath smears of gray, veins still branched along his own wrists. He touched the blade to one of the raised channels but couldn't make himself push. He moved it to the bulge of flesh beneath his thumb, sliding it diagonally across. A thin edge of skin lifted up as easily as the corner of a page, and a bulb of blood emerged.

He touched the blade back to his wrist and closed his eyes. She'd sliced where she knew the blood would run. Would one cut be enough? Or would he feel the pain, and then have to cut again?

His arms were weak. He could barely raise them.

If only he could cry. His face was hot, but his throat was clear. He could breathe. The air was the same air, and he dug into the ash around her, piling it up to her neck. When he got to her head, he stopped. He couldn't bury her face. Her eyes were closed.

"Talk to me," he whispered. *"Laura."*

He reached to wipe the ash from her cheek. Her head wouldn't stay still—it lolled back, a terrible weight atop her neck.

When the water came back, her body would wash downstream. Until then, it would swell in the heat like all the rest. He held the knife. How many times had he sharpened it on a rod when he could have been pounding it dull with a hammer?

It was too late to think about that.

Her head was out of the ash, but not by very much. No one would see it. If this was her grave, it was almost hidden. The sky was yellow and hot. He could feel it burning up the skin on his face and arms. His neck was moist again, and he cursed it. He was not yet close to dying.

He held the knife in both hands, like a sword he would drive into the ground. He wouldn't allow her body to swell. He would keep her down beneath the ash. He closed his eyes and pressed the tip into the mound of her chest, leaning until it twisted in and sunk.

"Oh, God," he cried.

He pulled it out and forced himself to lean down on it again and again. He wanted to feel as if the blade were forcing its way between his own ribs—for each incision to be an incision through his own flesh and lungs.

But he felt nothing but the heat of the day. The work of stabbing his wife was only making it hotter. He held the knife in front of him—a dull reflective silver—and tried to find his veins again, but couldn't. He couldn't even look. Steve McCarthy had said his systems would shut down, but his thirst hadn't even stopped. That would be the sign—when the thirst went away.

In front of him was the boy. He stood along the bank where the ash hadn't piled.

"Stay there," Eddie said.

The boy stood very still. He seemed held there by the weak filament of Eddie's gaze. Then he started to turn.

"No," Eddie called. "Wait!"

He ran, and Eddie raised himself from the ash, tumbling through until it was shallower underfoot. The boy picked his way along deep drifts like he knew them by heart. Eddie's knees bumped together. He wasn't ready to run yet.

At the bottom of the spillway, the boy ran across Route 29, to where the park picked up on the other side. Eddie saw the back of his burnt hair as he went down among the boulders following the streambed. There was sand where the pools had been—a streak in each, like a cat's eye. He felt his chest strain, but forced his legs to follow. When the trail leveled off, the ash was almost gone. There had been a sandy bank there. The boy was getting smaller in the distance and then he was gone.

"Hey!" Eddie called. "Come back!"

The trees up the hill were only burnt on the side facing the stream, so that each was two-toned. Near the streambed were blackened shrubs. He kicked one and it collapsed over his shoe. The air was close down there. He sat on a rock and looked at the scrape on his wrist. It hadn't even bled.

The knife was back on the trail. He'd left it there. He'd left everything. But when he looked into the woods, she was there, too—she was all around him—and when he pushed his fists into his eyes to dispel the image, she wouldn't go away.

He pushed harder, grinding down with his knuckles. He saw her hair—black and straight and moving around her shoulder as she turned her head. He could taste it in his mouth. The hopelessness in his stomach began to spread.

He hit his fist into his ear, and hit it again until an ache reached down his jaw and his skin went numb.

He thought of Steve McCarthy, who had talked of taking it slow—how that was the only way to survive. But Steve McCarthy hadn't really known how long a body could last in the heat without water because he'd been drinking all the while. Steve McCarthy had thought that moving slowly had been the key, but Eddie knew now that the key was moving fast. Eddie could see Steve McCarthy's shoulder bursting open. He could see the look on his face the moment the jug had dropped from his hand—as if he no longer shared a history with his own arms and legs. Eddie felt it, too. If his body was not his own, then he owed it nothing, depended on it for nothing, and was free. There was nothing to keep him there.

And so he ran.

If the boy was up ahead, Eddie would find him.

He ran and his legs did not give up. He would run until he caught the boy or until the thirst vanished and he could run no more. He was going as fast as he could go with his eyes open, but then a strange revelation arrived. He suspected he could go even faster with them closed.

It was true.

Seeing had only been slowing him down. With his eyes closed, the ground turned to air and his body made no sound. He couldn't feel his legs moving or his jaw aching. He couldn't feel the flutter in his chest.

He went until the toe of his shoe clipped an imperfection in the path and he shot forward in the manner of a base runner stealing third. The skin of his palms tore into white strips, and more blood welled beneath. His palms were already bruising, and he felt a healthy, functioning pain taunting him with its throb. He had stores of wretched life left in him.

If the boy was still ahead of him, he would have to rest, too. Eddie lay down on the rocks and saw above him the great metal underside of the Beltway. He'd already come this far. He remembered running this trail and hearing the groans of big rigs overhead thumping and tapering off. All was quiet now, even his heart—though it was beating gently. How many more miles before the trail emptied out and he was walking on the highway? It would be flat up there and maybe he'd see some drivers. Then it was Route 50 and over the bridge, and he'd be just eight miles from Laura's parents' house.

Laura's parents would treat him like their son, despite the tragedy he was part of. They would grieve for Laura together. She was all they had. But now they'd have him. They'd lost a grandchild in the past and this would be too much for them alone.

Next to him was a charred stump. It must have been a stump before all the rest was burned because the top was chainsaw-flat. Lying on the stump was a string of colored beads—butterfly shaped, a sorbet orange, green, and pink. Fishing line held it together. A little girl's bracelet. Someone else had placed it there, unkinked as it was. A lost and found right there in the woods, as though whoever it was had hoped the owner would be walking by and find it. He held it in his palm and ran his thumb over the indentations stamped into the bits of plastic. Then he laid it back down, a scar of color on the dirty wood.

His arms and legs were sore, but his vision was clearer than before. He got up and ran with his eyes open this time, and another bit of color bloomed in front of him. Thirty feet ahead of him a flower was poking from the ash. He stopped and put his hand on his knees. The flower's redness was evidence of something.

As he approached, though, the shape of it changed. It wasn't a flower, after all. It was the frill of a little shirt. A girl was there, her hair clumped up. Her cheek was coated in a film of soot. Eddie touched it, and in the track his finger left, the skin was swollen pink. The rest of her body was covered in dirt and ash. Two men were down ahead of her, but all their color was gone. One looked at the sky, his eyeballs dead and bulging.

Eddie walked around them and kept on going. After a while, the thirst arrived again and started spreading. Laura's parents were on a well, and if their power was out, then her father had surely rigged a system to get the water to the surface. That was a man who wouldn't let his wife go thirsty; Eddie was sure. He admired Laura's father: whatever his hands could build, he built it for his family.

Through the trees, Eddie watched the sky slide down like a patch of oil. It was amber at the horizon. Black shadows swam through the limbs and gave the impression of people running. Every few minutes, he stopped and stood still, looking around him, but there was no one there.

The ash was thinner, and he could see the trail again where it curved along the bank. The ground was soft and brownish gray. The shadows in the trees looked like children. He saw them running, but didn't believe he really saw them. It was just the amber light playing through the branches.

Soon, he stopped to take a piss.

"Ha!" he said, shouting at his zipper like a madman.

But nothing came out. He unclenched the muscle in his groin, and a warmth spread between his legs. He thought maybe he'd wet himself, but when he felt there, he was dry. His fingers tingled, but that was okay; his headache was okay, too. His headache protected him from the heat.

Another child streaked across his vision. It was just a shadow in the trees, but Eddie called out. Steve McCarthy had told him to sit and rest—that if he sat and rested the feeling would come back into his legs. But Steve McCarthy was a liar, and Eddie didn't have time to sit and rest. His window was closing. He needed to get to the bridge. He needed to get to Laura's parents' house.

He ran on wobbling legs, trying to ignore the children in the trees. One of them was gray and thronged with streaks of light, which blinded him, and then there was a single child, running. Eddie left the trail and followed him up into the tree line.

"Come back here!" he called.

The ash was heavy there, up to his shins. But higher on the ridge, the trees were trees again, unburned. They had a rotted, hollow look. The boy looked over his shoulder and zigzagged gleefully, as if Eddie had wandered into a game of tag.

"Stop!" he called. His voice was harsh. The boy turned and stood where he was.

Eddie kept his arms at his sides, as though any sudden movement would spook him. The boy's left hand was palsied and twitched at his hip in the manner of a gunslinger's. His hair still stood on end, his shirt the same color as his arms and neck, the cloth so tattered it looked like rotting skin.

Eddie tried to hold him with the sternness of his voice. "Where are your parents?" he called.

The boy clutched his arms at the elbows across his chest.

Eddie didn't move. "Why aren't you at home?"

The boy looked at him with muted eyes.

Eddie tried to walk, but his legs wouldn't follow. He pitched forward, and the boy ran. Eddie watched from where he'd fallen. There were dead leaves in his face so dry his chin made a powder of them against the earth.

"Wait," he called. The boy grew fainter in the woods, and Eddie squinted hard, hoping to find traces of motion that he could connect together into a path.

There was a sound that may have been branches breaking, but may have been no sound at all. He heard only his breath and then a buzzing.

When he opened his eyes, the buzzing was gone. The woods

were silent, but the sky had changed color. The amber at the edges was darker, and overhead was gray. He rolled onto his side and grabbed his thighs to get his legs beneath him. He leaned into the trunk of a skinny tree, and as he pushed himself up, the trunk broke like wafer candy. It was a tall tree and the upper branches whizzed through the air far away from him. The headache was gone. He could stand. He started slowly, but soon he could walk and then he could run again.

He ran in the direction the boy had disappeared, watching the ground to see where he'd disturbed it. His own feet left deep imprints among the leaves, but it was as if the boy had floated over them.

It was strange the way his energy left him—like a plug had been pulled at the base of his spine, all of it draining out. He imagined the boy in front of him, the way he'd looked over his shoulder devilishly—as if he'd been the one to pull the plug when Eddie wasn't looking.

First the sky above him went blurry and then he doubled over and couldn't lift himself up. He stumbled through the woods, his eyes so heavy he almost didn't see the refrigerator on the ground in front of him. He almost ran right into it. It was on its side, as white as a box of light. Four legs hung over it. Above the legs, two bodies sat.

The boy came out from behind the refrigerator and stood next to the two men's legs. He grinned at Eddie, as though he'd won by getting there first.

"Keep going where you're going, pal," one of the men said. He was shirtless and wore a heavy metal chain around his neck, the kind a bike messenger might use to lock up in the city, except a cross hung from it. The other man reached over the edge of the fridge and twisted the handle of the samurai sword that leaned against it.

Behind them, tarps were tied to the trees and Eddie could make out bodies lying beneath them on blankets. The tarps were brown and green and red, and strung at different angles like the rooftops of a far-off arid city.

The boy walked back and forth, catlike, between the legs of the two men, running his hand along the metal of the fridge. They didn't pay him any mind.

When the man with the chain bent over, the chain stayed motionless against his chest. Eddie stepped closer. It was a *tattoo* of a chain and a cross. The other got off the fridge and held the samurai sword. He addressed the tip to Eddie.

"What do you want?" he asked.

Eddie's throat was too dry to speak. The air hurt going in. He clutched at it with his hands as though he were choking.

The one with the tattoo tapped a knuckle next to where he sat on the metal door of the refrigerator. "This isn't for you," he said. "It's for us and the women."

Eddie pushed hard with his stomach muscles and made a squeaking sound. The effort forced him to sit, and he looked up at them from the ground.

"We got an arrangement with the moms," the tattooed one said.

"Nothing left for you," said the other. "Go back the way you came."

"Gary . . ." the tattooed one said.

"What? He's a dead man. Look at him. It's too sad."

He propped the sword against the side of the refrigerator and raised a canteen to his lips, tilting his head back. The canteen was green and wide, with a cap connected by a bendable plastic strip. Eddie had had one just like it when he was young. He used to play "lost soldier," hacking at trees with a pocketknife. The memory was strong enough to drop the walls from where he sat—so that he was nine years old again, deep in the woods behind his parents' house.

The two men stood up and Gary opened the refrigerator door, bending the upper half of his body into it. When he came up he was bear-hugging a watercooler jug against his chest. He leaned it on the side of the refrigerator and took off the cap.

"Give it here," he said, and the other man held the canteen. "Hold still," he said. He touched the lip of the jug to the lip of the canteen and poured out two pulses of water.

Eddie clutched his throat again and rasped. He skidded forward on one butt cheek, and then the other. The backs of his legs pounded silently against the earth.

"Get up. Get out of here," Gary said. "This isn't for you."

"You don't just get precious things for free," the tattooed one said. "Supply and demand. Get it?"

"If there's no supply," Gary said, "you don't get to demand it."

"And he works for a bank."

"*Used* to work."

"Yeah, used to. What do you do now, then?"

"This."

"Right. This."

They seemed to have forgotten Eddie for the moment, talking as they were.

He moved closer, legs out in front of him, trying to use his hands but his hands weren't responding. They flopped on limp wrists when he pushed them on the ground.

"What is this?" Gary said, his voice going high. "Go die somewhere."

"Gary . . ."

"He should have gone with the rest of them."

"Yeah, but they didn't come back," the tattooed one laughed.

Gary spat a loogie that landed near Eddie's hand. "At least they were trying to help themselves."

He put the heel of his shoe on Eddie's shoulder and extended his leg. Eddie fell to his side. He tasted the earth in his mouth. It tasted of fire. He flailed his hands and caught the crook of his elbow around Gary's shin.

"Get him off! Get him off!" he squealed, as if Eddie were a spider.

The tattooed one retreated behind the fridge and raised the samurai sword.

"Take your hands off him," he said. "I'll cut you with this thing."

Eddie squeezed his arm tighter and pulled himself along the ground using Gary's leg. He was close enough that Gary doubled over and leaned his hands on Eddie's back.

"Do it, Matt!" Gary yelled. "Do it, already!"

"I'll do it!" Matt yelled. "Get off him! I'll do it!"

Eddie pulled in tighter. He was trying to get close to the refrigerator, but wasn't having any luck. Gary's weight was keeping him pinned down.

"I'll do it!" Matt yelled again.

Gary squirmed around and soon his leg was free. Eddie's face was in the dirt again. He lay there in front of them.

"What the hell?" Gary said. "Why didn't you do it?"

Eddie heard the flat edge of the samurai sword click against the fridge.

"I didn't need to. Why would I do it if I didn't need to?"

"What do we do with him now?"

It was quiet for a while and Eddie closed his eyes and continued to taste the earth.

"Give me the glass one."

"The empty?"

"Yeah."

Eddie felt their steps beat on the ground as they approached him. One of them put a shoe into his ribs. He felt a blow at the back of his head, and the world closed in and was black.

WHEN HE WOKE, he was in another part of the woods. The dark swirled around him like hot oil, scalding his imagination. He would die here, he thought, or he was dead already.

But the longer he was awake, the clearer it became that he was living. The back of his head throbbed and he reached up and felt the stickiness there. The woods were so flat with darkness that he couldn't move. He tried to sleep, and did, dreaming of Laura's father—how he would drive across the bridge and down Route 29 when all of this was over, how he would park his car in the lot next to the spillway where the weekend hikers disembarked with their dogs and baby strollers. Eddie dreamt that he was there with Laura's father. How they would walk up the trail together and find his body where it lay on the ground. Laura's father would say, "You dummy," as he often did in his joking way. "You should have listened to that old guy and stayed where you were. You could have made it if you stayed put. Why on earth would you run?"

"My neighbor had a gun. He would have shot us."

"No, he wouldn't have. It's hard to shoot a person."

Laura's father had been a soldier once, though he never talked about it with Eddie, and so the way he spoke about shooting someone would carry weight.

Eddie wouldn't know what to say to that, and maybe silence would be best. For a while—early on in their relationship—he'd called Laura's father "Sir," but that hadn't lasted, thankfully. Now there was respect between them. They could be silent together when considering important things. If Eddie had stayed alive a little longer, Laura's father probably would have taken him aside one afternoon—when the women were out doing something together—and told him about Laura's little girl, about how precious she'd been to them and how young Laura had been when it happened. He would have become emotional, and for the first time spoken with Eddie about God and faith, in a way that showed he'd never before given those ideas much serious thought. But Eddie would see that those ideas—of God and faith—were in place for just this kind of thing—that without them, even the strongest people risked falling apart—how they made even the strongest people, in so many ways, seem ordinary. It would be a somber afternoon, certainly, but they would have endured it together, and by the time Laura and her mother got back from whatever they were doing, Eddie would love them all that much more. He would have been that much more a part of their lives.

When Laura's father left him, and it was just Eddie there, alone in the darkness of the woods, he dreamt about how cruel it was that he would have to live all the way to morning. If he were dead, at least the night would be over. But his mind ran with a turbulent depth, and time was like a stick gone beneath its current. He opened his eyes many times and the sky was black, but finally when he opened them, it was gray. The next time, it was the dull yellowish color of dawn.

He was able to get himself to his hands and knees and crawl toward where the sky was lightest. Rocks dug into his palms but there wasn't any pain. They pressed into the soft spots around his kneecaps, too, but his knees were as numb as foam balls.

He was crawling through the ash again, close to where the stream had been. Where he disturbed it, small clouds rose near the ground. He could see the shock of tawny sand, the brownish orange streak through the streambed. The bank was a few feet away, and it was steep. He had no choice but to tumble down—ash in his face, sand in his eyes and mouth.

At the bottom, the sand was as dry as if nothing had ever flowed above it. He touched the brown streak. It wasn't sandy but was like clay that had dried brittle in the sun.

He lay on his back and, without the trees obstructing, he could see the sky. It had the weight of thickening custard, as if the days were no longer repeating infinitely, but getting older—and that today was of a denser quality than the last.

Something snapped behind him.

Eddie lifted just his head, his chin touching his chest.

When he opened his eyes, something rose vertically in the corner of his vision. It was as murky as a smudge.

Then clarity. He saw it—a plastic bottle with a cap.

There was water in it.

He tried to cry out, but only grunted, flailing with his dead hands and slapping at the sand. With his elbows, he dragged himself forward on his stomach and bumped the bottle, knocking it on its side. He tried to upright it, but his fingers passed over the plastic like they were only nubs of rubber. He raked the bottle closer, trapping it between his forearm and his chest. Though he was shaking, he slowly levered it upward, so that he could press the top of the bottle against his stomach, and set it standing upright in the sand. He held his breath so that he wouldn't send it tipping over again.

There was still the problem of the cap. It was screwed down tight, and his fingers wouldn't work to grasp it. He squeezed the bottle's base between his forearms and bent his face over top, clutching the cap between his teeth and twisting his head until the threading gave way. Pain reached from his teeth back into his neck. A crystalline pain! Eddie felt like he'd unearthed a gem from the sand. He bit down harder and the pain spiked in the top of his skull. If he could get the liquid down, everything was recoverable. It would take a little while, like Steve McCarthy said, but it would all come flooding back.

His arms were shaking so much that his knuckles hit against one another. With the bottle between his forearms, he lifted it to his lips, but as he did, the shaking worsened, and his grip was no longer tight. There was nothing to catch the bottle as it rotated away, out of his grasp, to fall on its side. In four spasms, the water drained into the sand.

His idiot body! The hope he'd felt was trapped inside him like a toxin. Where the water had spilled, the sand was dark, and he dug at it with his elbows and then with his face, sucking up the grit between his teeth, feeling it pack inside his lips and nose.

He turned and lay on his back again, exhausted—too exhausted to brush the sand from his face. There was no sun, but the heat came from all around. If the sun were a yoke, it had broken and spread out over the great bowl of the sky—it had spilled into the outlines of the trees.

Why hadn't they struck him harder? It was a game they must be playing. To dangle a man's life in front of his eyes. They'd put the water next to him just to watch him flounder. His father-in-law was right. To kill was not an easy thing. But what kind of man would exact this kind of torture—to let him die slowly in the sand with this ringing idiot hope still pushing through his veins? He could taste it. His mouth was baked closed, but felt deliciously wet. Neither was more real. He pushed his imagination back. Something deep inside him insisted that he keep what was real real—to separate it from the rest.

When he tried his eyes again, he could see the cadaverous shore. There were rocks on the riverbank, and as the light reached them, thin streams ran down their sides.

He closed his eyes and opened them again.

He saw it there—the water, trickling.

"Oh," Eddie said, turning on his back. His mouth hung open. "Oh."

It would happen slowly at first, but then would come the rush. He focused his eyes, and looked again at the shore—silver streams dripping and reflecting in the sun.

There was a voice around him not his own.

"Here," the voice said.

Eddie looked up. The burnt boy was a blur against the sky, and Eddie squeezed his eyes shut, waiting for another blow.

But the strike didn't come. The boy moved around him and Eddie could see into his charcoal face—the eyes like glass, warped and made precious by fire. The sun broke around his body and pierced Eddie's vision. He could hear the boy's knees scraping in the sand. Something hard pressed against his mouth, and he recoiled, but the boy touched his face. Water broke against his lips, and Eddie lunged with his mouth to catch it, keeping his lips pressed against the plastic. It was a fresh bottle, and the boy kept it tipped. Eddie gulped and coughed, and the water spilled onto his shirt.

"Okay," he said. "Okay." He held his hand up and the boy's knees scraped back in the sand, and he stood above him.

Eddie's heart beat deeply in his chest. He could feel it in his ears. Soon, though, the pounding stopped.

The boy looked down on him with tight lips as if awaiting a command.

Eddie sat up and beckoned with his hand and the boy took a step closer and held the bottle out. He took it and drank deeply again. Then he gave the bottle back, and dropped his head between his knees.

It took a moment, but he remembered. The water in the rocks. It was just feet away from him, but he didn't lift his head. Instead, he kept it between his knees; the water had hurt his stomach where it landed.

When he looked up, he saw that the boy hadn't moved.

"Help me up," Eddie said, and offered out his hand.

The boy set the bottle down in the sand so that it stood upright. He squeezed a hand on both sides of Eddie's and leaned back. Eddie reached behind himself and got to standing. The boy slumped back and sat in the sand. He wore a bored expression.

"I'm going to save you," Eddie said.

The boy stood up, and Eddie spoke to him as if to himself. "Come here," he said. "Look."

He reached a hand into the air and steadied himself.

"It's this way," he said. "I saw it."

At the rocks, though, his chest tightened. He searched over the dark crevices. He got on his hands and knees.

"Help me find it!" he told the boy. "I saw it. There was water here!"

The boy got on his hands and knees next to him, and Eddie ran his fingers over the rocks. Some were pocked and some were smooth as eggshells.

Eddie began to dig. He forced his hands between the stones to feel for dampness, but felt only dry sand. The light overhead silvered a trickle of something to his left, and he sprung for it, releasing a noise from his chest that was high and false-sounding.

For a moment, he was able to believe that *everything* was false—not just the noise he'd made, but this spot where he was digging, that the flash of water he'd seen had come from somewhere else.

Then he saw it.

It was the pom-pom thread, unmoored and stuck at the base of a rock. Had it traveled this far from where he'd placed it? Or was he still this close to home?

It fell from his grasp and reflected the light in sharp slashes where it lay.

The boy stood close by, and when Eddie looked at him, it was like he was staring into the depths of an illusion—as if the boy's ribs had disappeared, and his heart and lungs were fluttering beneath his shirt.

Eddie closed his eyes, and when he opened them, the boy's shirt was still again.

If what he'd seen was false, then he'd lost the truth already. What was real was somewhere out in front of him, tangled in the air, the rocks, the ash. Laura. As if she, too, were only a reflection that the sun would soon illuminate. That she might appear up ahead, waiting for him to catch up—at the bridge already, making her way to her parents' house.

"She left it here for us," he said, and as the words emerged, he made himself believe them. He bent to pick up the silver thread, letting it fall again so that the boy could see him do it. "She wanted us to make it here. She's leaving me signs to follow."

He took the boy's shoulder to hurry him up off the bank. The shirt tore away in Eddie's hand, but the boy's skin was fine beneath.

On the ridge, they crouched beside a stump, and the boy put the bottle of water on the ground, his hands on his knees like Eddie's.

"I'm going to take care of you," Eddie told him. "She wants me to."

The boy continued his ghostly staring.

"You'll come with me," Eddie said. "I'll take you away from here. Okay? My wife," he continued, "you met her. Up at the house." He looked back down the hill to the bank, searching out the other silver thread, but couldn't see it anymore.

"Where did you get the water?" Eddie asked.

The boy pointed into the woods.

"Was it a jug? A big one?" Eddie stretched his arms out in front of his chest to show the size. The boy nodded.

"Show me," Eddie said.

Next to them, some of the ash had been trampled, exposing the ground beneath. There were footprints all around them, he saw.

"People were here," Eddie said. "Do you know who they are?"

The boy shook his head.

Eddie tried to think.

"It's not safe," he said. "We'll get the water when it's dark." He touched the top of the bottle. "We can refill this then."

There were still some bushes there, and they took cover crouching next to them. The boy looked down at the streambed without speaking.

After a while, a noise pulsed through the silence. Eddie turned and saw men breaking through the brush.

He got down low and pulled the boy close in next to him. The boy's breathing swelled and receded against Eddie's side.

"Stay still," he whispered, and the boy's breathing stopped. "You're okay. Easy. Easy now."

The men cut down beneath them, passing so close that Eddie could see where the ash had left marks on the backs of their legs. There were no voices, only footsteps, but the sound of them rushed through Eddie's ears like traffic.

The one in the rear carried a water jug on his shoulder like a tribesman who'd killed a translucent hog. Eddie squeezed the earth in his fists to keep from crying out.

When they were gone, he said, "Do they know where you are? Do they know you took some?"

The boy was silent.

"Where are they taking it?" Eddie said.

The boy looked down and studied the way an odd shape of stone broke from the ground in front of him.

Eddie allowed his hands to unclench. "What's your name?" he said.

"Dylan."

"Like *Bob* Dylan."

The boy continued staring at the rock. It looked like a nose protruding from the ground—like a face all but buried. Eddie waved his hand across the boy's field of vision.

"We're going to go to my wife's parents' house," he said. "They're on well water. Do you have any idea what that means? What I'm telling you?"

Dylan shook his head.

"I think we should sleep now. It's better to walk at night. Those are bad men, so we'll stay away from them. It won't be hard. We've got the whole woods here. Are you tired? Can you sleep?"

Eddie pulled the boy up by his wrist. With the other hand, the boy clutched the bottle of water to his chest.

"We'll get in the leaves," Eddie said.

There were trees up there, and the leaves were ankle deep. He mounded them between a boulder and a slope of stone. The lichen on the stone was now as crisp as insect skin.

"Get in there," Eddie pointed, and Dylan put one leg after another into the leaf pile. "Sit down. Let me cover you up."

He sat down and Eddie pushed the leaves up to the boy's neck. Only his head stuck out above the pile and he looked at Eddie, blinking as if having just emerged from darkness.

"Take a sip before you go to sleep," Eddie said.

Dylan's arms broke through the leaves and unscrewed the cap. He tilted the bottle to his lips, and the water rolled slowly down the plastic. As it touched his mouth, he tipped the bottle back. It looked like he hadn't swallowed any. He handed the bottle to Eddie.

"I'm good," Eddie said, and then, "Okay. A little." He took the bottle and gulped from it, then pulled himself away. He capped it and gave it back to Dylan. There was still a quarter of the bottle left.

"Close your eyes," he said. "You probably don't like to sleep when it's still light, but try, okay? We've got a long way to go. I don't want to have to carry you."

"You won't carry me."

Eddie looked down to where the men had come through and saw the faintest impression of their path.

"I'll stay up and watch. Don't worry about them. They're going in the other direction."

If anyone passed, they would pass downhill from him, where the walking was easier, and Eddie would be able to see them come. He leaned his back into the rock and felt comfortable. It was strange, he thought, that the stone at his back was a comfort. He didn't notice it, really—that was why. He picked up a handful of leaves that were light as air.

THE SKY OVERHEAD was a perfect blue, and his heart leapt. He swiveled in his chair and looked at the time in the corner of his computer screen. Maybe he'd be able to leave early. If he left early, he could grill up those chicken thighs, and he and Laura could have a picnic on the porch. If he stayed even another hour, he'd be too tired for that. There would be plenty of light, but that wouldn't matter. The traffic would do him in.

When he opened his eyes, it was dark and his breath adhered to his throat as though it were lined with tape. He gasped and squeezed his lungs and sucked at the air around his face. Then he remembered the boy.

Shadows had pooled between the rocks, and he leaned over to ruffle the leaves there. He patted with his hand and felt Dylan's bony head.

"Hey," he said. "Wake up."

The head didn't move, and Eddie thought maybe it wasn't a head at all. "Come on," he said, and the head rose from beneath his palm. Eddie felt the boy's shoulders and his hot, dry back.

"Give me another drink," Eddie said, and the boy handed him the bottle.

The woods were too dark to walk through, but they would have to try.

"We have to go. Give me your hand."

He reached down and the boy took his hand.

"We're leaving," Eddie said. "Say good-bye to all this."

They walked along the edge of the streambed, just inside the bank where the sand was still soft underfoot. Eddie let go of Dylan's hand and followed just behind him. It was as if they were walking toward a dark picture with a smear of gray at the bottom, and the smear of gray never came into focus. When Dylan slowed, Eddie touched him between the shoulders. "Left, right, left," he said. "March on, little soldier." They walked for a long time. The woods up the slope were so black they weren't woods at all—only something penetrable. Eddie gripped his fists, testing the strength in them, imagining what he might do if they were seen.

When Dylan stopped, Eddie stopped, too.

"We need to drink," Eddie said.

Dylan held the bottle to his lips again.

"Take more," Eddie said, but Dylan shook his head. "Give it to me, then."

He filled his mouth and let the water sit warmly on the sides of his tongue. His skull felt full of water, too, but it was water he couldn't reach. There were reserves he had no access to. He'd have to wait for them.

When he swallowed, the dryness was there again in his throat, as though his mouth had not, a moment earlier, been wet.

"Let me just hold it for a second," he said, and he held the bottle and let the pale light off the sand reflect inside of it.

Then they walked on into the silence. The smear of gray that was the streambed disappeared ahead of them, and when they walked to the end of it, Eddie saw that it hooked sharply to the right. Dylan sat down.

"Get up," Eddie said.

Eddie stood beside him and saw how the slope was graded. The trail next to the streambed was wide there.

"Okay, stay where you are, then," he said. "Rest for a little bit."

Up the trail was a guardrail for a road, and beyond it, the

dim lines of a crosswalk. Eddie stood at the trailhead, looking out into the street.

"This way," he called down. "Come on. This is the way up here."

He went down to grab the boy, to carry him if he had to, but felt him pass by his legs.

"Look for something silver," Eddie said. "She might have left it for us to follow again."

He ran his hands over the guardrail and kicked at the dirt by the road, but there was none of the silver thread.

"She knows I know the way," he said when he didn't find any.

The shoulder of the street was wide and empty, and the grass had been mowed close to the ground. It disappeared underfoot and left more dark footprints behind them. Eddie recognized this street. They were at the edge of the park, and if they kept walking, they'd come out near the exit for the highway.

"You stay close," he warned. "If you hear anything, you tell me."

The shoulder was shadowed by thick trees at its edge, and Dylan followed him, taking big steps to match his footprints. Eddie crinkled the plastic bottle against his hip to make sure that he was still carrying it.

The street opened out onto another and the streetlights hung darkly in the air overhead. Rectangular sections of the night sky were blotted out as if redacted where signs for the highway were attached to thick metal poles.

The on-ramp was ahead, curving up and over the highway. It was clean of debris, and they followed it, Eddie touching the concrete wall marred with fender paint.

He held up his hand to Dylan, and they stopped and surveyed the stretch beneath them. On the highway, there were a few cars at odd angles, but nothing was moving there.

"If we see people, we can go into the woods," Eddie said.

They circled along the ramp and emptied out onto the lane to merge. The asphalt seemed to shiver beneath their feet. Eddie imagined trucks bearing down on them. On the other side of the guardrail was a footpath, and Eddie stepped over onto it.

"Raise your arms," he said, and Dylan raised his arms up over his head. Eddie grabbed beneath his armpits and hoisted him up and over.

They walked along the path, and the highway stretched before them like a strip of prairie carved into the woods. Eddie's eyes were heavy. He looked behind him and saw Dylan wobbling.

"Come on," he said. "Sit here."

They sat on the guardrail. Eddie took another sip, and offered it to Dylan again, but he refused.

"When's your birthday?" Eddie asked, testing him.

He had to clench his brain like a fist to remember his own.

"Mine's in March," Eddie said, finally.

They kept going. Eddie's legs burned in his hips. He thought soon the sun would break over the horizon, but it didn't. The next time he looked for Dylan, he wasn't there. He was sitting down in the dirt behind him.

"Come on, pal," he said. "You stay in front of me now, okay?"

Dylan's legs were bent beneath him in a figure four, and Eddie stooped to lift him by his pits again, but his body was limp. Eddie stood him upright, but he only slumped back to the ground again.

"I need you, buddy," Eddie said. "I need you to be my scout. I bet you have eagle eyes. We're looking for a bridge. It goes all the way across the bay. There are *big* silver supports that go up into the sky, and wires that come off those. That's what you'll see first, okay? Those big metal supports. They're like towers. I need you to look for them."

This time, when he picked him up, he stood. And when Eddie prodded him between his shoulder blades, he walked. Eddie walked close behind, staring at his ashy back as if walking into the cast of his own shadow.

They went on and Eddie closed his eyes, but even then, they kept walking.

"EDDIE, WAKE UP," Laura said. "Wake up, Eddie."

Her hand was on his chest, rousing him as if for work. She stood next to him, wearing a green T-shirt.

"Keep going," she said. "You have to keep him with you. You can't just leave him behind."

She walked beside him for a long time in silence, and Eddie watched her. To her side, off the highway, the tree branches reached out into small leafless networks. There were buds on them. Even the air felt like spring. The woods were full of sound. Voices. There were people in the trees, and light streamed through them like water through a net. Ahead, the highway was obstructed by something Eddie couldn't see. He looked at the woods again, but the trees were just dead poles in the darkness.

As they got closer, he saw the obstacle more clearly. It was a wreck. Only one car remained, and its nose was crumpled in.

Glass and plastic were spread out over the highway and over the path where he walked.

A warm familiarity spread through his body. The wrecked car was *his* car. He knelt down in the path and began to pick up shards of plastic. Most were small, but a few were long and pointed. He put them in his pockets.

"What are you doing?" Laura asked.

He turned and looked over his shoulder to where she was standing, but it was only her voice. Her body wasn't there.

"I'm collecting it."

"Don't," she said. "You have someplace to be."

"I'll need proof for the insurance."

"What proof? You think that's going to be proof?"

He crouched there and looked at the destroyed car.

"Anyway, it's not yours," Laura said. "You weren't driving on this highway. This is the way to my parents' house. You were coming home from work."

Eddie looked out onto the wreck and saw that she was right. This car had been an SUV.

"Where's the boy?" she asked.

"Dylan."

"Where is he?"

Eddie looked behind, and then stood and strained his eyes ahead. The path was empty in both directions.

"I lost him," he said.

He backtracked down the path taking careful steps. He was afraid that Dylan had curled up somewhere and that he'd step on him or kick him accidentally. But the path was an uninterrupted gray line in the darkness.

"Dylan," he whispered. "Come on, pal."

He backtracked for longer than Dylan could have walked. Then he held on to the rail and vomited on the asphalt of the highway. It was only a trickle of spit, but he gasped and clung to the metal and cursed himself.

When he opened his eyes, the gray of the horizon was a lighter gray. He looked for Laura, but then he tried to keep himself from looking—from fooling himself. The world without Laura was lead-heavy around him. She was gone, and he'd been weak to let himself imagine anything else. He had to be strong. The path was still empty and the highway was empty going forward. He could see ahead where the woods on either side came to a point at the end of his vision.

He rested there on his knees to build his strength. Once he was standing, he could use his legs again.

If Dylan wasn't curled up on the highway, then maybe he was in the woods. Eddie looked back and forth as the day began to brighten. He tried to jog, but the wind in his ears was painful. If he spent time searching the woods, he'd never make it to the bridge, but the woods would be cooler and he could hide himself in the leaves in the daylight.

He walked as the highway sloped gradually upward. To his right, on the other side of the guardrail, the land dropped off, and he stopped to peer down into the depression between where he stood and where the woods started up again. Someone was sitting in a chair there. He could see the top of her head—the gray hair of an old woman. As she lifted her face to look at him, he thought he knew her, but didn't know from where.

Her shirt billowed out around her waist, and something moved in her lap. Dylan was curled up there.

Then he recognized her. It was Ruth Blackmon. His neighbor. Mrs. Blackmon. Just across the street.

Eddie stepped over the guardrail and put his foot on the edge of the slope, but before he could step to test its firmness, he slid on his heels and fell on his back and rolled. As the world turned over, he squeezed the plastic bottle tightly in his hand.

"You all right?" Mrs. Blackmon said.

Eddie stood up. The hill was soft and hadn't hurt him. He brushed the dirt off his face. Mrs. Blackmon was sitting in a folding chair, and Dylan's head was nuzzled against her chest. Mrs. Blackmon was in her sixties. She was retired, and Eddie's mother sometimes sent him over with a bowl to pick her grape tomatoes, or to help her net the blueberry bushes that the birds enjoyed assaulting.

But no.

That was when he was a child. When he looked again, he saw that it wasn't Mrs. Blackmon. It was Mrs. Kasolos.

"Where'd you get him?" Eddie said.

"He came to me," Mrs. Kasolos said. "You need to keep track of your son."

"It was dark." He examined her carefully. "What are you doing here?" he asked. "You're dead."

"I'm waiting. My daughter went off to look for people. She'll be back. We found this chair on the side of the road. Perfectly good."

"Dylan," Eddie said.

Dylan pulled his head from out of the folds of Mrs. Kasolos's shirt like a bird from beneath a wing.

"Why'd you run off like that?"

He looked at Eddie with dreary eyes.

"Well, I'm glad he found me," she said. "Because now you're here. I don't know when I've been this thirsty."

"You and your daughter don't have water?" Eddie looked at the bottle in his hand. There were, perhaps, three sips left.

"Not anymore."

"This is all we have," Eddie said. "We need it to get to the bridge. I've got family over there."

"And I have nothing. So who's ahead in the game?"

"Your daughter's coming back for you."

"This one's nice," Mrs. Kasolos said. She put her hand on top of Dylan's head. "Not too whiny."

"He needs to come with me," Eddie said.

"Of course," she said. "And I need a drink."

"He's my *son*," Eddie said, hearing himself say it.

Dylan looked up the hill at the highway above their heads.

"Come on," Eddie said. He took Dylan by the wrist and pulled him off Mrs. Kasolos's lap.

"Give me your hand," he ordered, and Dylan reached up.

"Let's go. Keep up. We have to go."

He began to run, and when Dylan turned his head to look back, Eddie jerked his arm like a leash.

It was slow going up the hill, and he struggled to keep his breath from blocking up his throat. When it leveled off at the path next to the highway, he stopped and squeezed Dylan's hand in his own. It was rubbery and loose. Ahead, the horizon was blank, but it could have been an illusion from the pitch of the land. The bridge could have been just beyond his sight.

He started jogging again, but something caught him, flexing thinly across his shins. He pitched forward and fell headlong, his palms hitting the dirt again. Dust spun into his mouth. Dylan stood above him and Eddie could see the tight white rope that had toppled him.

A woman stepped out from behind a tree. She held a stick with both hands, and thrust the sharpened end at Eddie's face. Eddie squeezed his eyes shut, and when he opened them, the tip was an inch above his forehead. The tip had been blackened in a fire.

"That was my mom back there!" the woman shouted. Her face was red and dirt had caked along the tendons in her neck. A wound on her forehead had dried as dark and crusty as a caterpillar. "It was a test! You failed it!"

A man and a boy about thirteen emerged from the woods. Each had his own sharpened stick.

"Give us what you got," the woman said. The man wore a shirt with the sleeves rolled up. It was unbuttoned halfway down the front, exposing red flesh beneath a puff of black hair.

"Why didn't you come for her before?" Eddie asked.

"Shut up," the woman said. "Hand it over."

Eddie turned to look at Dylan, but the woman touched his cheek with the side of the stick, straightening him out again.

"I need it for the boy," he said.

He rolled over onto the bottle and put his hand into his pocket. He felt the shards of plastic there.

Dylan sat down on the guardrail. His face was a doll's face with half-shut lids.

The woman planted her front foot next to Eddie's chest. The muscles in her calf twitched in fierce debate. Those muscles would decide the fate of her pointed stick—if it was going to withdraw or proceed directly into his face—and Eddie pulled his fist from his pocket and slammed the longest plastic shard into the soft spot behind her knee.

It stuck there, deep, and she howled and fell to the ground as the other two ran to help her. He stood up, scooped Dylan to his chest, and ran, the boy's legs overflowing from the basket of his arms. The road was flat as a runway, and when the weight of Dylan's body began to burn his shoulders and neck, he kept on running. He held the bottle in the vise of his hands beneath him as the plastic twisted his fingers until he thought that they would snap.

The sun was overhead, and they were alone. The white stripes on the highway were ten feet long, at least. Too long. His vision wasn't right. The green highway signs across the divide were huge and sparkling.

As he lowered Dylan to the ground, the boy began to scramble. It was an animal's recognition of a proximity to freedom. Eddie let him fall. He hit the ground and then stood and organized his shoulders.

"You're not what you said," Dylan said.

Eddie sat down in the dirt.

The boy began to walk back in the direction that they'd come.

Eddie stood.

"Dylan," he called. "Get back here!"

He walked quickly to him, and tried to grab his arm, but Dylan shook away. Eddie pressed down on his shoulders, and his little-boy body collapsed like a cardboard box. Eddie was on top of him, pinning him to the ground. Dylan squirmed, but Eddie leaned hard into his chest, and finally he was still.

"You have to come with me," Eddie said. "Sometimes you

have to do things you don't like." He planted his shredded palms in the dirt on either side of Dylan's body and pushed himself up, but Dylan stayed flattened where he was.

"Come on," Eddie said, but the boy didn't move. "Take a sip of this," he said. "Come on," but Dylan lay frozen on the ground.

Eddie took a sip and then another, and when he looked up from the bottle, Dylan was sitting.

Something had resigned in him, and Eddie led him to the woods. The leaves were thick on the ground, and he piled them up again. When Dylan sat, Eddie stooped to cover him up, but the boy tossed and kicked himself free of the leaves and began to whimper. It was too hot to be buried.

Eddie sat on the ground. It was soft, and he leaned back against a tree.

"Imagine that it's night," he said.

The sky was bright and bled beyond the branches that cut across it. When he thought of Laura, he had to tell himself, *These are her eyes,* and picture her eyes. He had to say, *This is her nose; this is the curve of her cheek.*

Points of light began to strike the inside of his skull like static against a screen. His skin was alive with itch, and when he scraped his nails along his arm, he thought he'd rip it open.

"Let's go," he said. "I can't sit here."

Dylan was up, peeing against a tree.

"Don't!" Eddie shouted. He stood and went to him but couldn't judge the distance, bumping his knee hard into Dylan's back.

"You peed," Eddie said. "You let it out of you."

Dylan stood back.

"That's okay. You had to."

At the path, the sun flamed at the top of its descent. It blinded Eddie to look ahead, and he hit the guardrail and stumbled against it.

Dylan sat and hung his head. The light had turned him into a few loose sticks of glare and shadow. His face was gone; the tips of his fingers bled out into the hot yellow air.

"Dylan," Eddie called, and then he said the name softly, testing his voice. He couldn't tell if he'd spoken out loud.

He went to him and lifted him to his chest again, entwining his fingers beneath the boy's rear end to keep him up. Voices around him made *W* sounds and *H* sounds. Then they began to shriek, but Eddie told himself they weren't there. Dylan shuffled in his arms as Eddie ran. Though the sun was in his eyes, he felt the closeness of the guardrail with his legs and he followed it as it turned.

"You track stars," he heard Laura saying. "You never get out of shape." He loved that she loved his body because it wasn't her own—that he was able to seek the mystery in hers. He loved that no matter how long he loved her, she would always be a separate person—that love's limit arrived before two people could press together into one.

Another voice was at his chest. Eddie ran harder when he heard it.

"It's there," the voice said.

He opened his eyes. The sun had dipped to the side of the woods, and up ahead was the great skeletal arch of the bridge.

"There."

Eddie's legs began to float, and though he couldn't feel them, he knew that his arms and head, his whole body, all of it, had lifted off of him like a shirt. He didn't care about his body—it was nothing to him—and so he ran.

There were tollbooths ahead, and the highway widened to accommodate the additional lanes. To the side of the booths, the sun was seeping through a stand of bulrushes, and beyond that the land broke off and there was sky. Eddie couldn't see what lay beneath it. There were people there in front of the bulrushes. They milled about in the deepening light as though they were neighbors to one another.

Eddie's mind, too, began to float above him, as if it longed to reunite with his floating body. It was different from the marathon he'd run his senior year—the year he hadn't trained. At the end of that race—having run too far, too fast—he'd thought that he might die, but knew he probably wouldn't. Now, with his mind high above him, he could only think of living.

Dylan was no longer a weight in his arms, but a buoyancy he clung to in the vast sea of air around him. The people stood, hands on hips, in T-shirts and in shorts, with hats or blown hair. As he approached, he saw a woman whose eyes caught his and were full of laughter, until they widened and her eyebrows peaked. The sun dipped and was gone and he let himself fall because there was no weight and he was floating.

HE WOKE FEELING something hard press against his lip, and then a warmth on his teeth.

"Drink," the woman said, and Eddie opened his mouth and let the water pass down into his throat. He coughed and heaved and rolled to his side to catch his breath.

"Easy," she told him, and tilted the glass to his lips again so that he could sip more slowly.

He closed his eyes and opened them. The day filled him in the way light leaps into darkness—a sudden clarity illuminating the shapes around him. Something had extinguished deep inside him, and he felt the hiss in the looseness of his mind, saw steam floating in thin gray columns that flattened and broke and disappeared along the horizon.

"The helicopters won't miss us this time," the woman said. "Not with those going."

Eddie tried to stand. They were on the ridge of bulrushes, and down below them bonfires burned. It was the smoke that he was seeing, but his eyes weren't right. He waved his hand as if to catch himself, but he was feeling around for the boy. Beside him was air so warm and thick he could have let himself tip over and still remained aloft within it.

"Easy," the woman said again.

She smiled sadly, the way she might over a horse with a broken leg. There was a hard and trembling grace in her eyes, and Eddie waited for her face to twist into something necessary—for the shot to ring out—as she put him out of his misery.

Slowly, she reached out her hand to him, but his heart released, and he unwound, bolting away from her and running into the dry woods beside the tollbooths.

He ran deep into the leaves until their raucousness beneath his feet forced him to stop and strain to hear that he was alone.

"Dylan," he said, but only softly. He didn't look behind any of the trees. The only thing moving in the woods was him.

His legs had worked too quickly and were as limp as dangling wire. He walked back to where the trees met grass before the asphalt of the highway.

Below him, the land dropped off to a beach where the fires burned, and great cement stanchions held the bridge where it lifted free from the land. Beyond was what he hadn't been able to see from the rise, where he had seen only the woman and the smoke in the sky.

It was the bay, full and wide, pierced along its breadth by the deep legs of the bridge. Close to shore, the water browned like a spill into the blue-gray surface and rippled beneath a wind Eddie was protected from among the trees.

Tangled piles of driftwood were mounded on the beach,

and a wheelbarrow heavy with split logs from someone's yard sat with its wheel pressed halfway into the sand. Men and women tended the fires, and a propane tank had been cut so that its two halves could be propped up on legs like cauldrons above the flames. There was some kind of contraption over top of them—corrugated plastic peaked like a roof, with gutters off the ends.

One of the men stood shirtless with his back to Eddie. The muscles around his shoulders pinched and depressed when he pointed at one fire and then the next. The others carried driftwood in their arms and heaped it at the bases of the fires. At the waterline, a group in shorts and pants rolled to the knee waded in with metal buckets and pickle tubs. They walked up the beach with their shoulders straining and the water sloshing over the lips of the buckets that knocked against their thighs. One woman expelled a laugh so sharp and sudden that Eddie jerked his head to see if a bird had fallen from the sky.

He watched as they helped one another tip the water into the tanks atop one of the fires and stood back as a man removed his T-shirt and knelt and fanned the flames with it until the smoke billowed up around him and the fire licked the metal black and blacker still. The steam gathered strength beneath the plastic ceiling and was as thick and white as paper. They stood next to one another and spoke words Eddie couldn't hear.

Beneath the gutters were plastic bins, and when the fires had settled, and the steam died down, they lifted one bin and tipped it so that a thin stream of clean water broke over its edge into a jar.

Eddie squinted through the twilight. There were tents and children on the beach, and he scanned their faces, looking for

Dylan. In an instant, he faltered and stopped his search, squeezing his chest to keep it from caving in where panic had blown a hole. He tried to remember, but couldn't—couldn't remember what the boy had looked like.

The harder he pressed his mind, the more the memory faded.

He crouched in the trees, looking out over the beach and the water.

Two little girls sat cross-legged on a towel on the grassy rise beside the tollbooths. They were closest to him, and he walked over the asphalt of the highway to them on shaky legs. The wind knocked grit against his ankles. There were plastic cups and scraps of paper all around them, and the girls warbled back and forth like parakeets.

Eddie stood above them, invisible for a moment against the sky before they craned their necks to see him. He tried to find his voice.

"Where are your parents?" he said.

"Over there," said one, pointing down at the beach. She had blond bangs, and her hair curled gold where it touched her shoulder. "It's a sleepover," she said, "with all the neighbors."

"Have you seen a little boy?"

She nodded.

"Where?" Eddie asked.

She pointed down toward one of the fires where a shirtless boy stood in dirty red shorts.

"That's her brother," she said, bopping her companion on the head to demonstrate the connection.

"Not him," Eddie said. He stared at the two of them as though they'd vanish if he looked away. "A different boy."

"I know a boy at school," said the other. "Aiden."

"He doesn't share," said the first. "That's why he doesn't get stickers." Her shirt was marred with fingerprints. Eddie watched her pluck an empty two-liter bottle by the neck from off the grass and place it in her lap. Her friend reached over and patted the plastic, saying, "Good kitty."

"What are you doing?"

"Pretending she's a cat."

"A cat named Button," said the second.

"Where are your parents?" Eddie asked again.

"I *told* you," said the first, flopping down and slapping the grass in exasperation.

Eddie left them and walked toward the bulrushes where a woman was standing by herself.

He saw that it was the same woman who had caught him, and he stopped where he was, but she beckoned him closer.

"You came back," she said, teasing just a little.

"There was a boy with me," Eddie said.

"A boy?" she said, leaning on a hip to consider it. "I didn't see a boy."

Eddie touched his forehead with the edge of his fist, and the pressure there was soothing. He closed his eyes and felt again what it had been like to float.

"It's worse back there, yeah?" he heard her say. "We've pretty much held it together here. We're a close community, so that helps. We all know each other."

"He was with me," Eddie insisted. "The boy," and when he opened his eyes, he saw that her face had hardened around the deep concern that she was holding for him.

"No," she said, firmly this time. "You were alone."

Eddie looked out onto the bridge. There were shapes moving there, but they were blurry and could have been anything—a shadow from a passing cloud just as easily as a little boy. He could look out into the coming evening and twist those shapes into anything he wanted, but none of that twisting mattered.

His insides wouldn't settle. Pain and ease flashed through his guts like light and dark on the water, but from the outside—to the woman standing right next to him—he must have appeared perfectly still. From as far away as the bridge, he was likely invisible above the shore, both real and unreal, there and without dimension. It didn't matter that all of this was happening to him.

"My wife," he said, and his tongue was thick again, but he collected himself.

The woman looked down at the grass that covered the short distance between them. She was silent for a while.

Then she said: "It's brackish water, you know? It has a salt content. Maybe that's why it's still here. We've got a couple of geniuses on our side. My husband's an engineer. If you boil it and let it condense, you can drink it. It's distilled."

Beyond the fires, the Bay stretched full and smooth beneath the two spans of the bridge. The sun was going down and the water was gray, but to the west it was bright as neon where the light was touching it.

"Look," she said, motioning to the fires and the people tending them. "All this in just two days. A day and a half, really. The human mind is really something when you need it to. be."

She glanced beside her and squinted against the last of the sun. The two little girls had gone off somewhere, and the grass was empty.

"When my kids were little," the woman said, "they used to love when the power went out. We'd read to them by candlelight."

She looked at him and her face softened to accommodate what must have been devastating his. She was standing nearer to him now. She hadn't touched his hand, though he felt that she would—that she would take it and hold it without thinking it a kindness.

Then she closed her eyes, as if letting the evening settle over her, and together they stood and faced the expanse of darkening water.

ACKNOWLEDGMENTS

I WOULD NOT have been able to write this book without the friends and family who read and reread its earlier drafts. Many thanks to Andrew Ewell and Hannah Pittard, Nick Soodik, Dr. Alex McQuoid, Patrick Somerville, H. Jerry Cohen, Jerry Gabriel, Mark Rader, John Watt, Rob Roensch, Ari Lieberman, Jeff Klein, Cathy Chung, Mikail Qazi, John Moses Jr., Thor Polson, Murray Warner, Dara Warner, and the Warner I live with, Joanna.

For their continuing collegial support and willingness to discuss books and writing, I'd like to thank Michael Downs and Andrew Reiner.

For her keen eye, attention to detail, and equanimity in working with a first-time novelist, I'd like to thank my editor, Lea Beresford, and the team at Bloomsbury USA for whipping this book into shape.

I'm also grateful to Christy Fletcher and Sylvie Greenberg at Fletcher & Company for their intellectual generosity and dedication to my work. Thank you both for seeing something special in these pages.

And, of course, a thank-you to my folks, Rona and Steve, who not only taught me and my sister to read and write, but with infinite patience did the same for middle school kids across the state of Maryland. For forty years.

A NOTE ON THE AUTHOR

BENJAMIN WARNER TEACHES writing at Towson University. *Thirst* is his first novel. A Maryland native, he lives in Baltimore.